BLACK MOON

VEILED INTENTIONS
BOOK 3

ELLE KEATON

ONE

MAT

Monday morning

Sheriff Mat Dempsey released a gusty sigh. The semipeaceful feeling he'd been enjoying before the 911 call came in evaporated faster than the morning fog. Mat flicked a quick glance at the man standing beside him before his gaze focused back on what lay in front of them. He grumbled, "We have got to stop meeting like this."

This was a body in the waters of Hidden Harbor—again. The second this year, and the second Mat was able to identify with a single glance.

"Duane Cooper," Marshal Soper said, lips pursed.

"Duane Cooper," Mat affirmed.

He tried not to feel resentful. The man was dead, after all. He'd had family who would mourn him. At least Mat thought so.

However.

However, even Mat, who was not a medical doctor like Marshal, had spotted what looked like a bullet hole in the chest when Foster Jennings had pulled Duane's body out of the water and flipped what was left of him over onto his back. Meaning the department had work to do.

Water dribbled from the remains, soaking the sheet and the gravel underneath it. There wasn't much glamorous about a waterlogged corpse.

Ironically, if Cooper had been alive (and not on the run from the law), he would've been the one doing the retrieval, as he had for Chastity Reynolds, the body discovered in February. Instead the task fell to Foster Jennings, technically one of Piedras Island's EMTs, who was certified in scuba and water rescue. Not that this was a rescue.

Mat stared at the body. It hadn't been in the water long; the fish and other underwater creatures hadn't had a chance to make much of a meal of him. Duane had most of his fingers and toes still, though one eye was missing. The remaining eye stared unblinking into the early-September sunshine.

"Well, fuck."

"Sir," Deputy Flynn, Mat's most valued employee, muttered from where she stood on Mat's other side. In a weird sort of déjà vu, she'd been the one to receive the 911 call about Cooper. She'd also been the officer on duty when the call about Chastity Reynolds came in months ago.

"I feel like 'fuck' is appropriate here."

Birdy shrugged but nodded.

Marshal retrieved a pair of disposable latex gloves from the evidence kit in his trunk and pulled them on before kneeling next to the body. The thing about bodies and water was that water and aquatic life tended to get rid of any helpful evidence.

Foster watched Marshal work for a moment. "I'm going to take off my dry suit. Do you need a hand getting him to the morgue?"

Usually, Marshal transported DBs in his rust bucket of a Land Cruiser, but Foster had arrived in the island ambulance, which made things easier.

Marshal looked up at him. "Sure. Thanks."

"I'll be back in a few," Foster said.

Mat turned to Birdy. "Mrs. Tenny called this in?"

"Yes, sir. She was walking her dog and saw the body in the water."

Mat could feel the press of the crowd of island residents behind him. News had spread quickly, as it always did, and those with nothing better to do were now rubbernecking from the other side of the yellow crime scene tape. Likely some of the people there did have something to do but had dropped it for the current spectacle.

Reluctantly, he turned around to look. Mrs. Tenny was at the center of the crowd. He could see her gesticulating as she, no doubt, elaborated on how she'd discovered the body.

"Flynn, get Mrs. Tenny to the station, and take a proper statement before she does any more harm. Did she recognize the body, do you think?"

Birdy, who had started to walk away, stopped and looked back at Mat with a thoughtful expression. "No, I think she would've said."

"Okay. Tell Holstrom and Radden to try to disperse the crowd—and since we know that won't happen, make sure they all stay on the other side of the tape. Send Jones up to the hospital to keep lookie-loos away. That's the last thing Marshal needs."

As he gazed at the crowd of curious islanders, Mat caught sight of Stu Dennis, the local historian. Yep, everybody had come out to see what was going on.

Mat turned his attention back to the marina. First Chastity and now Duane. What was it about the damn place? He reminded himself that Chastity had been strangled, and her body had likely floated on a current into the marina—although they didn't know where she had gone into the water. Duane had been shot. Had it happened here at the marina, or had he been shot somewhere else and dumped here? As far as he knew there hadn't been any reports of gunfire but Mat knew as well as anyone the multitude of reasons why shots may not have been heard or been mistaken for fireworks or a car backfiring.

He sighed and wished, not for the first time that week or even that day, that Niall was home. Not that Niall was part of the Piedras County Sheriff's Office, but as an ex-detective he had good insight. And Mat just plain missed his fiancé.

But, after a long training period, Niall had been assigned his first big case with West Coast Forensics, the consulting firm he'd accepted a position at. Mat was excited for him, but Idaho seemed a long way away right now, and their bed felt empty without Niall in it.

"I don't think an autopsy is going to tell us much more about cause of death. But…" Marshal's voice broke into Mat's thoughts.

"But what?"

"I'd like to do one anyway. There are some things I'd like to confirm."

"Like what?" Mat asked.

Marshal shook his head. "I'm not putting ideas in your head. If I can confirm my suspicions, you'll be the first to know, Sheriff."

"How long?"

"I'll try to call you before five."

Foster, having changed back into his EMT uniform, walked over to where Marshal and Mat waited. "Ready?" he asked.

"Ready," Marshal said.

Mat watched the two men load the body onto a metal gurney and cover it with another sheet before wheeling it over to the ambulance. Once the body was inside, Marshal said something to Foster. Then he peeled off his gloves, tossing them in a hazardous waste bin in the ambulance before heading to where his Toyota was parked.

"Don't call me, I'll call you," Marshal called over to Mat as he climbed into his car.

The crowd still milled around, but the hum of conversation had lessened, and Mat figured many were heading back to their usual morning routines. The diehards would stick around, though, and he wondered how long it would be before Stu Dennis cornered him to try to weasel some details out of him.

It was going to be a hot day. Mat tugged at his collar, already uncomfortable in his uniform. The morning sun glittered off the green-blue water of Hidden Harbor; sailboats and motorboats bobbed in the current. A couple of seagulls and crows down on the rocky beach were fighting over rock oysters. A flock of terns swept along the water's edge, a multitude of birds moving as one. The leader changed the angle of his wing, and the others followed. It was mesmerizing to watch. Mat wished the damn birds could tell him what they'd seen.

The gate to the marina was still open. Foster had needed access to retrieve the body, and Tom Bellows, the dockmaster, had left it ajar.

Mat crossed the parking lot to the marina office, a tiny building with a fresh coat of aqua blue paint. "I'm going to check the dock again," he told Tom. "When I'm finished, please lock the gate. Access is restricted until we release the scene."

Tom sighed and ran a hand across his billiard-ball-bald dome. "This is going to piss people off."

"Yes, well, we all would have preferred not to start the day with a dead body."

Tom had the grace to look embarrassed, but Mat understood his feelings. The Hidden Harbor Marina clients were demanding, and many weren't full-time island residents. Tom had some difficult personalities to deal with.

Mat's footsteps echoed across the water as he slowly walked along the main dock and down each side dock, peering into the water and at the boats moored there. None of the boats appeared to have been tampered with; there was no handy blood spatter. A few of the moorages were open; Mat made a note to ask Tom who had been in and out recently, but he didn't find anything immediately suspicious. After taking several pictures using his cell phone, he turned and headed back toward where he'd parked.

As he carefully inched his cruiser past the crime scene tape, Mat rolled his window down. "I'm heading back to the station," he said to Deputy Radden. "You stay here and keep the amateur detectives away from the scene. No one is to enter the marina, got it?"

Patrick nodded. "Got it, sir."

Mat had just entered the station when his cell phone buzzed. He dug in his pocket for it. Even before he glanced at the screen, he had a feeling he knew who it would be.

"Hey," he said, tossing his keys onto the corner of his desk.

"A body?" Niall sounded both astonished and outraged.

"What? No 'I love you'? No "I miss you'?" Mat teased.

"Mat," Niall growled, "you know I miss you. I was already suffering, and now I hear another body's been found?"

Ever since someone had tried to blow Mat up in the spring, Niall had been acting like a protective mother bear. At first Mat hadn't minded; he'd been recovering, and being on the receiving end of a bomb was serious. But now, months later, it was beginning to grate just a little.

He sat down in his chair and leaned back. "Yeah, another body. Tentatively ID'ed as Duane Cooper."

"Tentatively?"

"It's Duane. But, you know, official channels and all that."

"What happened?"

"Somebody got to him before we could. He took a gunshot to the chest. I'd say he'd only been in the water a few hours. Who'd you find out from, anyway?"

"The first person? Your mother. But I also got a call from Stu and a text from Birdy. Then Shay called and wanted to know what I knew. That was all in about a ten-minute span."

"Jesus Christ." Shay Delacombe was Niall's recently acknowledged half brother. They were like two alpha wolves circling each other, not wanting—at least on Niall's part—to admit they might need the relationship. Although in the last couple of months, Niall seemed to have lowered his guard when it came to Shay.

Mat shared what he could with Niall. He may not have been a medical examiner, but as a young beat cop in San Fran he'd been on enough water recovery scenes to form his own opinions, and Duane was in far too good of condition to have been in the water long.

When he finished, Niall grunted something unintelligible that could have meant "Good" or "Tell me more."

"Marshal took the body up to the morgue. He'll let me know more as soon as he can. I mean, cause of death was the gunshot, but Marshal was a little evasive about something."

"I don't like it," Niall said.

"Yeah, neither do I."

Their connection crackled. Mat heard the high whistle of some kind of bird—a hawk, maybe—and he wondered where Niall was.

"Why kill Duane now?" Niall asked. "And where has he been all this time?"

Mat had been wondering the same things. Where had Duane been? After the bombing, they'd all thought he'd managed to flee Piedras, but… it seemed not. Who wanted Duane dead, and why?

"Go stay at your mom's until I get back."

"What the hell, Niall." That was going too far, as if Mat needed to run to his mother whenever something went a little sideways. He opened his mouth to argue, but Niall beat him to it.

"Somebody already tried to kill you once. We all thought it was Duane. What if it wasn't—or if he was working with someone? Then the fucker who wants you dead is still out there. And you are not safe." His sentence ended with a growl.

"Niall, there's no reason for you to jump to DEFCON one here. Nothing has happened in the past few months, and there's no reason to think anything will happen now. Maybe whoever was hiding him got sick of it and shot him themself."

There was a long silence on the other end of the line before Mat heard Niall utter the word, "Please." The near-begging tone of his voice staggered Mat.

"Okay," he conceded, "but my mom's house isn't any safer. At home I have Fenrir and an arsenal of weapons at my disposal, and I'm a damn good shot." Niall was overreacting; no way was Mat in danger because Duane Cooper had been offed. If anything, he was safer. "If you really want me to, I will—but I'd like to point out that if there were any actual danger, *which there is not,* I'd be putting Mom and Riley at risk."

Niall ignored him. "I'll be home as soon as I can."

"You'll be home *when* you can."

Mat clicked off and set his phone next to his keys on the desk. Having Duane Cooper show up dead *possibly* put a hole in the theory that he was the one who set the bomb in Mat's cruiser—or, at least, that he'd been acting alone. If it hadn't been Duane, who had it been? And if Duane had done it under orders from someone, who was the shadowy figure they hadn't considered?

TWO
NIALL

Monday

"Can I talk to you in confidence?" Niall asked, at the same time
wondering why he thought calling Shay back was a good idea.

"Of course. What do you need to talk about?" Shay replied,
confusion lacing his voice.

Niall could hear the raucous calls of seagulls over their
connection, and horns honking. Shay must be in downtown Seattle. "I just got off the phone with Mat."

After ending his call with Mat, Niall hadn't put his phone
away, instead immediately calling Shay. Niall's hands were shaking. Why did this have to happen now, when he was on assign-
ment hundreds of miles away from Hidden Harbor?

He'd dragged his feet the rest of spring and into summer
before finally completing the training and extra licensing for
West Coast Forensics, hoping they would get a break and find
Duane Cooper... and it had to happen now? Had the timing
been on purpose? Had Duane's killer waited until Niall was
gone to put a bullet in him and dump him in the harbor? There

was little doubt in Niall's mind that whoever shot Duane had either put the bomb in Mat's cruiser himself or ordered Duane to do it.

"Is this about the body that turned up in the harbor this morning?" Shay asked.

"Yeah. The DB is Duane Cooper, and Mat says he was shot."

"Ah. I hadn't heard that, just that a body had been found."

"And, for the record, it wasn't me who put him there," Niall clarified. Although more than once, back in March, when he thought he'd lost Mat, he'd been willing to take matters into his own hands. Niall had never thought of himself as vengeful until someone had tried to kill Mat Dempsey. "But I need a favor."

"What do you need?" Shay asked.

"Do you have time for a minivacation on Piedras until I get back? With any luck, Leo and I will be wrapping up in a few days." Niall hoped so. He was sick of this tiny mountain town in the back of beyond, Idaho.

"Funny, that," Shay drawled. "I'm closing down my practice here in Seattle and moving back to the island."

Niall was shocked. Shay had been a prominent defense lawyer in Seattle for at least a decade. And he was very good at what he did. Once or twice, Niall had come up against Shay and lost; Tanya Nichols was the one that stuck in his craw. On the other hand, maybe it wasn't a surprise. Shay had been coming up to Piedras quite a bit recently.

He shivered. Wind gusted from the northeast, where the Sawtooth Range jutted from the earth, and the thin shirt he wore was no protection against it. It might be late summer, but—this morning, at least—Graniteville, Idaho, hadn't gotten the memo.

"Why? Not that, you know, I'm not glad." Niall was still getting used to the fact he had a living family member. And yes, he'd called Shay for help, but there were extenuating circumstances.

"Claribel's not getting any younger. I'm not retiring, just

slowing the pace a bit. It feels like the right time. I might actually enjoy having a social life—who knows?"

"Where are you going to live?"

"For now, I've rented a place out past Killegen's Point, kind of on the way to Brooch Resort. I'll have you and Mat out when you get back. Eventually, I'm planning to build a house on the land I inherited from my dad. It's just been sitting empty all these years."

A half smile formed on Niall's lips. "Nice," he said. And it was. Niall was starting to get attached to his older half brother. They'd known each other as kids but never suspected they were related until recently. Or, at least, Niall hadn't suspected.

"In other words, yes, I can keep an eye on Mat, although I'm not sure what good I'll be able to do."

"I know." It killed Niall to ask, to bare his soul to Shay, to admit he had a soft spot the very size and shape of Sheriff Mat Dempsey. "I know I'm overreacting. This... this is just harder than I thought it would be."

"I'll do my best."

The multiple homicide Leo and Niall were assisting on had occurred deep in the heart of Idaho. The bodies had been discovered in Graniteville, in unincorporated Valley County, which meant the case fell to the county sheriff's office.

Almost as soon as the sheriff arrived on the scene, he'd called for help. With only two deputies—much like Mat's department—and none of them with any kind of forensics training, they wouldn't be able to investigate properly. With budgets tighter these days, the smaller law enforcement offices had to make do with inexperienced applicants from community college or even vocational school. Niall wasn't knocking them, it was just a plain, hard truth. Mat dealt with it every day.

As luck would have it, Sheriff Dawson had recently been to a conference where he'd learned about WCF, and he hadn't been too proud to apply for aid—there was also no way he could afford to bring them in on his meager budget.

So here Niall and Leo were, deep in the Payette National Forest, unraveling the how and why behind a double murder. The sheriff had done his best to keep the scene clean, but the bodies had been removed before they arrived, and Niall and Leo were relying on photographs of the scene.

For the past week they'd been in residence at the best the tiny town had to offer, a four-room motel with sketchy Wi-Fi and a collection of VCR tapes spanning two decades of the worst of Hollywood.

Niall stalked back into the local tavern, which was also their unofficial headquarters; Leo was seated at a heavy pine table waiting for him. A large framed photograph hanging on the wall above the table was a picture of the tavern from the 1920s. It hadn't changed much since then, if at all. The tavern had better Wi-Fi than their motel, and the owner was letting them use the space before he opened in the evenings. He even made them coffee, although calling it that was generous.

"We need to hear back from that geologist," Leo commented as Niall sat back down across from him.

Niall nodded agreement. Reaching for his cup, he took a sip of tepid coffee.

"Everything okay at home?" Leo asked.

Leo had seen Niall's reaction to the slew of phone calls and was aware of the situation on Piedras.

"Yeah, for now."

"If you need to go…"

As much as Niall wanted to race home and make sure Mat was safe and stayed that way, he was not bailing on his first job with WCF.

"No. I called in a favor."

"Okay, then I'm going to talk to the hardware store guy again.

Marcus Langley," Leo said, standing up and pushing his chair away from the table.

"Okay." Niall dragged one of the files Leo had been flipping through across the table so he could read it again as well—for at least the thirtieth time. He knew why Leo wanted to talk to Langley; he'd discovered the victims and called it in, but so far there was nothing but Leo's and Niall's gut feelings to connect him to the crime. Which of course they were going to listen to, because Niall couldn't count how many cases he'd solved by paying attention to his instincts.

The couple had been discovered in an ancient walk-in freezer in the kitchen of the R-K Ranch, just outside of town. The bodies had been frozen solid, so... there was that. The first thought had been murder-suicide, as there was a Smith & Wesson M&P340 on the floor next to the man's body. The husband had confronted his wife in the freezer, and whatever the situation was between them, it had escalated, resulting in both their deaths. But Sheriff Dawson had thought the angle of the entry point on the man's forehead looked wrong.

It *was* wrong, and even though the bodies being frozen made the evidence a bit weird, Leo was a gunshot specialist. After examining the body and the photographs, he determined the size of the burn marks around the entry wound was too small for what was supposed to be a close-to-the-head shot—as a suicide might present.

No fingerprints except the victims', but, hidden underneath an enormous plastic container of pickles, they'd found a partial footprint that didn't match either of the couple's shoes, as if maybe the killer had fallen against the container and then moved it back, not realizing he'd left evidence.

Leo and Niall were waiting on Ryder Mann from the home office to (hopefully) identify the type of shoe. And on a forensic geologist Leo was recruiting, to see if she could tell them anything about the soil left behind.

Niall's phone vibrated on the table. He checked the screen—not Mat. He took a deep breath to calm his heart rate before answering.

"Hamarsson."

"Detective Hamarsson? This is Amelia Bjerke."

"Good morning, Dr. Bjerke."

"Good morning to you too, although I imagine you're more interested in what I have to share with you."

Niall knew from the tone of her voice that the forensic geologist had found something. He just hoped it was the something they needed.

"I'll cut to the chase. The soil you sent me has traces of—" She interrupted herself. "Do you want all the scientific terminology or just the outline?"

"The outline is good. You can send the details in an email."

While he listened to her speak, Niall stared at the black-and-white photograph of the Graniteville townspeople on the wall opposite him.

"Long story short, some of the sample you sent me comes from a very specific place in Idaho. The contents are not native to the region where the crime occurred, and there is no way for them to get there naturally."

"What I hear you saying is that the only way the soil could have gotten here is on the bottom of a shoe, tire tread, something like that?" Niall clarified.

"Yes. This ore is rare, found only in Shoshone County, in a relatively small area of the flood plain of the Coeur d'Alene River around the town of Prichard. The chances of it being found in Payette National Forest are next to zero—it is *very* rare."

"What about... a bird or animal?" Niall asked. Birds had messed up scenes for him before.

"No. I mean, I suppose a bird might carry a piece of ore in its beak, but not the three hundred miles from Prichard to Graniteville. Whoever left this at your crime scene stepped in a significant amount in Shoshone County and then carried it south with them in the sole of their shoe. I can tell you where it came from, within a mile or so."

"So we find the footwear and we've got them?" His chest tightened. They were close to this guy; he could feel it.

"I imagine you'll also find it in the footwell of whatever vehicle the perpetrator drove. If you don't find the shoes, find the car."

Niall nodded. Bjerke was right, of course.

"You can testify to all this?"

"Yes, sir. This is my specialty."

"Has Zelinsky convinced you to come aboard yet?" Niall asked.

She chuckled. "I'm considering it."

With the folder he'd been looking at gripped in one hand, Niall stepped outside and glanced up the street. Graniteville Hardware was a bit up from the tavern and across the street, and Leo was just coming out the front door. He waved and jogged over to where Niall waited.

In another life, Niall might have found Leo attractive—before Mat eclipsed everything and everyone else. Leo wasn't as tall as Niall and had blond hair a bit on the long side that gave him a boyish look, although Niall knew Leo was in his early forties. He had a charming and disarming way about him. Niall was certain it had worked in his favor more than once when he was interviewing suspects.

"What's up?" he asked when he reached Niall.

Niall waggled the folder in his grip. "Let's find out who has ties to Prichard, Idaho."

THREE
MAT

By five in the evening, Marshal hadn't called Mat with his findings as promised. Mat's fingers had twitched every time one of the phone lines in the station rang, sure it would be Marshal. But no, it had been calls about missing cats or parking tickets, and one from Stu Dennis asking if Mat had any comment Stu could post for the online newspaper.

The living took precedence over the dead, and if a patient had been admitted to the ER, Marshal would be dealing with that. Duane wasn't going anywhere. Instead of giving in to the urge to call him, Mat left the station to head home and then to his mother's, as he'd promised Niall.

First, though, he stopped at the marina. The station had fielded several calls from boat owners complaining about the gates being locked, and Mat knew he couldn't keep the place closed down much longer. Not when they didn't have any concrete information that Duane's murder had taken place there: no blood, no smoking gun. That he could've been shot near the ferry terminal and floated over was just one scenario Mat had come up with.

A second walk-through revealed no new evidence. When he stopped in at the office, Tom Bellows was still there, and he pushed several paper grocery bags stuffed full of small brown envelopes into Mat's arms. Mat stared down into the bags, wondering what he was looking at.

"Sorry," Tom said. "It's pretty casual here, kinda like camping. Folks just fill one of these out and pay cash for guest moorage." The envelopes had spaces for owners to enter their names, addresses, and phone numbers, as well as the vessel name, length, and draft. Tom shrugged. "We don't verify unless we get somebody who regularly skips out on paying. Or visits a lot, so we want to offer a discount and keep them coming."

Mat sighed. There were hundreds of the crumpled envelopes; Hidden Harbor was a popular destination. Tomorrow he'd pass the bags to Birdy and have her track down and confirm each vessel she could: boring but necessary work. Unlike his other deputies, Birdy could be trusted not to do a half-assed job. The likelihood of them finding something useful in this bag was damn low, but you just never knew.

"Thanks for cooperating, Tom," Mat said.

"Well, this kind of thing isn't good for business," Tom replied. "You got any leads yet?"

"Nothing I can share. As soon as we have something, we'll make a public announcement."

"It was Cooper, though?"

Mat figured that information wouldn't have stayed secret very long. Birdy had already called Duane's ex-wife with the news, also asking if she'd claim his body.

Mat was glad it had been Birdy, and not him, delivering the news. Duane had been AWOL for almost five months, and divorced for years, but Mat had heard the wail of anguish from the other end of the phone call.

"It was," he confirmed. "When was the last time you saw him?"

Tom's bushy gray eyebrows drew together. "He wasn't here too much, not unless it was a police call. He moored his whale tour boat at the public dock by the ferry terminal or, I guess, at East Bay."

East Bay was the marina that had burned down in April. That turned out to be the work of a jealous lover, but for a hot second Mat had considered Duane a top suspect.

Mat nodded. "Thanks again. If you think of anything or something comes up, don't hesitate to call the station or me directly."

After leaving the marina, there was nothing left for him to do but head to his mother's house—after stopping at home for spare clothes.

It still felt a bit odd for Mat to turn in at the Hamarssons' battered mailbox instead of continuing down the road to the home he'd shared with his mother for so many years. Mat, in fact, owned the house his mom, sister, and niece lived in. But as soon as Ella's divorce was final, he'd be changing that; Ella had grown up there too, therefore it was hers as much as his. Their other sister, while not estranged any longer, had no plans to ever move back to Piedras. Putting Ella on the deed was the least Mat could do for her.

Mat's cruiser didn't bump along the drive like it used to. A few months ago, Niall had had more gravel trucked in, smoothing out the bumpy, neglected driveway. He'd also replaced his grandparents' burned-out cabin with a yurt. He claimed the structure wasn't permanent, but Mat wasn't so sure. Niall had been asking for Mat's opinion about various cabin designs, but Mat felt awkward about weighing in. The burned-out cabin had been Niall's grandparents', not Mat's—Niall should be the one making decisions about its replacement. Niall argued they were getting married, so it was both of theirs.

The yurt was basically a cabin anyway. It had a kitchen area, a bathroom, an open great room area, and a bedroom. A pine deck wrapped around the yurt, and Mat and Niall had spent most of their time at home this summer stretched out on loungers on it, watching the world go by. They watched sunsets. They watched the tide come and go. They watched Niall's wolfhound, Fenrir, play in the waves with Mat's niece, Riley. The Perseid meteor shower had been a highlight of midsummer.

It wasn't the same with Niall gone, but Mat was going to have to get used to it. Niall was a driven investigator, and West Coast Forensics was the perfect fit for him. He'd be traveling a lot.

Mat slowed to a stop, parking his newly issued cruiser in his normal spot next to Niall's Subaru. The wind picked up, as it often did this time of the day, gusting against the walls of the yurt and making the branches of the Douglas firs along the edge of the property dance. An impatient woof sounded from inside. Smiling, Mat climbed out and headed to the front door.

Fenrir gave him a toothy grin and a tail wag before loping off to do his business. Within minutes the big dog was back, nosing his way through the partially open front door.

"That was fast," Mat said as he tossed some t-shirts and a couple pairs of jeans and whatnot into a duffel bag. "Do you want to go visit Riley?"

Fenrir twirled in pleasure at Mat's words. If Mat was going to be staying at the family home, logically Fenrir would too—besides, Mat didn't think he'd be let in the house if he didn't bring Fenrir along.

Mat sat back in his chair. It creaked slightly under his weight.

"Thanks for feeding me, Mom," he said, rubbing his belly and winking at her.

"*Pfft*, of course." Alyson stood and began to clear the dishes.

"Let me do that, Mom. It's the least I can do for imposing on you."

"You're not imposing," she insisted.

When he'd arrived, Mat had shared what he could about the discovery of Cooper's body and how Cooper turning up made Niall nervous because it meant an unsub might still be out there gunning for Mat.

Mat took the plates from his mom's hands and stacked them on the counter next to the sink. Riley and Fenrir were in the backyard. It had slipped Mat's mind that his sister was away too; she'd traveled back to Texas to pack up the things she wanted from her almost ex-husband. It was part of the divorce negotiations. Mat found it sad that what's-his-name cared more about possessions than he did about his daughter.

Turning, he leaned one hip against the counter and asked a question that had been on his mind lately. "Mom, was it hard being married to a law officer?" He'd never considered the question before; he'd never thought he would be getting married.

Alyson snorted and raised an eyebrow at him. "It's a little late to be asking that question, isn't it? Both you and Niall are in law enforcement and face danger every day. On top of that, you worry about Niall, and I know he worries about you. I can't even imagine how it feels for you. You're magnets pushing and pulling at the same time.

"But yes, it was hard for me. Your dad believed so hard in what he did. He thought he could make a difference in the community, and he did. He loved being able to help people, to catch the bad guys—not that there was a lot of that here then, mostly petty crime. Still, I worried. I thought I knew what I was getting into when we got married, but in all honesty, it does take a toll."

"You always seemed happy," Mat remarked.

"We were happy. Happier than most, I think."

"But…"

"But worry takes its toll." She cocked her head. "If you want some advice from your old mom, make time for yourselves. Take those holidays, use up your personal time. Cherish every moment. Let Birdy Flynn carry some of the load, see if the county will let you hire a few more deputies."

"The county has agreed to hiring someone, so there's that."

"Well, that's good."

Mat turned on the faucet so he could rinse their dishes. This was a comforting evening routine, something he'd done for years before moving in with Niall. Alyson used to wait for him, and they would stay up talking about their days.

"Flynn is going to be in charge while we're on our honeymoon."

"Have you two decided on a venue yet?" His mom tried to sound casual, but Mat heard the repressed curiosity in her tone.

Mat released a sigh but smiled. It was killing his mother not to be in charge of all the details. But he and Niall were firm about it: they were going to plan their wedding themselves—and now he chuckled, because they sounded like a pair of three-year-olds. "We're thinking about getting married in Hawaii, then having a reception here on the island later."

Of course, they hadn't yet bought their plane tickets or made reservations at a resort. Were they even resort guys? Most of Hawaii's appeal seemed to be distance from Piedras. As much as Mat loved his home and the community he served, sometimes it was nice for them not to know every minute detail of his life.

His mom was quiet for a bit, then said, "I'm going to make a pot of decaf so we can talk this over."

"Mom," Mat groaned. "Niall and I are the ones getting married."

She plugged in the coffee maker before pulling the decaf beans from the freezer. "Yes, but this is a cry for help if ever I've heard one." Reaching across him, she filled the carafe with water and then poured it into the coffee maker.

Rolling his eyes, Mat finished rinsing the plates and stowed them in the dishwasher. By the time he was done, his mom had the coffee started.

"Cookies?" she asked.

The back door banged open and Riley and Fenrir burst inside, bringing the musty pre-autumn air with them.

Riley eyed her grandmother with a decidedly predatory look in her eyes. "Is it cookie time yet, Grandma?"

Alyson took in her grubby granddaughter with a single glance. "First it's bath time, then you can have some cookies."

"Grandma," Riley protested, throwing her head back and looking at the ceiling as if her grandmother had asked her to do the most ridiculous thing in the world.

"Bath," Mom said firmly.

"Hmph."

Riley dashed out of the kitchen and down the hallway, and a minute later they could hear the bath water running. Fenrir padded out into the living room, where Alyson had a dog bed set up for him. Mat heard him as he turned around three times and settled with a thump, something that always made Mat smile. Why did dogs do that?

His mom turned to him. "So, about the wedding."

"No cookies until we let you help?" Mat teased.

"Something like that. Honestly, Mat, I won't do anything without running it past you first, but you and Niall are both very busy—too busy to plan your wedding. And Hawaii is ridiculous. If you really want to go there, go for your honeymoon. There are several places here on Piedras that would be lovely and affordable for the ceremony."

Alyson slid out a file folder that had been tucked in between her cookbooks and handed it to him. It was stuffed full of various venue brochures from around the San Juans and the mainland.

"Look at these while I pour coffee and set the cookies out."

It was a losing battle… and his mom was right. Neither he nor Niall had the time to plan a big event. He sighed; they should've eloped when they had the chance.

That night, Mat slept on the living room couch, as he'd given his room up to Riley when he moved out months ago. It was comfortable enough, and Fenrir slept on the rug next to him, his doggy snores keeping Mat company. It niggled at Mat that Niall didn't call, but he didn't have great cell reception where he was in backcountry Idaho. Before tucking his phone away, Mat shot him a text confirming he was staying at Alyson's; they could talk tomorrow.

FOUR

NIALL

Monday

Niall and Leo had installed themselves back at their table in the tavern, and Leo was looking on impatiently as Niall chatted with one of the analysts who worked from the WCF offices.

"Yes, it's a specialty hiking boot, pricey and popular. The tread is fairly unique, but it's the wear on this one that really sets it off." Ryder said, his tone confident.

"So you say, Sherlock. Is the perp six feet tall, right-handed, with a lisp and a southern accent?" Niall teased. He liked Ryder Mann and Scarlett Weaver; Leo called them the WCF home team. It was easy to get a rise out of Ryder, so of course Niall goaded him whenever he had the chance.

"Jackass," Ryder grumbled. "Give me all the crap you want, but I'm telling you, from the wear marks on this tread, I'd say that the owner has some kind of permanent injury or disability. The arch is far more worn down than the rest of the sole. Maybe he walks with a limp or a shuffle?"

There was a rustling sound, and then everything got muffled.

Niall glanced around the tavern. Eventually Ryder came back on the line. "Scarlett's got something for you guys. Have Leo call her line." He clicked off without saying goodbye.

"Scarlett's got something," Niall informed Leo after summing up what Ryder had told him about the boot print.

Now it was Niall's turn to listen to a one-sided conversation. Leo nodded as he listened, raising his eyebrows at something Scarlett said. Niall knew Leo had asked Scarlett to see if she could find a connection between Graniteville and Prichard. It seemed she had.

Leo ended the call and shoved his phone back into this pocket.

"Marcus Langley has a cabin outside of Prichard, close to the river. He also has a recreational mining permit."

"You think he brought that ore in?" Niall asked.

"The stuff Bjerke told us about, yep," Leo agreed. "Marcus is probably mining for gold or silver. Did you know Idaho is one of the world's biggest producers of silver?"

"Focus, Leo."

"There's literally a five-mile radius where that ore occurs in conjunction with silver deposits in Idaho."

"Let me guess. Langley's cabin is within that radius."

"You, sir, are the winner. We're gonna need a search warrant."

Four hours later, Sheriff Dawson was in possession of two search warrants, one for the hardware store—Langley lived above it—and one for his late-model Jeep, and they were headed back to Graniteville.

"How do you want to do this?" Niall asked Leo. As the newest team member, he didn't want to step on any toes.

Leo pursed his lips, focusing on the highway ahead of them. Graniteville was just a few miles away. They'd accompanied Dawson to McCall in case the judge wanted to talk with them. She hadn't. The sheriff had done a great job of presenting the evidence against Langley.

"Dawson's had his deputies keeping an eye out while we were

gone. One of them is stationed in front of the store, the other is in back. Dawson will serve the warrants, and we'll back him up."

Dawson didn't think Langley was a flight risk. "His family is here. He's a bit of an odd guy, but," the sheriff had said, shrugging, "so are a lot of us."

Graniteville Hardware was situated in an old two-story clapboard building that had seen better days. The structure may have been white once, but over time it had faded to a dingy shade of gray. There was little left of the original paint, and a few pieces of siding needed to be replaced.

The front door was recessed between two large windows. At nearly four in the afternoon, the rays of the late summer sun reflecting off the watery panes of ancient glass were blinding. But Niall remembered from his previous visit that one side of the window displays had things like climbing ropes, carabiners, and gloves, because Langley catered to hikers and campers who stopped in the tiny town. The other window had rakes, hoes, bags of lawn seed (why, Niall wondered), shovels, and, randomly, what seemed to be empty paint buckets.

It was an unsettling walk back in time as the three of them pushed through the door. A bell hooked to the door handle chimed, announcing their presence. The store was dimly lit, the aisles narrow and the shelves packed with goods of all kinds. On a top shelf against one wall, Niall spotted an ancient and dust-shrouded clothes dummy lying on its back, one handless arm lifted into the air as if asking for help. A stack of MREs had fallen or been left on the floor. Niall's booted foot hit them, and he winced as they scattered across the aisle. A fly buzzed loudly, bumping its body against one of the windows.

Langley's office was in the back, but he didn't come out to meet them.

"Are we sure he's here?" Niall asked quietly.

Leo nodded, "His Jeep is still in back, and he hasn't left through the front or back door. He's been here since we left."

A tingling between Niall's shoulder blades was alerting him that something was not right, but he couldn't put his finger on it. He grazed Leo's wrist with his finger to get his attention and made eye contact. Leo nodded again. He felt it too; the store was too quiet. The fly had stopped bumping against the window. Somewhere, a clock ticked.

Sheriff Dawson was about five feet ahead of them. "Langley?" he called out.

Langley didn't answer. The tingling between Niall's shoulder blades intensified. Some primal instinct screamed, "Danger." They needed to get out, *now*.

"I think we should—"

The building exploded. There must have been sound of some kind, but Niall didn't hear it after the first monstrous detonation. Around them, in a kind of slow motion, shelves began to collapse, the inventory vomiting off the metal shelving and onto the cement floor. Years of dust plumed into the air, making it impossible for Niall to breathe or see, and he still couldn't hear. What he remembered later was how the clothes dummy slowly teetered back and forth before finally tumbling off its perch to land behind a display of uncut keys that glittered in the afternoon sunshine. What a weird thing to notice, he thought.

Then the back of his head exploded with agony. He shut his eyes against the pain, but he could see stars as the ground lifted up to meet him. He tried to open his mouth, to say something to Leo, but everything went dark.

FIVE

MAT

Tuesday

"Mat." His mother shook his shoulder. "The phone is for you."

Mat sat up, groggy. It had taken him forever to fall asleep, the sounds of the house he'd grown up in no longer familiar and comforting. The tendrils of a dream clung to him, strands of a spiderweb he couldn't brush away quickly enough.

"What?" He realized Alyson was holding his phone out to him." Who is it?" He took the phone from her, pressing it against his chest. His brain still wasn't working right. "What time is it?"

He got up from the couch and padded into the kitchen. The stove clock read 3:20. He'd been asleep about two hours. His dream wouldn't dissipate. Irrationally, it seemed like answering the phone made it stickier and more ominous. Maybe he'd heard the ringing and hadn't been able to wake himself up? He was that tired; he shook his head again to try to wake himself up a little more.

His mom followed him. "I don't know who it is, they wouldn't say. I'll make coffee."

Nodding thanks, Mat sucked in a deep breath and brought the phone up to his ear. "Dempsey here."

His mom busied herself at the sink, but Mat was aware she was listening to every word of his side of the conversation. Her movements were careful yet sharp; Mat wanted to tell her to go back to bed but knew she wouldn't. If the worst had happened— if *something* had happened to Niall—Mat didn't know if he could handle the comfort she'd try to offer him.

"Sheriff Dempsey," a younger, worried, male voice replied, "my name is Ryder Mann. I work with Leo Zelinsky and Niall Hamarsson at West Coast Forensics."

Mat's stomach lurched; he was going to vomit. "Has something happened?" he managed.

"Sort of, but first—both Zelinsky and Hamarsson are going to be fine, from what Leo's told me. But they were admitted to the hospital last night for observation."

The relief was so overwhelming, Mat nearly collapsed into one of the kitchen chairs. Instead he just grabbed the back of one to hold himself steady. He had so many questions. The first one was, why hadn't he been notified right away?

"I'm sure you're wondering why it took so long for me to call," Mann said, "or why Investigator Hamarsson hasn't called you himself. My apologies. Field Lead Zelinsky has authorized me to share the information I have about the situation."

Mat heard Mann take a deep breath, then he began to speak. "Zelinsky and Hamarsson were assisting in the service of a search warrant yesterday evening, in a hardware store in Graniteville. As they entered the store, the suspect detonated a homemade bomb. The guy had made the structure into a booby trap. Hamarsson and Zelinsky were hit on the head by flying debris and both were unconscious for a time, so the EMTs admitted them for overnight observation.

"Their cell phones were destroyed, which is why we couldn't contact you immediately—and it took longer than any of us here in the office liked to find out about the incident. In my opinion, those fuckers out in Idaho took their time on purpose. I can't prove anything, of course, but Leo has a big-ass tattoo of a rainbow merman on his arm. And," Mann added, "I didn't think you'd want this call on the Piedras County Sheriff's Office emergency line. As soon as Hamarsson was able to, he gave me this number." He rattled off the number of the hospital and Niall's room number. "I just talked to him, so I know he's awake. If you dial direct, he will answer, but at this time of night the switchboard won't put you through. And don't worry, I'm getting new phones to them ASAP."

"Thank you…" Mister Mann? Mann? Mat's brain would not cooperate.

"Just call me Ryder. It's easier. And you're welcome."

"You mean," Mat clarified, because something Ryder had said was just beginning to compute, "the hospital dragged their feet because Niall and Leo are gay?"

"Like I said, I can't prove anything," Ryder replied.

"I just… don't understand that kind of hate."

"Me either."

He disconnected, quickly punching in the numbers Ryder had provided. The phone rang once before Niall's growly voice came on the line, and for the first time in five minutes, Mat could breathe. He sucked in a shuddering lungful of oxygen.

"I'm fine, Mat." Niall's voice cut through Mat's lingering panic.

Relief at hearing Niall speaking—and grouchy as fuck—coursed through Mat's veins. "What the hell happened?" he demanded, standing up again and pacing to the kitchen door and back to the table.

Niall cleared his throat before replying. "I'm sure Ryder told you, but the perp set up a booby trap and we walked right into it. The entire building came down on top of us. Leo and I got off easy. The sheriff was trapped in the rubble, and they had to dig him out. He's having surgery on his leg."

"The perp?" Mat asked, but he thought he knew the answer. He padded to the back door and looked out over the yard he knew so well. Dawn was still an hour or so away. Mist clung to the grasses and draped elegantly along the tops of the fir trees that surrounded the lot. He shivered. The coffee pot gurgled and the first drops of coffee landed in the bottom of the carafe with a splat and a hiss. He watched as his mom opened a bag of bagels, sliced one, and dropped it in the toaster. This is what happened: regardless of people living or dying, you slept, had coffee, ate breakfast. For all his years in law enforcement, Mat had never felt it so keenly before.

"The fucker took the easy way out. Blew himself up," Niall ground out, bringing Mat back from the rabbit hole he'd fallen down.

It may have been the easy way, but the fucker had almost taken Niall with him, and that shook Mat to the core. Especially after the conversation with his mom last night.

"Okay, um..." Mat caught his mom's eye, mouthing "He's okay" to her, even though she had to know already. "I'll call Birdy in and start heading your way. You don't want to fly with a concussion." He looked around the kitchen as if his car keys were going to miraculously appear. "If I catch the first ferry, I think I can get to you by early evening." It was a grueling eight-hour drive if traffic cooperated, which it never did.

"Mat, I don't have a serious concussion—the doc thinks maybe not one at all. I was just knocked out," Niall growled, interrupting his panicked planning. "Ryder's got everything taken care of. He's already on his way. He and someone else from the office are coming to get us. I guess Ryder got the short stick, because he's driving me to Anacortes. I'll walk on the ferry from there."

If Niall thought Mat wasn't meeting him at the Anacortes ferry landing, he was several cards short of a full deck.

"Ryder and company should be here in a couple hours. They're flying in and then renting cars."

Mat didn't go back to sleep. By the time he'd argued with Niall and finally hung up the phone, the clock had ticked over to four a.m., and he'd been wide awake. He and his mom had sat in the kitchen sipping coffee and talking about everything *but* losing a partner to violence.

He went in to work early and spent most of the day at the station, digging through the envelopes he'd been planning to hand off to Birdy. It had slipped his mind that today was her day off, and his other deputies were not investigators. Thankfully, the Island County Council had finally authorized the hiring of another deputy and posted the position a few weeks earlier. He'd already interviewed a few candidates.

While he was staring at his desktop, the screen flickered. He quickly clicked Save.

There were so many visiting boats; Hidden Harbor was a popular destination. By midafternoon, Mat resorted to the reading glasses he kept tucked in the top drawer of his desk. Was he slightly vain? Yes. But the damn glasses made him feel ancient.

He'd created an Excel doc and was laboriously entering the information from each envelope, translating various scribbles and chicken scratches into data. What he was looking for he didn't exactly know, but in his experience as an investigator it was things like this, the tedious stuff, that often led to a break in a case.

Now it was after seven in the evening, and Niall was arriving on the next ferry. Mat chuckled to himself because apparently Niall hadn't been able to shake his chaperone in Anacortes. Ryder

Mann had been given strict instructions to get Niall home, and dropping him off at a ferry dock didn't count. And, yeah, Mat was grateful for Ryder sticking to the plan.

"Hello?" Shay Delacombe's voice cut through his wandering thoughts. Mat swiped the glasses off his face and stood from his desk, waving Shay over.

Shay was dark and tall, like Niall, although not quite as heavily muscled. Now that they knew Shay and Niall were half brothers, the similarities between them seemed obvious, and Mat wondered that no one had noticed over the years. It was amazing to him how often people only saw what they wanted to see.

"Come on back. What's up? Want some coffee or something?"

Shay stepped around the barrier and into the bullpen—calling it that was a bit of a stretch, though, since it housed five desks and two or three officers at a time at the most. Mat noticed Shay wasn't wearing one of his usual suits; instead he had on blue jeans, sneakers, and a comfortable-looking dark green sweater that reminded Mat the weather was getting more and more fall-like every day.

"Good coffee, or the stuff everybody else drinks?"

Mat nodded toward their tiny break room. "I'll make a pot of the good stuff."

Shay followed him and leaned against the door of the nook-sized room. "I heard the news."

Mat glanced over his shoulder, meeting Shay's dark gaze. "Are you here as an attorney, or..."

Shay's wolfish grin flashed. "Niall called me."

"Niall called you?" Christ, it was even worse than he'd thought.

"Apparently he thinks you need a sitter while he's gone. Seriously, though, he's very concerned about Cooper showing up dead right now, and I can understand why."

With careful, methodical movements, Mat prepped the coffee and pushed the On button before turning back around and leaning one hip against the counter. "Unbelievable." He shook his head.

"What?"

"A perp blew up a building yesterday, and it fell on Niall and his new partner. I think he's the one who needs a guardian angel."

"He's okay?" Shay asked sharply, his expression full of concern.

"They kept him overnight for observation, but he's on his way home. He should be on the next ferry. The suspect didn't survive, and other agencies are taking over now."

Shay crossed his arms, leaning against the doorjamb. "He's a damn lucky man."

"Don't I know it. So, Niall wanted you to... what?" Because Niall was going to hear from him if he thought the sheriff of Piedras County needed a bodyguard.

"I don't know, exactly, but I was headed up here anyway. I'm closing my office in Seattle and moving back here. In fact, it's done already."

"Wow, Shay, that's great." Having Shay on Piedras could be a good thing, Mat thought. Shay and Niall were slowly getting to know each other, and the move would make it easier.

The coffee maker beeped. Mat twisted around, grabbing two clean mugs and filling them with the hot brew.

"There's creamer in the minifridge if you need it," Mat offered. "Moving here is a big change for you, right?"

That reminded him, they'd received an application that came with high recommendations, and he'd scheduled an interview for the following afternoon. If Soren Jorgensen interviewed as well as his resume indicated and he accepted their offer, he'd be moving to Hidden Harbor from Skagit, a small town on the mainland just south of the Canadian border. Mat desperately needed another deputy. The island's population was expanding, and his department was already stretched thin.

Shay took the mug Mat offered him, sipping at the hot liquid before answering Mat's question.

"Not really. I've been thinking about it for a while now. Claribel isn't getting any younger, and even though I'm only her great-nephew, I'm the one who watches out for her. Not like her useless sons can be bothered. I've rented a house out past Killegen's Point, for now."

Mat was sure when Shay said house, he meant a very nice home. The rentals past Killegen's Point were high-end, and Mat couldn't imagine Shay settling for anything less than the best. At the far end of Piedras, a mile or so past their small airstrip, was Brooch Harbor Resort. The harbor there was actually more protected than Hidden Harbor, but it was smaller and privately owned.

The Brooch was upscale, owned by one of the oldest families on Piedras—not Delacombes or Dempseys, surprisingly. They even hired their own private security. That was fine with Mat; he didn't have the time to send a deputy out there every time somebody lost a diamond earring.

"Have you found anything out about Cooper?" Shay probed, bringing Mat back to the conversation at hand.

"I talked to Marshal earlier. As I thought, death was caused by the gunshot to the chest. He'd probably been dead twenty-four hours, give or take, but Marshal thinks less because the body hadn't been, uh, nibbled on much. And he wasn't a true floater yet, he'd been dragged by the tide. This is off the record, by the way." He raised an eyebrow at Shay.

"I'm a lawyer, not the press."

"You know what I mean." Opening the fridge, Mat pulled out the milk and poured some into his coffee mug. He needed the caffeine after getting less than three hours' sleep.

"Yeah, I won't say anything. What else?" Shay prompted.

"He was in bad shape, and not just from being shot. Marshal said he was severely underweight, as if he hadn't been eating."

"If he's been on the island all this time, it would've been hard for him to hide without help. Everyone knew to be on the lookout for him."

"I guess." It bothered Mat, though. Where had Cooper been hiding, and why was he killed now? Had he become a threat or perhaps a burden?

Mat's cell phone vibrated. He pulled it out of his pocket and read the text. Looking over at Shay, he said, "The ferry is about twenty minutes out, and Niall's on it. Want to ride over there with me?"

SIX

NIALL

Tuesday

Ryder was driving Niall up a fucking wall. The kid was nice in small doses, a great person with a sharp mind. But after a ten-hour car trip with a nagging headache, Niall was at his wit's end. Ryder seemed to think he needed to speak for both of them, all the time, for the entire drive. Every single fucking minute.

Niall had pretended to be asleep for an hour or so, but his head ached enough he couldn't quite nod off for real. Furthermore, the car Ryder had been able to rent on short notice did not accommodate Niall's long legs. The doctor in Idaho had said keeping him overnight had been a precaution but he still needed to take it easy for a few days. Niall pondered what the definition of "taking it easy" actually was.

Normally, the ferry ride would've soothed him. Niall loved being on the water at night, loved watching the San Juan Islands slide by, the dramatic evergreen trees defying gravity, trunks jutting off of cliffs, rugged silhouettes catching the light of the moon. But there was no moon tonight. In fact, Ryder had informed him just minutes ago that this was a black moon, the third new moon in a season with four moons. Who the fuck knew that kind of shit?

The moon *was* absent from the sky tonight; the only light visible was from the faraway stars. It was a perfect night for smuggling and other nefarious goings-on. A thought struck him. Why he hadn't realized it hours ago, Niall didn't know. "Where are you staying?" he asked his chaperone.

This was the last ferry of the night that would sail all the way back to Anacortes. There would be one more inter-island ferry but none to get Ryder to get back to the mainland. And it was the tail end of tourist season, and likely the ferry line was backed up for fucking miles. They'd only made it on this run because Ryder had flashed his WCF ID around like it was government issued. Whatever, it got them on the boat.

"Um." Ryder glanced at Niall, his brown eyes wide behind the thick horn-rimmed glasses he wore. "I figured I'd just grab a room somewhere. I was going to look online"—he waved his smartphone around—"but there's no service out here."

Another thing Niall liked about the long, normally quiet ferry ride: no cell service until about ten or twenty minutes out of Hidden Harbor. But in any case, Ryder wasn't going to find a room this late in the day.

God, he was such an asshole, but all he wanted was to collapse in bed with Mat's arms around him and let his lover take care of him. He didn't want to deal with Ryder Mann and where he was going to sleep tonight. But he owed it to Leo—and to Ryder, who'd driven a hell of a long way to help him out.

The crackly announcement that all drivers needed to head back to their cars came over the ferry's sound system. Niall and Ryder slowly made their way to where the car was parked and got inside, waiting for the ferry to dock.

After what seemed like hours to Niall, the big boat bumped against the pilings and settled against the dock. They watched a dockworker on the land side throw out a massive rope toward the deckhand waiting at the front of the ferry. There was an audible thud when it hit the deck. The woman grabbed it with both hands and jogged forward, looping the rope around a huge post. Niall wondered if it would actually hold the ferry or if the ritual was just for show. He knew from experience that the water around them was churning from the ferry's engines.

"Where am I taking you?" Ryder asked as he turned on the engine and began to follow the car ahead of them off the ferry and into Hidden Harbor.

Niall gestured to the right, toward a small gravel parking lot that acted as a waiting area, usually for picking up walk-on passengers. Two figures stood next to a police cruiser. He recognized one of them as Shay. Standing next to him was the person Niall wanted to see most in the world right now, Mat Dempsey.

Who would've thought, a year ago, that Niall Hamarsson, the tough Seattle homicide detective, would move back to the island he'd done most of his growing up on and fall in love with the local sheriff? He snorted. Someone who read too many romance novels, that's who.

"Pull in there," he said to Ryder.

"Jesus, Niall, you look awful," Shay blurted.

"Thanks, Shay, that's what happens when a building falls on you," Niall growled as he eased himself out of the rental car. After being jammed in the car for hours and then sitting on the ferry, he was sore and stiff, and not in the way he most enjoyed.

Ryder came around the front of the car. "This is Ryder Mann," Niall said. "Ryder, my partner, Sheriff Mat Dempsey, and my half brother, Shay Delacombe."

"They grow you guys big out here," Ryder joked, waggling his eyebrows at them. He was five foot seven or eight, so a few inches shorter than Mat and a head shorter than Niall and Shay. Definitely the outlier among them.

"Shay, thanks for coming out," Niall said, ignoring Ryder's comment.

"Yeah, about that," Mat began, his eyes narrowing.

"So hey, does anyone know where I can stay for the night?" Ryder interrupted, which this time Niall was grateful for. He held up his phone. "I just checked on Hotels.com, and everything seems to be booked up. I can understand why," he added, looking around. Even in the growing dark, Piedras was beautiful and peaceful.

Niall sighed. Looking at Mat, he asked, "Do you think Alyson would put him up for a couple nights?" Because so help him god, if he had to spend more time with Ryder today, there was going to be a fourth homicide this year on Piedras.

Ryder opened his mouth, probably to argue, but Niall kept talking, shooting him what he hoped was a sufficiently quelling look. "Leo asked me to make sure Ryder took a couple days before he dropped off the rental car and hopped a plane back to the Bay Area."

Ryder snapped his mouth shut, eyes wide. Clearly, he'd had no idea about Leo's request.

"From what Leo told me, Ryder hasn't taken a vacation in years."

As they were talking, the other cars in the small lot began pulling out and heading toward their homes. Across the street, the lights went out in Harbor Barber, owner Kim Carr closing up for the night. Niall had the nebulous thought it was about time for him to get his hair cut.

"But…" Ryder began.

"I wouldn't argue, if I were you." Niall glared at his coworker. "Accept the damn hospitality."

Ryder snapped his mouth shut.

"Niall." Mat's soothing tone washed over him. "I don't think that's how we treat people who just traveled across multiple states to bring you home. Let me call my mom. I'm sure she'll say yes."

"Don't bother," Shay interjected. "He can stay with me."

Ryder's head swiveled toward Shay, his eyes wide.

Mat frowned at Shay. "Do you even have furniture? Have you actually moved in yet?"

"Let's not argue with the man," Niall said. "If Shay's offering, we're accepting. All I want is to have you take me home. My head is pounding. I want to lie down, and I want you to be there with me. I don't want to deal wi—er, see Alyson tonight. I love your mom, but I'm done. Except for Fenrir. Where is he?"

Ryder said, "I think that's the longest sentence I've ever heard you string together." He glanced at Shay again, assessing him. "If you're positive?"

"My place is huge. I won't even know you're there," Shay assured him.

Niall grumbled, "I'm certain that's impossible."

"Okay, it's time to get you home." To Shay, Mat said, "I'll call you tomorrow."

Niall's skull throbbed again, and all he wanted was to be lying down with Mat next to him. That's all. Was it too much to ask? Mat moved to his side, seeming to understand Niall didn't want help, but he *needed* Mat to be right there.

"Wait!" Ryder cried out after them. "Sheriff Dempsey, Hamarsson's bag is in the trunk."

Niall was tired enough he managed to doze off during the drive home from Hidden Harbor. After he eased his aching body out of the cruiser, he leaned on Mat as they slowly made their way inside.

"Fenrir's at Mom's," Mat said. "I'll need to either leave to go get him or ask her to drop him by. Or we can get him tomorrow.

It's not as if he's any trouble. He and Riley are probably planning their takeover of the world."

Niall collapsed onto the bed with a groan. He was too old for this kind of shit. Mat moved into his space, wrapping his arms around Niall's shoulders, and Niall let his head rest against Mat's stomach. Mat's sheriff's uniform was scratchy against his face, but Niall didn't care. The now-familiar scent of Mat enveloped him, and he was able to relax for the first time since he'd woken up in the hospital the night before.

"God, Niall," Mat whispered into his hair.

Niall understood the weight behind Mat's words, had himself suffered in the spring. He kept his head pressed against Mat's body, his arms wrapped around Mat's waist. Mat's scent, the low-key gurgle of his stomach, the remote beat of his heart, all worked in tandem, making Niall's aches and pains fade to a dull hum.

Finally Mat pulled away. "Let me help you undress and then I'll grab you something for your head."

Minutes later, Niall was ensconced in their bed naked, because that's how he slept best, with the lights off. Mat padded back in carrying a glass of water and a couple acetaminophen. Taking the pills from him, Niall swallowed them dry and lay back against the pillows.

Mat set the glass on the bedside table. "You need to stay hydrated. It will help."

"Any news on Cooper?" Niall asked as Mat moved around in the bedroom, using the dim light from the kitchen area to undress and find a pair of sleep pants and a T-shirt.

"Oh, yeah," Mat said, his words muffled as he pulled the shirt over his head, hiding the scars from the bombing from Niall's view. "I talked to Marshal. It was definitely the gunshot that killed him, but"—he walked back over to the bedside and sat down carefully—"he was underweight. As in almost starving."

"Huh," Niall grunted. That was interesting.

"Yeah. If I had to guess, I'd say he weighed around 190 last I saw him. Marshal said the body weighed about 160 pounds. Thirty pounds is a lot to lose in just under five months. His muscle mass was definitely depleted. Where was he all this time?" Mat mused.

"Huh," Niall repeated. Where *had* Cooper been? After a while, they'd assumed he'd managed to flee the island—but maybe he'd never left.

"And" —Mat's tone changed— "this time, I'm going to let it slide that you called Shay to keep an eye on me while you were gone. I'm not even going to dwell on the fact that this time it was *you* who was hurt."

Niall would've rolled his eyes, but it was too much effort. And it hurt.

"You are going to rest until Marshal clears you for work." Mat stopped, flashing an odd sort of guilty look at Niall. "And, um, Mom is helping us plan the wedding."

SEVEN

MAT

Wednesday

Mat left while Niall was still in bed the next morning, the comforter protecting him from the slight nip in the air, a prelude to the fall weather approaching. He'd extracted a promise from Niall that he would take it easy. Mat wasn't sure he believed Niall's agreement, seeing as a bored Niall historically led to trouble. He'd tried to make a case for staying home, but really, it wasn't an option with everything going on.

Niall had insisted Mat go to the station. He claimed his head didn't hurt as much as it had the day before, but Mat wasn't taking any chances. Before he left, he called his mom and asked her to please drop Fenrir off at their place... and, of course, with that would come some powerful Alyson Dempsey love.

"He says he feels better, but I don't want him driving or anything until Marshal says it's okay." Maybe having Fenrir around would keep Niall grounded. Mat hoped so, anyway.

Then Mat left a message on Marshal's phone asking if he had time to stop by and check on Niall.

. . .

Mat had a busy day ahead. As much as he wished it not to be, as much as he'd wanted to stay home and take care of Niall, today's checklist could not be delegated to Birdy. He hated dumping the remainder of the envelopes in her lap, but at this point they were the only lead they had. It was as if Duane's body had shown up out of the blue.

"I sent you the Excel doc I started yesterday," Mat said to Birdy when she arrived. "When we have a complete list, we can look for… something. I'm guessing we won't find anything, but once they're all entered, let's concentrate on the dates around the bombing and this past month or so."

"What about February, when Chastity Reynolds was discovered?" Birdy asked.

Mat leaned back in his chair, mulling over the idea. Could Chastity's death be connected to Duane's somehow? Jeffrey Reynolds had confessed to her murder, but was it possible the events were related in a way they hadn't linked yet, if only because there had been nothing to indicate an association?

Something one of his old sergeants used to say floated to the surface of Mat's memories: "When the shit hits the fan, turn it off." What McCallum had meant was slow down, breathe, throw away assumptions and take the evidence piece by piece as objectively as possible, and then rebuild the puzzle.

"Good thinking, Birdy. Finish entering the information on the envelopes, then start a year back and move forward to the most recent entries. Let's see if we find a pattern, a boat or person who stands out—jeez, I don't even know, but if it's there, we'll know it when we see it."

Then, of course, the phone rang, throwing all his carefully laid plans for the day into chaos.

. . .

"Jeffrey Reynolds wants to talk to you."

Amanda Tate was Reynolds's current lawyer. Mat didn't like her much. He was never a fan of lawyers trying to get the guys he arrested out of jail.

Reynolds, aka Trey Jackson, was being held pending trial for the murders of Chastity Reynolds and Mat's older brother Sean. The case against him for Chastity's death was solid, so solid the judge hadn't granted bail. The deeper investigators dug, the higher the pile of evidence linking Jeffrey to Chastity grew, but the key was the colorful scarf that had been wrapped around her neck. A scarf gifted to Jeffrey by his unsuspecting boyfriend. Mat's brain skittered past that fact; he didn't want to think about Reynolds being anywhere near Niall.

"Why would I want to talk to him?" Mat asked, even though he had just been thinking about the man before she called.

"He claims he has something to tell you'll want to know."

Tate's tone grated on Mat's last nerve. She was just the most recent in a line of several public defenders… and the most persistent. Another reason why Mat found her irritating. She was doing her job, after all. Persistence was a great trait for the defendant, but Mat was tired of dealing with her and the public defender's office.

"I thought you weren't his lawyer anymore." He'd heard Jeffrey had fired his attorneys and was planning on defending himself.

And why, after months in county jail, would Reynolds want to talk to Mat now? Was it coincidence, after Cooper's body appearing two days ago, that Reynolds was asking for him?

Tate sighed into Mat's pause. "I'm doing you a favor, Dempsey. Whatever problem you have with me, I suggest you put it aside. He claims you'll want to hear what he has to say."

"Do you know what information he's got?" Mat asked her.

"All he would tell me is that it's something about your father's death. I thought that might get your attention."

His father? That was not what Mat had expected to hear. A feeling of foreboding settled heavily in his stomach; he tapped his sternum, trying to make the response disappear.

His father had been killed over ten years ago in a boating accident. What information could Jeffrey Reynolds possibly have about him? Mat quickly did the math. Jeffrey would've been in his early twenties when Sean Sr. died, and Jeffrey hadn't grown up on Piedras. If he knew something about the death of Sean Sr., he must have learned it more recently.

"Fine. I'll meet with him."

"The justice center, today, twelve thirty." Amanda disconnected before Mat could reply. He hated it when people did that.

Jeffrey Reynolds was one of ten or so perpetrators being held for trial in the Piedras County Justice Center–slash–courthouse. Prisoners weren't always held there these days, but a concession had been made for Reynolds. Mat didn't know who'd made it happen, but Jeffrey should consider himself lucky, because accommodations in Anacortes were much grimmer.

Mat and Deputy Flynn made their way down the metal staircase to the basement of the justice center, their footsteps creating a cacophony that echoed all around them. The stairs were dimly lit by fluorescent lights that must have been hung in the 1970s and only added to the unpleasant atmosphere.

At the bottom of the stairs, Mat pushed through the door and walked swiftly down the long hallway to the rear of the building where the cells and interview rooms were located—as far from the courtrooms as possible. Deputy Flynn kept pace at his side.

A figure Mat recognized as Amanda Tate waited, one heel propped against the cement wall. She likely had heard their arrival and moved to intercept them before they arrived at the holding cells.

"Dempsey." Amanda stuck her hand out, and Mat shook it

automatically. "Deputy Flynn, it's pleasant to see you," she said to Birdy.

"Tate," Mat said, "why are we here?"

She shrugged. She wore an expensive-looking dark gray suit that complemented her dark hair. Mat wondered why she bothered when she was on Piedras.

"I don't know any more than I did when we talked earlier, but he seems sure of himself. Whatever he's got to say, he thinks it will get him something."

"What does he want?" Mat pressed.

Another shrug. Someone should tell her shrugging ruined the lines of her suit. "He says he wants a deal."

"Jesus Christ."

Mat had no authority to offer Jeffrey Reynolds, or any other suspect, a deal. Anything like that would have to come from the prosecutor's office.

"I've advised him not to talk to you without an offer, but he's insisting." She sounded extremely frustrated with her client.

Mat nodded. He did want to know what Jeffrey had to say. And he'd brought Flynn along because he didn't trust himself around the guy.

Jeffrey waited in interview room one. Birdy moved past Mat to stand behind Jeffrey, her back to the wall. The rooms had not aged well. The walls were bare, and several layers of paint did nothing to hide the water stains and grime that oozed from the very skeleton of the old building. In terms of furniture, there were two chairs inside the room and that was it. Mat didn't like having a table between him and possible perps. Body language was almost more important than any words, and a table hid reactions from him: things like tightening fists, wringing hands, or any other tension. Mat took the chair across from Reynolds.

"Mr. Reynolds."

Jeffrey's knee was bouncing up and down. He was either nervous or excited, as Tate had predicted. The slightly too large orange uniform provided by the county made him look somewhat cadaverous. He'd been housed here for almost six months; his perfect hairstyle had grown out, and it looked like he'd been biting his nails. Mat wondered how much Jeffrey was bothered by less access to personal hygiene than he was used to. If Mat were a betting man, his money would be on "quite a bit."

"Sheriff." Reynolds sneered; maybe he couldn't help it.

Mat leaned forward, not letting Reynolds avoid eye contact. "Why do you want to talk to me, Jeffrey?"

"I like 'Trey' better."

"Yeah, well, I like potato chips, but the doc says I need to cut back."

"I want to make a deal." Reynolds's knee still bumped up and down, and he was tapping his fingers against his thigh.

"We can't make any kind of deal," Mat began. "For one thing, I don't know what information you have, and secondly, the district attorney has to okay it. You should be talking to them, not me."

"But you're the one who's going to want to hear this." Jeffrey's leg bounced rhythmically and now his hands were clasped together as if he was trying to keep them from moving.

"I can't offer you a deal," Mat repeated. "I can listen and then tell the DA. Right, Tate?"

Tate was standing next to Flynn. She locked eyes with Mat for just a moment before nodding. "Yes, Mr. Reynolds, Sheriff Dempsey is correct. He's not allowed to make a deal with you. It is up to you whether you share your information with him or share it with the DA instead. As your lawyer, I recommend you talk to the DA's office."

"Fuck the DA."

"Language," Flynn interjected.

"Do we need bitches in here?" Reynolds asked Mat.

"Tate represents you, and Deputy Flynn is here to make sure I don't do anything foolish," Mat replied. One thing they were certain about: Jeffrey Reynolds truly hated women.

"Fine." Reynolds's knee bounced even faster, and he leaned forward, whispering, so Mat had to lean close to hear him. "It wasn't an accident."

Mat sat back, frowning. "What wasn't an accident?" He glanced over at the public defender. Amanda Tate's shoulder moved with her signature shrug.

"July 3, 2009. It wasn't an accident." Jeffrey had Mat's attention again. "You go do some detecting work or whatever it is you do, and when you figure out what I'm talking about, come back and see me. And then I'll get my deal."

The blood froze in Mat's veins. He tried not to show how Jeffrey's words affected him, but by the smirk on the man's face, he didn't think he was successful.

"I'm done. I want to go back to my cell."

Amanda stuck her head out of the small room, summoning an officer Mat didn't recognize.

As jail security escorted Jeffrey out of the room with Tate following right behind them, Mat's thoughts spun. There was one significant incident in Mat's life that had occurred on July 3. The reason he'd moved back to Piedras Island. The reason he was sheriff.

"Are you okay?" Tate asked.

Tate was back already, or Mat had been standing there lost in thought long enough she'd had time to walk back from Jeffrey's cell.

"Fine."

But he wasn't fine, because Jeffrey Reynolds had just said that his father's death was no accident.

Outside the courthouse, the day hadn't changed. Dappled sunshine shone through the green leaves of the maples planted around the justice center. A few leaves were turning yellow; the others would soon follow. The kids were already back in school, and island life was continuing in the same rhythm it always had. Yet, with only a few words, Reynolds had managed to turn what Mat had always believed about his father's death on its head. He felt bare, stripped down, unprepared for what he'd heard. Why it made such a difference—his father was, after all, still dead—Mat couldn't put a finger on.

He and Deputy Flynn paused at the top of the steps. As Mat gazed out over the town and island he was charged with protecting, he asked, "Birdy, you were, what, fifteen when my dad died?" Jeffrey would've been somewhere around twenty.

She nodded. "About that. It was the summer before my junior year in high school. I already knew I wanted to go into criminal justice by then."

"Did you hear anything?" What he imagined a teenager might have heard about his father's death, Mat didn't know.

"Not really. I mean, I heard about it, of course. We all did. It was such a shock. Your dad was larger than life here on the island. He knew everybody. I mean, you do too, but you're different. Quieter. I think..." She looked back at the grimy building, clearly struggling for the right words. "I think your dad liked being the big man on the island, whereas you don't care about that part, but you do care deeply about the people who live here. You collect little facts other people miss, like that Miss Sandy's ailing, so you drive by her place almost every day, way over on the other side of the island. Or that Harry Harrison may be a grump, but he likes it when you stop and have a cup of coffee with him once a week or so."

Mat wondered how Birdy had figured that out. He did check on Miss Sandy on a pretty regular basis.

Birdy continued, "But as far as I know, everybody believed Sheriff Dempsey's death was an accident."

EIGHT
NIALL

Niall stayed in bed until the sound of Mat's cruiser crunching its way up the drive disappeared. He did feel better today. The doc in Idaho had said his concussion was very mild. He wasn't 100 percent, but at least functioning.

Alyson Dempsey was stopping by with Fenrir, and Niall expected her sooner rather than later. When Niall had solidified his relationship with Mat, he'd gained a mom. Alyson was good at it too; she read Niall well. She'd know he needed his dog by his side.

Gingerly he sat up, eased off the mattress, and padded over to the closet to pick out a pair of extra-worn, comfortable Levi's, a T-shirt from a training he'd attended years ago with a graphic of the all-seeing eye on it, thick socks, and his favorite ratty sweatshirt.

He'd been up and about for ten minutes or so and was waiting for the coffee maker to finish while he made a list in his head of things he needed to take care of, when he heard the sound of a car approaching.

It was likely Alyson. The biggest drawback of the yurt was the lack of real windows. At first, Niall had been so glad to have a space of his own again he hadn't cared about that… but now? Now he wanted to rebuild the cabin and sell the yurt back to Stu's grandson or maybe to someone on the island who might use it as a rental or something. Not being able to see out properly made him twitchy.

A tentative tap sounded against the front door, the only spot where there was a small glass window. He could see the top of Alyson's head through it. Niall crossed the living space to open the door, and Fenrir shot inside, followed by Alyson.

"Good morning," he said to his soon-to-be mother-in-law. "Hello, dog," he said to Fenrir, running his palm over the dog's head and back; he loved the feel of Fenrir's shaggy, wiry coat. Satisfied with Niall's greeting, Fenrir trotted to his food dish and sniffed it. He glanced over his shoulder at Niall. "Where's breakfast?" his expression said.

"He's eaten, don't let him fool you," Alyson said, moving past him.

Realizing he wasn't getting anywhere, Fenrir snorted and went to plop on his dog bed.

"It's good to see you, Niall," Alyson said, giving him a big hug. "You gave us a scare. You look like you were run over by a truck."

"Ah, just a building." Stepping back, he ran a hand across his face. "These nicks and bruises will disappear soon enough." Niall shut the door and asked, "Would you like a cup of coffee? Fresh pot."

"We're all so glad you're okay. You gave Mat and me quite a fright. I mean, it was only for a few minutes, but…"

She shrugged out of her lightweight jacket and draped it over the back of their futon couch. Another thing Niall wanted to change. He and Mat needed furniture that could withstand the wear and tear of two big men. The futon was fine, but one of these days it was going to fail.

"I'd love a cup, thanks. I also want to show you these brochures."

She pulled a manila file folder out of her large purse and offered it to Niall. It—the file, not her purse—was full to bursting with glossy brochures, slick menus, and internet printouts. Niall held back a sigh, recalling now that Mat had told him he'd caved and accepted Alyson's offer to assist with their wedding.

He understood, even if internally he rebelled against her offer. For Alyson Dempsey, their engagement was a bright spot in a bad year. She was over-the-moon excited that her remaining son was getting married. Her oldest, Sean Jr., had been killed a few months ago, and even though she and Sean hadn't been close in years, his death had been a terrible blow to the family. She kept her sorrow to herself, but Niall saw it in her eyes when she thought no one was looking.

Or, possibly, he was just more attuned to the specter of loss than most.

They were sitting across from each other at the round wooden table that served as a spot for Mat and Niall to eat all their meals. And, since Niall worked from home, also as his office. Yet another reason to look more seriously into designs for the new cabin. He needed an office.

"I know you two want to keep it small, so I only looked at venues that hold two hundred people or less."

Niall groaned. Two hundred guests? "Alyson, I have like two friends off the island I'd consider inviting, and I don't know if I'd actually send them an invitation. Everyone who comes is going to be there for Mat and the Dempseys."

"Pshaw, what about Shay? What about some of your old colleagues?" She smiled at him.

Niall didn't know how to tell her he had no real friends from before, from his time in Seattle.

She took his silence for acquiescence, flipping open the folder that lay on the table between them. Niall sipped his coffee, watching as she sorted the brochures into three stacks.

"After talking with Mat the other day, I've narrowed down the choices. I think you won't want to have the ceremony on Piedras because, as Mat said, all the residents will show up whether they're invited or not. This stack is"—she pushed it toward him—"places within driving distance between the border and Seattle. This stack"—she nodded toward the other brochures—"they're not my favorites, but maybe you'll like them. And the last are places in the islands but not on Piedras." That was the thickest stack. "We are a wedding destination area, so there are quite a few locations to choose from."

Niall sighed, wondering if she'd believe him if he told her his head was bothering him. It wasn't yet, but it would be after looking at all of these.

"Take a look at the first ones while I'm here, and if you like any of them, I'll call and see what their availability is."

He knew it was the only way he'd get Alyson to leave him alone... and they needed to make some kind of choice, at least set a date on the calendar. Maybe this would give them the impetus to start planning the damn thing.

He flipped through the brochures. They all looked the same to him: pretty buildings with arbors for the ceremony, large seating areas, and places for guests to linger afterward. Was it bad he honestly didn't care? He just wanted to be married to Mat already.

The brochure at the bottom of the pile caught his eye. In the bottom corner of the first page was a rainbow, and the couples featured on the front were same sex. He flipped it open. It was actually a tasting room for a place called Walker Winery, but they had a beautiful, even to Niall's eye, facility. It looked like the owners had remodeled an old barn. It wasn't too far from Piedras but definitely far enough so gate-crashers wouldn't make the trip.

"That's my favorite too," said Alyson. "When the kids were little, we used to take them on day trips to Skagit. There were places you could pick pumpkins, ride in hay carts, have hot spiced cider."

Niall frowned. "Couldn't you do that here?" The islands, especially Lopez Island, were dotted with small—and large—family farms.

"Yes, but here, everyone knows the sheriff. In Skagit we were just another anonymous family. It's really quite a lovely little town—and LGBT friendly."

Niall pushed the brochure across the table to her. "Do you mind calling them?"

Once Alyson left, promising to call Walker Winery and let Niall and Mat know what she found out, Niall called Leo. They needed to debrief.

"Niall, how are you feeling?" Leo's low-key California voice came across the line.

"Probably a lot like you are. Battered and bruised but glad to be alive."

Leo huffed a laugh. "Yeah, I ache in places like—my shins. Why are my shins sore?"

Niall chuckled. "How's Dawson doing?"

"Last I checked, his surgery had gone well. He has a long road to recovery, but he'll have both his legs and be able to walk."

"Jesus Christ, that was close." Niall shuddered. If they'd been any closer to the sheriff, their injuries would likely have been much worse—they could easily have died, which was probably what Marcus Langley had intended. "You know, I thought being a consultant would be a lot safer than being a street cop."

"You're telling me. Although this is the first time anyone from WCF has been injured by a building. Kimball took a bullet a few years ago—but he walked into a situation knowing the perp was armed and dangerous."

"Fuck."

"Yeah, tell me about it."

Leo and Kimball were close friends, Niall knew, having come up with the concept of WCF together several years earlier. Kimball had started the company, and Leo had joined when he retired from the Seattle police force. Niall had heard through the rumor mill—Ryder Mann—that Leo was buying in to the company.

"How was the ride back?"

Niall groaned, slumping in his chair. "Ryder can talk."

"He can. He's a good guy, though. Has some serious smarts, as I'm sure you figured out."

"Yes. I now know about types of crows, South American tree frogs, and the great flood that created Dry Falls and thus the topography from Montana to the Cascades."

"You must make him nervous if he's breaking out all those facts."

"Me?"

"Yes, Niall. You can come across as a bit formidable."

"I'm just a big teddy bear."

"Heh," Leo snorted. "Nooo, you're more like a scare bear."

"A... what?"

"Never mind. Let's go over Langley so we can close the file."

An hour later Niall's cell phone battery started to complain, and he and Leo disconnected. They were both off active cases for a couple weeks, but Scarlett or Kimball would be sending Niall cold case files to look over. These were files forwarded by small police departments and sheriff's offices in the hopes that WCF would be willing to take them on and give a family closure.

Niall was glad for the time off. As much as he *needed* to work —and loved what he did—until they figured out who killed Cooper and why it happened now, he had no intention of heading to San Fran and leaving Mat on his own. It was a weird, painful kind of kismet that Marcus Langley had tried to kill them, as it meant he could stay at home guilt-free.

He was down at his beach with Fenrir, watching the waves tumbling into the shore and Fenrir trying to herd them back out to sea—his eternal battle. The big dog was definitely mostly wolfhound, but Niall wondered if he didn't have a bit of sheepdog in his genetic history. It would explain much of his non-wolfhound-like behavior.

The day was chilly, and the wind was doing its best to sneak underneath his parka. The toque he'd pulled down over his ears wasn't keeping them warm, but he wasn't ready to go back inside. Mat was the center of his heart; he grounded Niall, loved him for who he was and brought him back into the light. But this beach was the center of his physical universe. It was where he was able to quiet his thoughts, where he visited his grandparents in his memory. Niall took another lungful of the cold, salty air, letting it fill him up and chase his headache away.

From behind him, the crunch of gravel reached his ears. Turning to look over his shoulder, Niall spotted a shiny, extra-large black SUV coming slowly down the drive. He spotted Shay in the driver's seat and Ryder sitting next to him.

Today the beach was also going to have to provide him with patience.

The SUV's doors popped open, and Ryder slid out. Shay followed more slowly. Was it Niall's imagination, or did Shay give him a bit of stink eye? He chuckled to himself.

"Wow," Ryder gushed, turning in a circle, trying to take in everything at once. "This is beautiful!"

Fenrir noticed their guests and let out a loud woof, bounding toward them. Ryder didn't flinch. In fact, he went down to his knees and greeted Fenrir with enthusiasm. Why had Niall thought Ryder's reaction might be different? Dammit, he was going to have to start liking the kid.

"What's your name, you sexy beast?" Ryder ruffled Fenrir's fur, and Niall thought Riley might have a competitor for Fenrir's affections.

"Fenrir."

"Oh, the son of Loki and Angrboda. 'Much I have travelled, much have I tried out, much have I tested the Powers; from where will a sun come into the smooth heaven when Fenrir has assailed this one?'"

Shay and Niall both stared at him.

"What?" Ryder protested. "I love Norse mythology."

Niall opened his mouth but then realized he had no response and shut it again. Shay caught his gaze, and this time Niall was certain he saw mirth.

"Nice hat," Ryder commented.

"It's a toque," Niall corrected.

Ryder narrowed his eyes. "A what?"

"Are you telling me this is something you don't know about? This"—Niall pointed at his knit cap—"is a toque. I picked it up the last time I was in British Columbia. The woman who sold it to me informed me I was never allowed to refer to it as a hat or a beanie. It is, in no uncertain terms, a toque."

"Huh." Ryder didn't sound convinced. "It's a beanie," he grumbled, continuing to pet Fenrir.

"Not a beanie. Subject closed. Anyway, what are you here for?"

"I'd run out of answers for Ryder," Shay joked.

Niall couldn't help himself; he burst out laughing. Ryder

looked surprised and then joined in. Shay watched and shook his head like they were both from another planet.

"I'm heading back tomorrow," Ryder said. "I asked Shay to bring me by to let you know, since you weren't answering your phone... and I'm nosy, so I wanted to see where you live."

"Well"—Niall turned a little, so he was facing the water—"this is it. This is my little piece of paradise."

"It's gorgeous."

"Do you want to grab some lunch? I bet you haven't eaten today," Shay said.

Niall's stomach growled at his words, reminding him he hadn't had anything but coffee and Tylenol. "Sure."

"How about the Hook? We could show Ryder a little of the island before he has to leave," Shay said. "If you have time?"

Niall suspected that even if he was too busy, Shay and Ryder would find a way to get him out of the yurt. "Sounds good," he agreed.

Shay drove them, pointing out a few landmarks along the way, like the supposedly haunted woods a mile or so past Niall's property. As they cruised into Hidden Harbor, he pointed out the high school he and Niall had attended, the camping goods store that had been in business since the 1950s, and a few other places. Ryder was so busy taking in the sights he didn't have time to talk. And of course, there was the Hook itself, which, while touristy, was also quintessential Hidden Harbor. Stu Dennis was sitting at the counter. He nodded to the three of them as they came inside.

"Where's Fenrir?" the waitress asked.

Niall was fairly certain that most residents liked his dog better than they liked him. That was fine; Fenrir was nicer. "At home."

"Well, I'll be sure to make him up a little doggie bag."

Niall rolled his eyes, and Shay chuckled.

"Is Fenrir a celebrity?" Ryder asked as they sat down at a four-top next to one of the picture windows that looked out onto the street and the harbor beyond.

"He's become quite popular," Shay answered for Niall. "The city council is thinking of having t-shirts and sweatshirts made with Fenrir's face on them. We're going to be bigger than Forks."

"Forks?" Ryder looked confused.

"Where that vampire movie was filmed," the waitress offered as she filled their coffee cups without being asked.

"What?"

"You're a millennial," Shay said. "The glittery vampire love story from a few years ago."

Niall had no idea what they were talking about, but he wasn't about to admit it now. Having Ryder not know another fact was making his day.

But then, of course, the light bulb went on and Ryder's face lit up. "Oh, *Twilight*. That's not my cuppa, but some of my friends loved it."

Niall thought it was funny how Ryder sprinkled his sentences with odd words like "cuppa." As far as he knew, Ryder had grown up in SoCal, not England.

The waitress waited for them to decide while they looked over the menu. Niall ordered a short stack of pancakes and Shay a vegetarian omelet. Ryder lingered, seeming to want to look at everything before making a choice.

"We serve breakfast all day, if that's what you want," the waitress said. "We're known for our club sandwiches. And we have a BLT and A that's to die for. It's the house specialty."

"A what?" Ryder asked.

"Bacon, lettuce, and tomato with avocado."

Ryder handed her the menu. "That sounds great. With a salad, please."

Silence fell between them, but Niall knew from experience it wouldn't last for long.

Ryder leaned his elbows on the table, resting his chin on his hand. "So you guys are half brothers? How was it finding that out?" He turned to Niall. "Shay told me a little about you guys this morning."

Shay chuckled. "When I could get a word in edgewise."

Niall had a window seat. People watching was one of his favorite sports. He figured it was a mix of being an introvert combined with years on the police force—it had become habit.

A large blond man he didn't recognize strolled past on the sidewalk.

"Whoa," whispered Ryder, saving Niall from having to come up with an answer about Shay.

"What?" Niall asked, still watching the stranger, who'd stopped just past the Hook and was ordering a coffee drink of some kind from Corridor Coffee, proudly known as "the smallest coffee house in the state." Something about the man—his stance, the way he kept his attention on what was going on around him —screamed law enforcement to Niall.

"That guy," Ryder stage-whispered. "Are the guys *all* big out here? Check him out, he must be at least six four. And look at those thighs, jeez." His eyes were comically wide.

Probably because all three of them, Shay included, were staring out the window at him, the stranger turned his head and caught Niall's gaze. He nodded, accepted his to-go cup from the barista, then continued on his way.

Not that someone from law enforcement couldn't take a vacation in Hidden Harbor, but Niall didn't think that guy was on vacation. He'd been wearing khakis, with a button-down shirt underneath his leather jacket, and he was carrying. Most men dressed down on vacation, not up... and left *most* of their weapons behind.

Their food arrived, and Niall allowed the conversation—the stream of chatter Ryder kept going, asking and answering his own questions—to flow around him. It felt nice. A year ago he never would've imagined himself having a meal with either of these men. He'd lived a lonely, head-down existence in Seattle. Except, he reminded himself, for his ex-boyfriend Trey, who had turned out to be a murderer.

His cell phone vibrated. Reaching into the pocket of his windbreaker, he pulled it out and glanced at the screen to see a text from Marshal Soper. Another new person in his life he could call a friend.

Marshal wanted to know how Niall's head was feeling and would he stop by the hospital. Niall thought about saying no, but Marshal would tell Mat, and… this caring-about-people business was complicated. Grudgingly, he agreed to let Marshal check him over. At least then maybe Mat would quit worrying about him.

"Can you drop me off at the hospital?" he asked Shay. "Soper wants to give his own opinion about the concussion, and he's free in twenty minutes."

"Any double vision? Headache so painful you can't sleep? Does it hurt when I do this?" Marshal pinched the top of Niall's arm, which was bare since he'd just taken Niall's blood pressure.

"What? No." Niall swatted his hand away. "Leave my arm alone."

Marshal sat back on his wheeled stool, grinning. He was very pleased with himself. "Sorry," he said, not sounding sorry at all. "Doctor humor. I think you are well on the road to recovery. You don't have any weird symptoms like the sudden appearance of a sense of humor."

"Ha, ha, ha." Niall rolled his sleeve back down and stood up. He grabbed his coat from where it hung on a hook on the back of the exam room door.

"Seriously, Niall." Niall turned back around while he shrugged into his jacket, and Marshal continued, "I'm really glad you're okay. Not just for Mat's sake. It's kind of nice having you on the island."

"Am I supposed to thank you?" Niall grumbled. No way would he admit to Soper he liked being back on Piedras as well. It was obvious anyway, wasn't it? What with the rebuilding of the cabin and the upcoming wedding?

Marshal shook his head. "Nope. Call me if your headaches get worse or any other symptoms arise. A concussion is nothing to fool around with."

NINE

MAT

Wednesday

Birdy's observation stuck with Mat all the way back to the station: *as far as anyone knew, his father's death had been an accident.*

Mat himself had certainly accepted the findings; the coroner who examined his father's body didn't note anything odd. Sean Sr. had hit his head, likely on the bulwark of the boat, and been flung into the water, where he'd drowned.

Now Mat had doubts, and they were there because of Jeffrey fucking Reynolds. Duane Cooper had been the one to pull his dad out of the water. Cooper had been the only witness. Ten years ago, no one had suspected Cooper had a dark side.

"Shit."

Birdy was quiet, and Mat knew he must be worrying her if she didn't scold him for use of poor language.

He parked, and together he and Birdy walked into the station. Deputy Radden was at his desk and a blond man Mat didn't recognize sat in the visitor chair nearby.

The man stood when Mat entered the room, sticking his hand out. "Sheriff Dempsey? Sorry I was a little early. Soren Jorgensen. I'm here for an interview."

Jorgensen was about Niall's size, maybe even a bit taller. Where Niall was dark and had olive-toned skin, Jorgensen looked like he'd just ridden the Bitfröst from Asgard to Earth. Except, of course, instead of pelts, or whatever Viking gods wore, Jorgensen was wearing slacks, a plaid button-down, and a black leather jacket.

Shaking Jorgensen's hand, Mat said, "Welcome to Piedras. Thank you for making the trip out here." He looked around. "Let's chat in one of the interview rooms. Coffee?"

"Thanks." Jorgensen lifted a to-go cup. "I picked something up on the way here."

"Didn't trust the station coffee? Good instincts."

"So, your resume is strong," Mat began. "I see you were involved in the takedown of a human trafficking ring a while back. And one of your recommendations is from the head of the FBI field office in Skagit."

Jorgensen nodded as he leaned forward and set his coffee on the table. "Yeah, that was intense." He shook his head. "Trafficking is a real problem. I don't think the general public understands how bad it is."

"With your recs you could apply anywhere. Why here?" Mat asked.

Jorgensen looked up at the ceiling a minute before answering, "It's not like I don't have ambitions; I do. But I don't want to move to a big city. I'm a small-town guy."

"Why leave Skagit, then? I talked to your Lt, and she's sad to see you go."

Jorgensen sighed. "I need a change. That whole case"—he waved a hand, encompassing a whole lot of things left unsaid—

"and some personal stuff make it hard to be in Skagit. I've thought about it a lot. I don't want to move far, and Piedras seems pretty perfect. Also," he said, leaning toward Mat, "I know from the grapevine that you're gay. I am too, and I'd like to keep working in an LGBTQA-friendly environment."

Mat tucked that fact away and veered the conversation back to Jorgensen's experience and motivations for being a cop. He was surprised to learn it was kind of the family business, as Jorgensen's uncle had headed up SkPD for a number of years. Jorgensen rushed to assure Mat he was not like his uncle at all, just another thing he wanted a potential employer to be aware of. Mat made a note, wondering what the hell Jorgensen's uncle had been into.

As the interview wound down, Mat already knew he wanted to hire Jorgensen, but there were more hoops to jump through before he could offer him the position. If he could, he'd make the offer then and there.

"Are you headed back this afternoon?" Mat asked as he walked Jorgensen to the front doors of the station.

The younger man nodded. "It's not too bad a trip. A nice relaxing ferry ride, and once I'm out of Anacortes, it's only about an hour's drive."

Mat stuck his hand out. "Thanks again for coming all this way. We'll be in touch. I think you'd be a good fit here." That was the best he could offer, knowing the man would take it for the tacit approval it was. Jorgensen's smile reached his sky-blue eyes. Jesus, when the gods had been handing out favors, Jorgensen had been at the front of the line.

At least one thing had gone well that day. Mat sat down at his desk, feeling a little more positive as he powered up his desktop. As Birdy watched him get settled, he said, "Jorgensen seems great. We'll run all the official deep checks. That hopefully won't take too long and we can offer him the position."

"Most of them are already completed, sir. We're just waiting on one last check to come back."

"Excellent."

Birdy shooed him out of the station a little earlier than usual. "Go home. Check on your fiancé."

Mat didn't argue. He needed to see Niall.

"I talked to Trey Jackson today," Mat said when he'd drawn close enough for Niall to hear him.

He'd found Niall down at the beach, throwing rocks into the water. Fenrir was likely close by, although Mat didn't see him.

"What did he want?" Niall asked, his voice full of suspicion. He picked up another rock and chucked it far out into the gunmetal-gray water.

Mat frowned, stuffing his hands into his coat pockets. The wind had a knife edge to it. "How do you know he wants something?"

"He's in jail. He wants out. Therefore, he wants something. Also"—Niall gestured at himself with his thumb—"cop, remember?"

Mat sighed. Niall's green stare bored into him. Jeffrey absolutely wanted to make a deal and thought he had information that would make it happen. Mat's shoulders slumped a little; he knew the subject of Jeffrey Reynolds would put Niall in a bad mood. "He wants a deal."

It was Niall's turn to frown. "Of course he does. What does he have as leverage? And why did he wait so long to say anything?"

"He said, 'July 3 wasn't an accident.' And that, once I figure out what he's talking about, to come back and see him. I didn't get to ask why he's only coming forward now. He didn't seem to want to spend a lot of time chatting."

"Maybe he heard about Duane Cooper," Niall said. "But what does July 3 mean?"

"That's the day my dad died."

Just at that moment, Fenrir came bounding back from his foray into the bushes, looking very pleased with himself. He was carrying something in his mouth, and it wasn't a stick. As he gamboled closer, Mat peered at the object clamped between his jaws, wondering what it was, but Niall beat him to it.

"What the fuck is that?" he asked.

It's not a human bone. Yeah, and if you repeat the words to yourself enough times, you'll believe it, Mat thought. Statistics weighed heavily against the remains Fenrir had discovered in the shrubs along the southwest edge of Niall's property being human, but Mat didn't hold out much hope, not with the way things had been going lately.

The bone looked old to Mat; it was definitely weathered. He'd been looking forward to a quiet dinner, and now they were digging the crime scene tape out of the cruiser's trunk and tromping around the woods and among Oregon grape and prickly blackberry, trying to figure out where Fenrir had found the bone. The dog had not been impressed when Niall ordered him into the yurt, but they didn't need his help. If there were more remains out there, Mat wanted to find them where they lay.

"It could be bear," Niall said from behind him.

"A bear?" Mat scoffed. "We don't have bears."

"That's not true. They've been known to swim here from the mainland. It could be dog, or something else. It doesn't have to be human remains."

"I don't know why you're arguing. You were just as freaked out as I was when he came out of the woods. My gut is telling me this is human."

Niall sighed, and Mat knew it was because he was right. Why, just once, couldn't they have a normal, quiet, *regular* day? He must've been muttering out loud, because Niall snorted. "You'd be bored."

Before heading into the woods, Mat had snapped a few pictures of the bone with his cell phone and sent them to Marshal. Very likely, the Piedras County volunteer coroner and ER doctor would be able to identify it. Hopefully sooner rather than later.

"Whatever they are, they've been out here for a while," offered Niall.

"I know."

But still Mat forged his way into the dense undergrowth. It was much darker here, the only light coming from errant rays of the sun, which had begun its inexorable descent toward the horizon.

"It wasn't until you arrived that Fenrir disappeared over here. Before that, he was on the beach. Think about it—he was here for maybe ten minutes, tops. I saw him at the edge for a little while, so that makes it more like seven minutes. He couldn't have gone too far."

Mat flicked on his flashlight, shining it back and forth ahead of them. All he could see were shadows and dark. The trees were thick here and the undergrowth even more impassable. Niall was right. They'd come too far.

He turned around to backtrack and slammed into Niall, who was much closer than Mat had anticipated. He stepped backward, and a branch or root caught him up. He grabbed at Niall for purchase, but they ended up tumbling to the forest floor with Niall breaking Mat's fall.

"Jesus, are you okay? Your head?"

"My head is fine. I didn't hit it," Niall grumped, trying to squirm out from underneath Mat's weight.

Niall was slightly taller than Mat, but Mat had the advantage of being on top. It had been a stressful week, even before Niall had almost been blown up, and then with Niall's headache they'd hardly kissed last night. Suddenly the bones didn't seem as urgent as they had. Niall was right; they'd been there a long time.

Where they lay, the forest floor was covered with pine needles and, when Mat put his hand down against it, surprisingly dry. With purpose and forethought, he ground his pelvis down against Niall's, needing the other man to understand how much he wanted him, how glad he was that Niall was alive and in his life. The damn bones could wait a little longer.

"Jesus, Mat," Niall whispered into the quiet of the woods. The words weren't a protest, they were a plea.

Slowly, so if by the slimmest chance he was wrong about Niall wanting Mat as much as Mat wanted him, Mat lowered his head to taste him, to experience the silken glide of Niall's lips, the prickly rasp of his beard shadow against his cheeks.

Niall quit moving under him. His hands moved from Mat's chest, where he'd been trying to push him off, to the back of Mat's head so he could pull him closer. Their lips met with a crash, and Mat was immediately lost. It had been too long. Even though he was on top, he was in no way in control. Niall wrapped his legs around Mat's calves and ankles, holding him down and rhythmically moving his hips against Mat's.

It was cold, damp, and nearly dark. Somewhere close there were remains, possibly human. Above them branches swayed, soughing against each other as the wind found its way to the interior. Mat didn't care. All he cared about, all he *wanted* was the man underneath him.

Niall moaned and bucked. Mat forced himself half onto his knees for better purchase. He was going to have to take a shower after this no matter what happened; he might as well take it to the finish. He threw one hand out to better support himself, thinking he'd use the other to unbutton Niall's jeans and feel his erection against his palm again.

His hand, the one not groping Niall's dick, landed on something slick, cold, and definitely not a root. "The fuck."

He sat back on his haunches, straddling Niall's thighs, and groped around, found his flashlight where it had fallen next to Niall, and shone it in the direction of whatever he had touched. The empty eyes of a skull stared back at him.

Later Mat would swear he didn't make a sound, but Niall insisted he yelped.

All Mat could think at the time was that he was being cock-blocked by a dead person.

Niall blinked up at him, his demeanor changing at the expression on Mat's face. "What?"

"We found them."

"Found—oh, shit. Let me see."

Niall snatched the flashlight from Mat and scrambled onto his knees to shine the light underneath the root ball of an enormous Doug fir that had been uprooted sometime in the past. Not too far past, though, because there was no secondary growth, no small ferns or fungi growing on the exposed earth.

"Well, shit."

Shit was about right. Mat's cell phone vibrated in his pocket. He considered ignoring it but pulled it out of his coat pocket. It was a text from Marshal, responding to the photo he'd sent minutes earlier.

I'd have to see it in person but tentatively human.

For Mat, that was enough. Marshal would never come close to tentative unless he was pretty damn sure, and anyway, now they had a skull to go along with Fenrir's discovery. Leaning forward while Niall had the flashlight trained on it, Mat snapped a couple pictures of the skull and tapped Send.

Crawling on his hands and knees, Niall backed out of the scene and stood up. "One of us is going to need to stay here while the other goes and gets tape. There's no point in doing anything tonight. If anything, we'll destroy any evidence left—what we didn't destroy already. Tomorrow we can come back and see what we can do. Brush yourself off. You look like you've been fucking around in the bushes."

"You don't look any better. Turn around so I can clean you off. And we *have* been fucking around in the bushes—at least, we almost were," Mat responded. Niall did as he was told, and Mat did his best to brush the pine needles, dead leaves, and dirt from Niall's parka.

"You know, you really know how to take a guy on a date," Niall snarked.

"Shut up, asshole."

"And such romance. Old bones, a dark forest—you were going to take advantage of me."

"Niall," Mat growled, "if you don't mind your manners, I'm gonna throw you down right here and finish what we started."

A broad grin stretched across Niall's face. Mat didn't know that he'd ever seen the man smile like that. Not in the time he'd been back on Piedras, and certainly not in high school.

"Only if you can catch me. Give me your keys, and I'll grab the tape. I'm not hanging around in the creepy woods with some old bones."

Chuckling, Niall left Mat to wait in the murky dark with the skull, loping off with catlike swiftness to their parked cars. The alarm beeped, and Mat heard his trunk open and shut. Then the light from his flashlight preceded Niall, bobbing as he found his way back to where Mat waited. Together they strung the tape up, around, and over the tree roots, then around a few other trees, clearly marking the area so they'd be able to find the scene the next day.

"Ah," Niall said as they made their way back out of the wooded area, "a cop's perfect dinner date. You are such a romantic. Wait, is this one of those mystery theater things?"

Mat rolled his eyes. Niall was ridiculous.

"Mom invited us for dinner over there, but now you look like you were rolling around in the mud making out with someone, and I'm not sure you can withstand her questions."

Niall slowed his pace as they drew closer to the yurt. "I'm pretty sure I can handle your mother—can you handle me?"

He was a wicked, wicked man. No, Mat couldn't handle Niall. He was a bolt of lightning Mat was trying with all his strength to hang on to.

TEN
NIALL

Wednesday

In the end, they decided to stay home. Niall hoped Mat understood. "I love Riley and your mom," he explained, "but I won't be very good company."

The bones in his backyard made him uneasy. And, if he was honest with himself, they were something he really didn't want to deal with at the moment—and that made him feel terrible and selfish. Whoever this person turned out to be, a family—a spouse, parent, sibling, child, or other loved one—had probably been waiting years for them to come home. For closure. Or it was possible that whoever it was no longer had family, in which case Niall knew he would feel obligated to make sure they were mourned with a proper Viking send-off. Maybe it wasn't too late for their spirit to reach Valhalla.

He watched Mat as he puttered shirtless and barefoot in the cooking area, opening a couple of cans of chicken soup and pouring them into a saucepan before placing it on the stove. Niall enjoyed watching him move. Mat was leaner than Niall, but he was still muscled and had broad shoulders that tapered down to his waist. He insisted he'd gained weight since a new bakery had moved in next to the station, but Niall didn't think so, and frankly, he didn't care.

"So," Niall began, "Jeffrey Reynolds thinks he knows something about your dad?"

Mat turned from stirring the soup to face Niall, leaning one hip against the counter. The scars from the bombing were still red and angry looking, and seeing them made Niall's blood pressure rise.

"He must. Or, as you said, he thinks he does."

"The fact that Cooper showed up dead must have something to do with it. It can't be a coincidence."

Mat frowned and rubbed the back of his neck. "Probably not. I just…" He sighed. "I don't think my dad walked on water or anything, but I've spent a lot of the day trying to wrap my head around the idea that maybe he was involved in something that led to his death. What if he and Cooper had an illegal side job going and it got him killed?"

Niall grunted. That thought had come to mind when Mat had first told him.

"Dad was a small-town sheriff with four kids. Granted, I was in my midtwenties and Sean was almost thirty when Dad died, but both of my sisters were still at home. My folks managed to pay for college for all of us, owned a home, had decent cars. We didn't live the high life, exactly, but…"

The yurt was silent but for the ever-present sound of the waves hitting the shoreline and the wind in the trees. Mat turned back around, stirring the soup before pouring it into bowls and bringing it to the table.

"Let's eat."

Fucking Jeffrey Reynolds. What was his motivation at this point? The more Niall thought about it, the more suspicious he became. Reynolds was, in Niall's opinion, a dickbag who thought the world owed him something, and he was going to try to use Mat to get what he wanted.

He had to be after some kind of leniency, and that stuck in Niall's craw. Yes, it happened all the time, a 100 percent guilty person trading information for a lesser sentence. Niall should be used to it by now. But he wasn't, and his sense of justice bristled at Jeffrey's... boldness. Whatever information he had must be good.

"Stop that," Mat said.

"What?"

"You're brooding, tapping your spoon against the side of your bowl instead of eating. Finish your soup, and then we can go relax in bed."

By relax, Niall was fairly certain Mat meant something else, something he was very on board with. But he could feel bits of leaf and grime where they had snuck down the back of his shirt. "I need to take a shower first."

"Sure, fine. I'll clean up in here."

"I can do that."

"Niall." Mat shot him a look. "It's a pot and a couple bowls. I think I can handle it."

Reason number three to move forward with new cabin designs: the shower was too small for the both of them. *Technically* they both fit, but it was tight and not fun—they'd tried.

With the hot water beating down on his shoulders and back, Niall fantasized about a shower-tub combo big enough for the both of them. About pressing his naked body against Mat's, maybe going down on his knees and taking him into his mouth.

"Babe, you're going to use up all the hot water, and I'd kinda like a shower too." Mat peeked around the shower curtain. "Oh."

Niall looked down his body to his cock, which was enthusiastically greeting his lover. He locked eyes with Mat and wrapped his fist around his shaft, pumping it just once, and the heated expression in Mat's eyes had his balls lifting and tightening.

"Fuck this tiny shower," Mat said. "Hurry up, I need you."

As quickly as he could, because he didn't want to end up in the hospital again, Niall rinsed and toweled himself dry. Soper had said all activities were fine, and that definitely included sex.

Leaving the towel to dry on the rack, Niall left the bathroom and padded naked across the open living space to their bedroom. *Their* bedroom. The thought hit him in a way it hadn't before, and he stopped moving. Not that he was unaware of the commitment he and Mat had made to each other, but the fact that he, Niall Hamarsson, had a life partner—someone who was as committed to him as he was to Mat...

Fenrir thumped his tail against the plywood flooring as if to say "Duh," spurring Niall back into motion.

"It's your turn—oh."

Mat was waiting for him, sprawled out underneath the comforter Alyson had gifted them. Niall knew he was naked.

"I'll shower later. Just gonna get dirty again anyway," Mat said, wicked grin plastered on his face.

Lifting the blanket slightly, Niall slid onto the bed and up against Mat's warm body. Skin against skin, hip against hip. So good.

"God, Niall."

Mat threw one leg over Niall's thigh and rolled on top of him, pressing Niall into the mattress. It felt good, life-affirming to have the weight of Mat's body on his, Mat's erection slotted against his own at the apex of their legs. It felt right, incredible, perfect.

"Don't move. Don't do anything," Mat ordered.

More often it was Niall doing the bossing around in the bedroom, but every once in a while—like tonight—Mat asserted himself and Niall could do nothing except obey.

The covers slid off Mat, exposing them both to the chilly evening air. Keeping eye contact with Niall, Mat leaned down and drew one of Niall's nipples into his mouth, alternately sucking and nipping, driving Niall wild.

"Mat," Niall groaned.

Mat let out an evil laugh before turning his attention to Niall's other nipple.

Niall bucked his hips, wanting Mat's attention elsewhere. Mat chuckled again and sucked harder. Relenting slightly, he snaked one hand downward to wrap his long fingers around Niall's cock. As he sucked Niall's nipple, Mat caressed Niall's erection, running his fingers up and down his hard length. It was torture. Niall felt himself slowly edging toward orgasm, but it was never going to happen at this pace. He groaned again, pushing up into Mat's fist, asking for more.

"Hmm, not yet."

But Mat did slide farther down Niall's body, stopping, thankfully, at his cock. Niall felt a drop of precome leak onto his abs. Mat kept his fist around Niall's shaft but didn't take him into his mouth. Instead he rubbed his face into Niall's pubes, breathing him in deeply as if the scent of Niall was all he needed to come.

Niall spread his legs as wide as possible, forcing Mat to crouch between them. Their lovemaking was generally quiet. Niall wasn't one for unnecessary conversation when he could be fucking. So Mat's "Spread wider, I need to taste you," surprised him. Niall was pretty sure Mat didn't mean his cock.

"In fact, turn over and get onto your knees."

Niall did so. He pushed his pillow to the side so he could breathe, his forehead pressed into the mattress as he offered Mat his ass, his hole. Rimming had never been something he'd felt comfortable with, but Mat had permission to do whatever he wanted with Niall's body.

Mat stilled for a moment, and Niall tensed with anticipation. Fingers, tongue, what was it going to be?

Gently Mat parted Niall's cheeks, murmuring, "You are incredible. If someone had told me I would someday be allowed to do this—to touch you like this—I would've told them they were out of their mind."

Then, one finger began to massage Niall's hole. "Yes, like that. Open for me."

Niall moaned into the mattress and pushed his ass backward; Mat was going to be the death of him.

Mat massaged and crooned for a few minutes, allowing Niall to relax into the sensation and anticipation that soon there would be more. His cock was heavy and hard. It throbbed, and he clenched because he wanted, needed, to come. Mat shifted, and then instead of his finger, it was his tongue.

"Fuck," Niall practically sobbed.

Mat licked and probed, stiffening his tongue and entering Niall, lingering at the ring of muscle there. Niall forced himself to relax even as he pulsed precome, and he shifted so he could touch himself.

Mat batted Niall's hand away. Niall groaned. He visualized how they must look right now: Mat's face jammed into his ass, Mat's tongue in Niall's hole while he still, too fucking slowly, pumped Niall's hot, weeping shaft. Mat's ass would be raised too, in a sort of invitation, Niall thought. His control snapped.

"If you don't fuck me right now, I'm going to flip you over and pound into you so hard you'll feel it for days."

Mat ignored his demand, releasing his grip on Niall's cock, which made Niall whimper with regret. Mat's tongue also left his hole, and Niall thought soon he'd feel the pleasure-pain of Mat's erection pressing against his entrance, inside him. But it was fingers Niall felt. Two fingers questing, pushing, probing inside where Mat had loosened him, where his ass was begging for more. Mat was the only lover he'd ever let do this. He'd never imagined he'd allow himself to be this vulnerable with anyone.

A jolt of pure electricity shot through his synapses. "Jesus Christ, fuck."

Crooking his fingers more, Mat rubbed across Niall's prostate again. And again, and again. Until Niall was a shaking pile of human cells who could hardly remember his own name. His balls hung heavy and tight; one more pass and he'd be coming.

Gently Mat pulled his fingers out.

"Fuck, Mat," Niall whined, lifting his head and glancing over his shoulder.

"Yeah, that's what I want. I want you to keep your promise. I want you to fuck me so hard that while I'm sitting in my office chair at work tomorrow all I'll be able to think about is your dick in my ass."

Mat flopped next to him on the bed and pulled his knees underneath him. Niall's cock throbbed. Sitting up on his haunches, he gripped himself and tried to recite the alphabet backward, because he was that close to coming.

He knee-walked to position himself right behind Mat.

"Fuck, lube."

Leaning over, he grabbed the lube off the bedside table and squeezed a shit ton into his hand. He didn't have the time or desire for finesse, but he wasn't going to hurt Mat. Quickly he rubbed the slick around Mat's hole and inside him. Mat moaned, and it was Niall's turn to laugh—except he was still so aroused he really couldn't. His shaft hung thick and heavy between his legs, his balls ached with need.

"Enough. Now," Mat demanded.

Shuffling as close as he could, so the backs of Mat's thighs rested against his own skin, Niall guided his red, demanding cock toward Mat's hole. He tapped against him and Mat relaxed, opening himself so Niall could slide into the heat of his body. There was a hint of resistance, but the muscle eased enough that Niall could push farther inside his man. Niall tried to be gentle, although he didn't know how long he'd manage—but Mat didn't want gentle. Instead he heaved himself backward, forcing Niall's cock inside him, all the way to his hilt.

Niall took, like, half a second to admire the glory of his cock stuffed into Mat's ass before he let loose, his hips jackhammering. Mat was speaking, but Niall couldn't understand him. He didn't know if it was because Mat was babbling nonsense or because he was so gone, he'd lost the ability to understand the English language.

"Harder, fuck me harder."

Niall pounded into Mat, aiming for his prostate and knowing he was hitting it when Mat gripped the sheets as if he might levitate. Mat reached underneath his body, and his arm started to move as he jacked himself. There was no warning, just Mat propelling himself backward again, then his hole clenched around Niall as he started to come. Niall lifted his lover so he was up on his knees, tight against Niall's front as he pushed into him. He snaked a hand downward and grabbed Mat's balls, gripping them as he felt himself tumble over the edge.

He shuddered spasmodically into his lover, one arm wrapped around Mat's chest, his other hand between Mat's legs. Come dripped down Mat's stomach, and now Niall felt it dripping from between his ass-cheeks as well. Niall's face pressed into Mat's neck; he could smell them, the sharp scent of their come. His cock pulsed one more time as he bit down on Mat's neck. Not hard enough to leave a mark, but not because he didn't want to.

He was just drifting off when their dinner conversation popped back into his head. Mat had rescued the sheets and comforter from the floor to cover them, and now Niall was pressed against Mat's back with one arm wrapped around his waist.

"I can hear you thinking," Mat muttered.

"Jeffrey Reynolds," Niall grunted. "What the fuck does he think he's up to? What does he know?"

"Well, obviously, he thinks he knows something about my dad's death. And he thinks it could get him a deal—though I doubt he's right about that. What he implied today was enough to get me to look into it again. I don't need him. It also makes me think he heard about Cooper. Why are jails and prisons always hotbeds of gossip?"

"Boredom on both sides, the guards and the prisoners, but... yeah." Niall shifted, tugging Mat even closer. "I don't trust him."

"I don't either, but there's nothing I can do about it right now. I'll look at the files tomorrow."

"Let me do it."

Mat flipped over onto his back, peering at Niall. "What? Why?"

Niall tapped Mat's chest with his index finger, letting his touch turn into a caress, the fresh scar tissue out of place under his fingertips. "Because you're too close. Let me talk to Leo and Kimball. I'm already on leave, and WCF has resources the sheriff's office doesn't have."

Mat sighed. "I guess. I mean—yes, I know that. But I have a feeling that the cases are connected. As I investigate Cooper's death, it seems we are just on either end of a long rope. The further we get, the closer together the two cases will be."

"I agree, but that doesn't mean I shouldn't start with your dad. In fact, I think it makes my argument stronger. I'll talk to Leo tomorrow, unless you're really opposed."

"I'm not... opposed, just worried. Nervous, I guess, about what we're going to find out. Does this mean my dad was involved in something, or at least that he knew about whatever Duane was up to and chose to look the other way? I always idolized him, and I guess... I *know* he wasn't perfect, but I'd still rather not learn he was involved in criminal activity."

"Whatever your dad did, or didn't do, doesn't reflect on you. You know that, right?"

"It kind of does, though. What I mean is, if my dad was involved in whatever Cooper was into, he wasn't the man I thought he was. And when I came back here to take my dad's place, I meant to be as good and fair as I believed he was. I became sheriff because of my family name, not because of my personal job record."

"Maybe in the beginning, when you were first appointed—elected, whatever." Niall flapped a hand. "But now, more than ten years later? You've made your own mark here, and the citizens know it. They know *you*." He tapped Mat's chest again, right above his heart.

The residents of Piedras loved Mat—for fuck's sake, every flower shop within fifty miles had sold out their stock when Mat had been injured in the bombing. His damn hospital room had been stuffed so full they'd started sending overflow to the geriatric center.

"I'm thinking about getting some tattoos."

Niall blinked at the abrupt change of subject.

"Sure, where?" He knew where. "Do you have something in mind? Kim at Harbor Barber is damn good."

"I'd like to cover the scars." Mat ran his hand over his own chest. "I dunno, maybe it's silly."

"Mm." Niall rolled on top of Mat, rotating his hips against Mat's. "Not silly. Tattoos are sexy as fuck and will only make it even more impossible for me to keep my hands off of you. It's not right that the sheriff looks so sexy in his government-issued uniform, I can't walk into the station without getting hard. Knowing you have tattoos underneath..."

Laughing, Mat reached up, pulling Niall down for a heated kiss.

Much later, they were both lying on their backs again, fingers intertwined as they recovered. They'd kicked the covers off, and Niall's overheated skin was starting to turn to goose bumps.

"So that's a yes to the tattoos, I guess," Mat murmured, turning onto his side.

Niall tugged the blankets back over them and snuggled into his back.

"Yes," he managed before sleep claimed him.

ELEVEN
MAT

Thursday

"I'll see you in a couple hours," Mat said as he slid into the front seat of the cruiser.

Fenrir woofed at a sparrow on his way down to the beach to do doggy things. Niall chuckled and leaned in through Mat's open window, and Mat eagerly accepted one more kiss before he had to leave. He'd never get used to Niall being his, never take it for granted.

"I'm going to call Leo in a little while," Niall said a few moments later. "Is Marshal coming to check out the remains?"

Mat nodded, still a little addled from the kiss. "Yeah, but I don't know when. And I'll be here too—I'll bring Flynn along. It'll be a learning experience for her."

Niall stood back, moving away and shoving his hands into the front pockets of his jeans. Mat put the car in reverse, adding, "Keep the damn dog away from the bones."

Niall rolled his eyes but headed the same direction as Fenrir, whistling sharply to get his attention.

. . .

Mat was the first person at the station. Once his desktop was powered up, he quickly created a file for the remains they'd discovered and uploaded the photos he'd taken. A professional photographer he was not, but they'd do for the time being.

"Sir, you're early," Birdy said as she strode into the bullpen and plopped her lunch bag onto her desk.

Mat leaned back, looking over at her. "We found some remains on the Hamarsson property last night." He held up a hand at her expression of horror. "Old—at least ten years, I'd say, maybe quite a bit older. Marshal is going to head out there later and check them out, and we'll meet him there."

Birdy sat down. "Do you have any ideas who it could be?"

"It was too dark last night." He shrugged. "I'll need you to pull up any missing persons—go back as far as you can. I don't think we've had any since I've been sheriff."

"Yes, sir, and I don't think so either."

Mat rolled his eyes at the "sir." "Let me know what you find."

She swiveled her chair around to face her computer, turning it on. "And if I don't find anything, sir?"

"Then we'll have to go to the community. You know as well as I do that missing persons aren't always reported. I'm hoping Marshal finds something that at least gives us a time frame, a decade to work with." He sighed. "But I have a feeling it's not going to be that easy."

"What about the evidence from the boats? Do you want me to work on that?"

Mat groaned. He'd locked the paper bags of tickets in a filing cabinet last night and put them out of his mind—but Duane's murder took priority over bones that had been buried and forgotten for years.

"Add what's left. I think there's just one more bag. I cannot believe that in this day and age they are so cavalier about keeping track of who moors there."

Birdy snorted.

"What?"

"'This day and age.' You sound like my grandmother."

He chose to ignore that; he was too young to be a grandfather. "Whatever. Anyhow, they're the only lead we have at this point."

"What about talking to Sharleen again?" Birdy suggested. "She saw Duane pretty often—he was at the East Bay Marina on a fairly regular basis. I think, no matter what she says, she knows a lot more about Cooper than she wants to let on. I mean, yeah, Joella Wainwright started that fire, but... there was still hinky stuff going on."

Mat raised an eyebrow. "Hinky?"

"The latest in investigative terminology," she replied primly.

Mat nodded, because Birdy had a point—not about "hinky" but about Sharleen, the former dockmaster of the East Bay Marina.

"I'll swing by her place today or tomorrow," Mat said. "If she does know something about Cooper, she probably thinks we've given up on her at this point—and I don't think she's going anywhere."

After Merle Wainwright's wife found out about the affair between Merle and Sharleen, burned down the marina, and tried to kill Merle, Mat had the impression Sharleen and Merle were no longer seeing each other. Mat thought he would've heard about it through the island grapevine.

As if reading his mind, Birdy commented, "Sharleen just stays holed up in that big house of hers. I think Merle called it off between them."

"You knew her better than me. Do you really think she knows something?" He was thinking about Birdy comforting Sharleen the night of the marina fire.

Birdy shrugged. "I knew her as a kid. I mean, Devon had a

boat at the marina for a while, and I used to go and play there while he worked on it. Run up and down the dock and get into trouble, chase seagulls, that sort of thing. I don't really know her well."

"Okay." Mat nodded. "She's on our list of people to talk to about Cooper. Anyone else we need to add?"

"What about Tom Bellows?"

"Yep. I have a hard time believing he didn't know Duane. Let's assume for now that Cooper and Chastity Reynolds are somehow related. I have a hard time believing that, after years of nothing more than petty crime, arson, accidental death, and other nonmurderous offenses, we suddenly have two completely separate homicides and they both end up in Hidden Harbor Marina. I'm going to go back through Chastity's file and make a list of everyone we talked to, and we'll go interview them all again."

"That means talking to Martin Reynolds," Birdy reminded him.

"It does. We'll do him together."

Because talking to Martin Reynolds was always the highlight of Mat's day. The man was useless, yet dangerous. Martin had been clear during the investigation into his sister's death that he believed wholeheartedly in QAnon, spending days at his computer tracking down conspiracy theories. He was also violent and volatile.

"We could ask him to come here. Or—he's back working at the Hook again," Birdy said. "We could stop in there."

"Is he in today?" Mat asked.

She nodded. "I saw his car parked in back on my way in."

Since Martin was just up the street, they decided to start with him. Besides, interviewing him first would get it out of the way.

Birdy preceded Mat into the local greasy spoon. They'd decided for casual. If there was space, they'd sit at the counter and have coffee. Martin wouldn't be able to avoid them, and he might feel less like they were confronting him. Probably not, but then again, Mat didn't really care what Martin thought.

Just as they walked in, two stools opened up at the counter. The waitress, a new girl named Brenda who Mat didn't know—she was probably not from the island—approached them to take their order, her little paper pad tight in her grip.

"Just a couple cups of coffee," Mat requested as she got closer.

Martin was in the kitchen; Mat could hear his voice and see him through the pass-through. He wore a dingy white t-shirt and checkered chef's pants partially protected by a white apron tied around his waist. He must've heard Mat's voice because he turned and glared at them through the small window.

Brenda looked over her shoulder, her eyes widening at the expression on Martin's face—it was not pleasant.

Mat called out, "Martin, can we chat for a moment?"

"Why do you gotta come into my place of work and cause trouble?" Martin whined through the tiny window.

"We're not here to cause trouble for you, Martin. We just have a few questions."

Martin pushed through the swinging doors that separated the kitchen from the dining room and stood at the end of the counter, his burly arms crossed over his chest. "I don't have time for this shit."

"Did you hear about the body at the marina the other day?"

Martin's eyes narrowed. Of course he'd heard. The islanders were likely talking of nothing else.

"Yeah, what of it? I was at work, ask anybody."

"It was Duane Cooper."

Martin didn't flinch at the name. "Yeah? And?"

"You know a lot about what goes on around Piedras. Have you ever heard anything about Cooper?"

Brenda sidled over to them, dropping off two mugs of coffee and a saucer with creamers stacked on it before gliding away. Mat drew one of the mugs closer to him, grabbed a creamer, peeled back the lid, and dumped it into the hot brew.

"If I do know something, will it keep you guys off my back?" Martin demanded. "I didn't know Cooper. He was way older than me, we didn't run with the same crowd." His glance moved right and left. Martin had something.

"But...?" Mat probed.

"Well." Martin waggled his head. "If a guy wanted some sockeye or something out of season, I heard Duane could hook you up."

That tidbit didn't surprise Mat. It had been almost fifty years since the Boldt decision affirmed Native Americans' right to fish in their traditional waters in Washington State and keep 50 percent of the annual catch, and non-Native fishermen were still pissed about it. The case basically went all the way to the Supreme Court but had been upheld.

Martin's information didn't necessarily mean anything. It could have been that Cooper was on good terms with one of the tribes and they gave him fish. On the other hand, it could've meant Cooper fished illegally, which... he'd had the equipment and the opportunity.

"Nothing else?"

Martin shook his head. "If you're done wasting my time, I got orders to cook up." Without waiting for a reply, he stalked back into the kitchen, the doors swinging behind him.

Mat paid Brenda but left his half-finished coffee; Birdy hadn't touched hers. By mutual agreement, they left the Hook and walked back toward the station. It was a short walk, and Mat enjoyed the chilly edge to the air. Fall was his favorite season.

"It's like he can't help being a jerk," Birdy said.

"I think the word you're thinking of is 'asshole.'" Mat nodded toward the marina. "Let's head over and see if Bellows has anything to add about Cooper."

. . .

The dockmaster looked surprised to see them at his door; his bushy eyebrows rose toward his nonexistent hairline.

"Good morning, Sheriff, uh, Deputy. Come inside."

They crowded into the small office. Bellows moved to sit at a wooden desk crammed into one corner, big enough there was no room for extra chairs. The walls were covered with dog-eared marine charts of the islands and locations farther afield. Piles of papers and an older laptop sat on the desk. Bellows was obviously one of those people with his own special organizational skill set.

"Thanks, Tom." Mat leaned against the frame of the open door. "We just have some more questions about Cooper."

"Sure, sure." Tom turned slightly so he was facing the two of them.

"I know you said you didn't know Cooper well."

Tom nodded. "He didn't keep a vessel here."

"Right. Wondering, though, what you knew about him. Had you heard anything… that seemed out of the ordinary?"

As they were talking, it occurred to Mat that Tom *was* the right age, that he and Duane Cooper probably had known each other for decades. Even if they hadn't been friends, it was impossible to live on Piedras for any length of time and not know *something* about just about every resident.

Tom's eyes shifted ever so slightly.

"He's dead," Mat said, "and we'd like to bring his killer to justice. We know he was involved in some illegal activity."

"I wasn't involved." Tom was nervous as hell now.

"Okay," Mat said reassuringly, "but you figured it out somehow?"

Tom latched on to the lifeline Mat had tossed him. "Yes, that's what happened."

"What was he doing?"

"I don't know the details—I didn't want to. Cooper paid me to look the other way." His words were rushed. "If I saw him, or his friend, here, I didn't record it. I just let them moor and stay. They never stayed long, maybe a night or two, and then they were gone again."

"Who was his friend?" Birdy asked, her tone gentle, as if she was only curious.

Tom squeezed his eyes shut. Fear, Mat thought, flashed across his face. "I didn't know his name."

"Have you seen him recently?"

He shook his head. "No, not for a few months."

"Would you be willing to describe him for us? From the sounds of it, this person is not someone who lives on the island."

Minutes later, Mat and Birdy left with a fairly vague description: a White male maybe in his forties, tall, maybe heavyset—but he'd been wearing a sweater the one time Tom had seen him on the dock—with dark hair and a beard. Tom had never spoken to him and never seen him close up.

"Great. It could be almost anyone." A beard was something that could come or go. Mat wasn't going to concentrate on that descriptor, and besides, it applied to most of the men on the island, both residents and visitors.

"As long as they're a middle-aged White male," Birdy said.

"That's still about half of the people who visit the islands. I wonder if we should try to get him to come down to the station so we can try to put together a composite."

"Yeah, but..."

"It's the only lead we have—of any kind. Dammit." Mat ground his teeth together in frustration. "Maybe I need to talk to Jeffrey Reynolds again." The last thing he wanted to do was talk to that creep.

"Sir," Birdy said as Mat pulled the station door open and they walked inside, "I'm not convinced he has anything more for us. Even if he does have information that proves your father's death wasn't an accident, is it worth it to help him get some sort of deal? I'm not saying Sheriff Dempsey's death wasn't a tragedy, but it happened a long time ago, and wouldn't opening up the case again also open old wounds?"

"I don't believe my father was a saint. I know he wasn't perfect. But if he was somehow involved in this same scheme Cooper was—smuggling? I don't know. I think it will come out anyway."

He needed to talk to his mother. More than anything, he did not want her hurt. If it turned out that his father had been... at least looking the other way, and at worst involved enough that Cooper or one of his cohorts had him killed, she needed to know before the entire island was talking about it.

TWELVE

NIALL

Thursday

Just after the noon hour, Shay dropped Ryder off with a glance at Niall that said he'd done his part for the cause for now. Niall had figured it was just as easy for him to finish up the last of the paperwork for the Langley case while Ryder was on Piedras as it would be to do it after he left that evening.

"I'll talk to you later," Shay said through his rolled-down window. "I'm heading over to help Claribel with some paperwork."

"Better you than me," said Niall. He and the matriarch of the Delacombe family had an uneasy relationship. Shay rolled his eyes at Niall before driving off, and Niall turned to Ryder.

"Your place is amazing. I can see why you stayed up here instead of moving to the Bay Area." Ryder's eyes were wide. He seemed to be trying to take in everything at once. "What's up with the crime scene tape? Are you practicing? You know, keep up the skills so it drapes just right?"

"Funny." Niall raised an eyebrow at his coworker. "Mat and I found some old bones in the woods last night."

"You're kidding me, right?"

Niall shook his head. "Nope. Marshal Soper, the volunteer coroner, will be here in just a few minutes to decide if it's a body dump or—unlikely—a Native American burial."

Niall wouldn't have thought it was possible for Ryder's eyes to grow wider, but they did.

"Can I watch?" Ryder asked, somewhat breathlessly, as if he was getting to see the Book of Kells firsthand, or possibly the Holy Grail.

"Behave yourself. No pictures or blabbing about it." Niall knew Ryder wouldn't say anything, but he enjoyed the younger man's indignant expression and was unable to keep from baiting him.

"Dude," Ryder squeaked, "I can't believe you think you have to tell me that! Have you told Leo and Kimball?"

No, he hadn't mentioned the bones to Leo, as the man had been injured worse than Niall and was recovering from an actual concussion, not just the possibility of one.

The sound of tires crunching against gravel reached their ears. They turned to see Marshal coming their way, driving his prehistoric, faded red Land Cruiser.

"Ooh," Ryder exclaimed, distracted. "That's a serious vehicle!"

"It is. He's very proud of it. Don't say anything, or we'll spend twenty minutes hearing about its provenance."

Marshal opened his door and climbed out. "Afternoon. Mat's going to join us in a few minutes. Does everyone have gear?"

Mat and Deputy Flynn arrived minutes later. Leaving Fenrir inside the yurt—and not happy about it—Mat and Niall led the others to the location about 150 feet in from the tree line. Even at midday the wooded area was dimly lit, the sunshine throwing odd shadows that intersected each other at wrong angles.

At the site, Marshal tugged on latex gloves and made sure his camera was fully charged. He also grabbed a bag of small tools, and they all pulled on plastic booties over their shoes so they wouldn't track more foreign matter around the scene.

"All right, let's do this," Mat said.

The Douglas fir harboring the remains had fallen or been blown over recently, exposing its root ball. The area around the tree was covered with pine needles, scrubby shrubs, ferns, and lots of nettles. They were lucky they hadn't landed in the nettles last night.

Marshal stood there for a moment, looking down at the partial skull and the other bones.

"It's been a while since I've done anything like this. Here." Setting his bag down, he unzipped it and grabbed a wad of gloves. "Everybody put a pair of these on. We'll do a quick zone search to try and determine if this is all we have to work with or if there are pieces spread farther away. Since the remains are old, I don't expect to find much… but you never know."

Marshal took hundreds of photographs as he worked, starting at the skull and working outward in three-foot-square blocks. The terrain was not conducive to discovering much. Niall was fairly sure the skull, the femur, and what looked like a hip bone were all they were going to find. The smaller pieces had been absorbed into the earth or taken by animals.

So, of course, it was Ryder who found it. It had taken over an hour, but he and Niall had made their way about nine feet from the fallen tree, deeper into the wooded area. Ryder was, Niall had to admit, very thorough and professional. They were sifting through pine needle debris and other plant matter when something caught Ryder's eye.

"What's that?" Ryder scooted forward, brushing at the thing with his gloved hand.

Niall leaned forward to peer at the object. "Huh, I don't know. It doesn't look like a root or rock."

Mat stopped what he was doing and came over to where they were kneeling.

Something decidedly not animal or vegetable was half hidden underneath a mass of root tendrils. Niall thought the twisted shard was a zipper. It was definitely a twisted, rusted piece of metal.

Marshal came around to kneel next to Niall. Shining his flashlight on it, he said, "Ah, a zipper." Glancing around, he said, "Likely the remains are modern—at least, not earlier than the 1930s. Probably much later. I think we can rule out Native American remains."

They all stared at the jagged piece of metal.

"Could the zipper have come from something else?" Ryder asked.

"Sure," Marshal said, "but for now we're going to assume due to the age and proximity to the body that it was part of what the person was wearing. Mat, it's your call. Do we disturb the remains further, or do we call in someone from the state to exhume them?"

Niall sighed. He knew the answer, and it was the right call, but now he was going to have strangers stumbling around his property, disturbing his peace and quiet and generally fucking with his peace of mind.

After carefully covering the area with a tarp and tying it down so it wouldn't blow away, they trooped back toward the parked cars.

"I could be wrong, but from what I could see of the hip, I think the remains are male. Which also means they were past puberty."

Marshal's words sent a shock of relief through Niall. If the remains were male, they couldn't be his mother. After finding them last night, his first secret thought had been that, somehow, she'd ended her life in those woods.

He didn't have a difficult time imagining his gruff, quiet grandfather burying his own daughter. Not taking her life, but if Ana had returned and overdosed or… something, Od and Jo would have mourned her privately. Niall knew his grandparents had loved their only child, but Ana had spun wildly out of control and left them wondering where they'd gone wrong—if there'd been something they could have done for her. And in the end, or at least the last time Niall had been in contact with her, she was nothing like the happy, smiling girl he'd seen in the few family albums he'd inherited and the photos Shay had sent him last spring.

After twenty years in police work, Niall knew Ana's troubles weren't his grandparents' fault. She had fallen into a drug habit all on her own. But once she'd started, she'd been unable to stop, and no one could help her.

He shook his head, pushing aside his macabre thoughts. The bones weren't Ana's. Od Hamarsson had *not* been forced to bury his daughter alone and in the dark of night. Niall was ashamed for even thinking he might have. But now they needed to figure out whose remains they were.

They were coming around the front of the yurt when Mat stopped him with a hand on his shoulder, letting the others go ahead.

"It's not your mother," Mat said, pulling Niall closer. They were just out of sight from everyone. Mat stared into Niall's eyes, cupping his face between his hands, which were warm from wearing gloves.

"I know." Niall grimaced. "*Now* I know."

He allowed himself to look deeply into Mat's blue eyes. They were full of love—something Niall was still getting used to—and worry.

"Why didn't you say anything?" Mat asked.

"I don't know. If I said it out loud it might come true?" He shrugged.

"God, I love you."

Mat leaned in and captured Niall's lips with a hot, claiming kiss, as if he knew that what Niall needed right in this moment was to be owned, to be Mat's and only Mat's.

His lips parted, letting Mat inside. Their tongues brushed against each other, the start of a captivating dance. Niall let his hands come up and rest on Mat's hips. He felt himself starting to get hard… and, *Jesus*, this wasn't the time. As much as he needed Mat to calm him, Mat had a job to do.

Reluctantly, Niall pulled away. "You need to go find bad guys," he grumbled.

"Yeah, you're right. But…" Mat quickly kissed him again. "Tonight we'll restart this discussion. I have some phone calls to make, and Flynn and I are going to stop in and talk to Sharleen Dixon. I won't be late."

Niall cocked his head. "Sharleen?"

"I'll fill you in tonight," Mat assured him. Then he squeezed Niall's ass and continued walking toward the cars. Niall followed after first adjusting himself. No one needed to know the sheriff had given him a hard-on.

THIRTEEN
MAT

Thursday

Mat didn't want to leave Niall, even though Ryder and Marshal were still at the property. He'd suspected Niall was worried the remains might be his mother's but hadn't realized just *how* worried until his man had noticeably sagged after hearing Marshal's words.

Living or dead, Ana Hamarsson was a specter. She haunted Niall's life, a permanent ghost. Niall couldn't mourn her properly, and neither could he confront her about the choices she'd made. She was the reason Niall woke up with nightmares about fires and being locked in small places... but she was also the reason Niall was a tenacious investigator who took every lead to its finish, who refused to give up. Mat knew Niall still dwelled on the cases he hadn't solved while with Seattle PD.

"Are we still going to stop by Sharleen's?" Birdy's voice cut through Mat's thoughts.

"Yes, thanks." He snapped himself out of his reverie and

flipped the turn signal from indicating left out of the driveway to right, toward Sharleen's house.

Mat parked the cruiser next to Sharleen's banged-up old truck. They got out, glancing around before crossing from the driveway to climb the porch stairs. The property seemed a bit more… rumpled than it had when he and Niall had been there a few months ago; the lawn was shaggy, and the flower beds had an air of abandonment to them. They definitely needed to be cleared out. Invasive weeds had taken over, crowding out the more delicate native plants.

The separate garage and smaller garden shed looked to be locked. A lone shovel lay where it had fallen or been carelessly dropped by the last user.

"When was the last time you saw Sharleen?" Mat asked.

Birdy bit her bottom lip, considering the question. "Probably April or May? I think I saw her once at the farmer's market, maybe?"

Mat lifted his hand to tap on the door, but before he could knock, the door opened and Sharleen peered out at them, her expression wary. Her cheekbones were prominent, and Mat wondered if the already wiry woman had lost weight from illness or if it was stress.

"Afternoon, Sharleen," Mat said. "How are you?"

"I'm doing fine. Why are you here?" Her gaze ping-ponged between Mat and Birdy.

"Can we come inside and ask a few questions about Duane Cooper?" Mat asked.

"I told you before, Duane and I weren't friends."

Mat met Sharleen's gaze and held it. Sharleen blinked. Her grip on the doorknob tightened, her knuckles white under her skin, which was tan from years of being exposed to the sun.

"Duane Cooper's body was found yesterday, and we're just asking questions of the people who... were closest to him."

"I told you months ago, and I told you again just now, we weren't friends." Now she sounded exasperated.

"That's fine, Sharleen. You did know him, and he spent time at the marina. Do you mind if we come inside and ask a few questions?"

Sharleen must've realized they weren't going away. She opened the door wide enough Mat and Birdy could slip inside and quickly shut it behind them.

The inside of the house was worse than the outside. Mat peered around as she led them to the living room. There were piles of things everywhere: grocery bags, envelopes, unopened mail, empty boxes. And not as if she was moving but as if she'd come into the house and just dropped things and let them lie where they fell. He glanced into the open kitchen as they passed by. A cloud of fruit flies hovered over a sink stacked high with dirty dishes. The faint sweet stench of rotten food hung in the air.

"Something to drink?" Sharleen offered, pushing a pile of clothing from an overstuffed chair onto the carpeted floor and sitting down. She motioned for Mat and Birdy to take seats on the couch.

"No, we're fine, thank you." Mat didn't want anything that might come out of that sink. Ugh. He and Birdy sat. Birdy had to move a heap of magazines to the already-piled-high coffee table in order to sit down. Cobwebs hung from the blades of the ceiling fan over the great room. They moved lazily in a draft Mat didn't feel. They'd agreed on the drive over that Birdy would do the questioning, as Sharleen seemed to like her.

"We don't want to keep you too long, Sharleen. Can you go over your relationship with Duane? Just"—Birdy glanced at Mat —"go through what was a normal exchange between the two of you, how often you saw him, that sort of thing."

Sharleen clasped her hands together in her lap. "I... don't

know what you want to hear. Duane stored a couple boats at the marina, along with the one he used for rescue. If there was a call, he didn't stop at the office. He and the officer responding with him just jumped in the boat and roared off. If he was using his other boat, he'd often stop and talk to me, ask about the weather, sailor gossip. He's really dead?"

Mat had a hard time believing Sharleen hadn't heard the news yesterday, but Birdy just did her thing. "He is." She reached over to squeeze Sharleen's arm in sympathy before continuing with their questions.

"Did Duane have any unusual habits? Were there ever people with him you didn't recognize? Someone maybe you didn't know, not from the island? We're interested in anything you can think of that might be of help. It might even be a small thing, something that may seem trivial."

Sharleen bit her lips together, shifting in her seat, her gaze again jumping between the two of them. "Once in a while I would be at the marina late in the evening, stopping by to check on things—especially in the summer when it was busier—and I saw Duane taking the other boat out. There's nothing wrong with taking a boat out at night," she hastened to add.

"No, there isn't. What struck you about it?"

"Once or twice there was someone with him I didn't recognize."

"Can you tell us what he looked like?"

"It was dusk, almost dark, but I think younger than Duane by the way he walked, and big."

"What do you mean big?" Birdy pressed.

Sharleen shot Mat a look. "Big, like Niall Hamarsson—but it wasn't him, of course."

"Did you ever see the man's face?"

"No, I wasn't close enough. And I had a feeling they didn't know I was there, and I didn't want to say anything..." She didn't meet Mat's gaze, instead staring past him at nothing.

Something about the man had made Sharleen nervous, or maybe she was hiding something. Likely it was both, but, conveniently, the marina had been burned to the waterline by Sharleen's lover's wife, so Mat and Birdy couldn't head that way and ask questions there. They were just lucky no one had been killed in the blaze.

Mat asked, "How's Merle?" both out of curiosity and to see what her reaction would be.

Her lips thinned. "Fine, I suppose. I heard he'd recovered from his injuries." The twisting of her hands in her lap belied her true feelings.

Mat stood up, and Birdy followed suit. "Thank you, Sharleen. If you think of anything else, please don't hesitate to let one of us know. You can call the station line, and someone will transfer you to Birdy or me. We'll let ourselves out."

As they were getting back into the car, Mat's phone vibrated.

"Marshal," he said.

"Sheriff Dempsey," Marshal responded.

"What do you have for me?"

"A request for you to not keep me quite so busy. I'd like to spend some of my time with Trevor and Caleb." Marshal had a teasing tone to his voice, but Mat knew he was serious.

Marshal was a caring man with a huge, giving heart. After being rejected by his family, he'd spent years living only for his job and to help others—until a pint-sized kid asked him to help his dad, and the rest was history. Marshal and Trevor, Caleb's dad, were a couple now. Stronger together and all that. A lot like him and Niall.

"Look," Mat replied, "I understand, believe me." All Mat really wanted to do was to stay at home with Niall and make sure he was okay, that he rested and didn't overdo it—regardless of Marshal declaring him fit.

"Yeah, I know. Anyway, I'm releasing Cooper's remains. His ex-wife is taking care of them. And, as far as the bones you and Niall found, I'm fairly sure they're not Native American, but I don't have the time or expertise to extract them properly, so we're going to need to call in the state archaeologist. And I'm warning you now, they don't move fast."

"Fuck."

"Sir," Birdy admonished from the passenger seat.

"I'll drop five bucks in the swear jar."

"What's it going to this year?" Marshal asked. He knew about the station swear jar and Birdy's attempt to clean up the language they used at work.

"Marshal wants to know what the swear jar fund is going to," Mat said to Birdy.

"Not sure yet, Dr. Soper. Either Toys for Tots or one of the women's shelters," she answered loudly enough for Marshal to hear.

"I'll drop in a fifty if you call me Marshal instead of doctor. But, back to the bones, maybe you could talk to the guys Niall works for? I'm fairly sure they do extractions like this one—or know of experts who could help us out."

Mat turned to Birdy. "Speaking of which, has anyone had time to look through missing persons… What do you think, Marshal? How far should we go back?"

Their connection crackled. Mat heard, "—last twenty years to start. The zipper seems newer to me, rather than older."

They disconnected, and Mat shifted the cruiser into drive, slowly heading away from Sharleen's toward the road. Glancing in the rearview mirror for a moment, he thought he saw a curtain twitch. Sharleen had been watching them leave.

FOURTEEN

NIALL

Thursday

"You should consider some protective wards."

Niall glanced up from sliding his debit card through the card reader. He was at Chester's Grocery-Mart picking up a few things for dinner. He and Mat might end up eating with Alyson and Riley, but if not, he didn't want canned soup again. He wasn't the world's greatest cook, but he could make a mean chili. Of all the things about being in love, the most unsettling to Niall was his need to protect Mat and take care of him—to do shit like make dinner.

He frowned at her. "What did you say?"

Sage, Chester's manager, head cashier, and everything else, watched Niall with a sharp gaze. "I said, you should consider some protective wards."

Sage, Niall knew, was a practicing Wiccan. He didn't have a problem with it. He figured Wiccans had just as much right as Christians to practice their beliefs, and Wiccans didn't trespass on his property trying to give him pamphlets.

"Why?" he asked as he entered his PIN and slid his card back into his wallet.

"I've been concerned. First Sheriff Dempsey was hurt badly by that bomb, and then you were hurt too."

"How did you find that out?" There was no use denying he'd been hurt; scrapes still covered his face from the explosion. The many bruises were covered by his clothing, but no doubt he was moving a little slower than usual.

"Shay Delacombe was in this morning, with the young man you work with."

"Ryder Mann." Niall rolled his eyes.

"Yes, Ryder, a very nice person as well."

He was going to kill Ryder, possibly with his bare hands. Unfortunately, he'd dropped him off at the ferry *before* stopping in at Chester's.

As if Sage could read his mind, she said, "It was Shay who said you'd been injured. I just think it wouldn't hurt to ask for extra protection. Fall equinox is almost here. I could gather a few of the witches on the island, and we could have a small ceremony. It would be very simple." As she placed his items into a bag, she continued, "No one wants to see you, or Sheriff Dempsey, hurt."

Whether it was the recent head injury, the fact he'd missed Mat, or the memory of those terrible hours after the bombing, Niall wasn't certain, but he found himself nodding. What would it hurt? "I'll run it by Mat and see what he thinks."

After all, he'd spent a good part of his childhood soaking in his grandfather's tales about the Norse gods. The goddess Eir was who the ancient Norse had applied to for help when ill, wounded, or in need of protection.

Niall suspected Od had made up the stories he told about Eir, as Niall had never found other evidence of them, but they still resonated with him. He had a tattoo of Fenrir on his chest. There was no reason not to let Sage and her friends have a protection ceremony—he and Mat needed all the help they could get.

. . .

They did not go to the Dempsey household for dinner that evening. When Mat arrived home, Niall knew with one glance he had too much on his mind. Spending the evening with Alyson and Riley was not what he needed.

Mat tossed his keys onto the table, where they landed with a clatter.

"How about I make chili and corn bread?"

Mat collapsed into the chair opposite Niall. "That sounds... incredible."

"Go get changed, and we can talk about the case if that's what you need. Or I can come up with other ways to distract you."

"Mmm." Mat waggled his eyebrows. "Both?"

"I can do both."

While Mat was showering and changing, Niall pulled the ingredients for his chili out of the refrigerator. He listened to the shower as he chopped onions and poblano peppers, adding them to the ground beef browning in the pan. Once the beef was cooked, he added a can of tomatoes and a can of black beans. The flavors could mature while he put together the corn bread.

Ten minutes later the shower turned off and Mat reappeared, now wearing a worn 49ers sweatshirt and a pair of cotton sleep pants.

Niall glanced at him and growled, "I hate that sweatshirt." He wasn't a huge football fan, and Mat only wore the sweatshirt when he wanted to get a rise out of him. So, he complied.

Mat waggled his eyebrows. "I can take it off, if you like."

"If you don't take it off, I'll take it off for you," Niall warned.

"Is that a promise or a threat?" Mat teased.

"Both."

Niall turned the stove down and covered the chili—it could simmer while he took care of business. "I don't know why you bothered getting dressed."

He padded across the floor, closing the distance between them. With a smirk on his handsome face, Mat retreated until his back met the wall behind him and he could go no farther. Niall crowded in against him, caging Mat in with his larger body. Lowering his head, he nipped Mat's ear before tracing a line with his tongue down Mat's neck to the juncture with his shoulder, where he bit down—not hard enough to leave a mark, but hard enough for Mat to feel it. Niall needed to claim him, to make sure Mat remembered whose he was. That even when Niall was away, he was thinking about Mat. Loving him.

"Jesus, Niall." Mat's head thumped against the wall, his eyes filled with lust.

"I warned you," Niall muttered against his skin, breathing in Mat's scent all the way to his soul, reminding himself how lucky he was.

As Niall reached down to lift the hated sweatshirt over Mat's head, Mat thrust his hips forward. Mat's thick erection brushed against Niall's, hot even through their clothes.

"You'd better be naked under those."

"Mmm."

Niall figured that was a yes. He tugged off the sweatshirt and flung it aside before going to his knees. Reaching up with suddenly trembling hands, Niall pressed his palm against Mat's cock. Mat groaned and thrust his hips into Niall's touch.

"Niall," Mat begged.

He'd been intending to take care of this in their bedroom, but here seemed perfect now —at least to start. Tugging Mat's sleep pants down over his hips, Niall was rewarded by the sight and scent of Mat's cock. Mat was fully erect, and not small. As Niall watched, a bead of precome seeped from his tip. Niall's own cock pulsed in response.

Taking Mat in his fist, with his other hand on his hip to keep him still, Niall licked Mat's shaft up and back down, pausing at the bottom to suck his balls into his mouth.

"Niall, oh, fuck."

Niall loved the feeling of Mat's erection in his grip: the heat of it, how responsive he was, the vein that throbbed underneath his palm. Niall's own cock was fully erect in response, and he took a second to adjust himself through his jeans. Fuck that; he unzipped and pushed his pants down so he could take himself in hand.

"Niall, I'm not going to last."

"Yes, you are." He tightened his hold on Mat, right at the base.

Then he took Mat into his mouth, engulfing him, running his tongue under his mushroom cap. His cheeks concave, he slowly wetted him with his tongue and his spit until Mat was lodged against the back of his throat. Still, he kept his grip tight. He didn't want Mat coming yet.

"Niall, Niall, Niall," Mat chanted.

Relenting, Niall pulled off him slightly, still lapping at him, tasting the precome that was now dribbling out at a constant rate. Easing off, Niall moved up so only Mat's tip was in his mouth.

"Shit."

Niall sucked, his lips a circle encompassing Mat, his tongue pressing inside his slit. Niall needed to taste his man for real.

Reluctantly—except he was looking forward to what was coming next—he let Mat's erection slip from between his lips. As he stood up, Niall kicked off his jeans and ripped his t-shirt off, tossing it next to Mat's sweatshirt.

Mat watched him, his eyes half closed, precome dripping onto the floor. He was so hard his shaft was an angry red—as if coming couldn't happen soon enough. And yeah, Niall wanted to come too, but he also wanted Mat to forget his own name.

"Get on the bed."

• • •

Mat lay on his back. One of his hands began to stray toward his cock as if he was going to try to get himself off. Niall knocked it away as he crawled onto their king-size bed.

"That's mine," he growled, tapping Mat's hip. "Turn over."

Niall sat back on his haunches and took in the beauty that was Mat's ass. Between Mat's thighs, Niall could see his heavy cock pointing down toward the mattress. Sometimes he had a hard time believing Mat was his. In a sort of slow motion, he reached out with one hand, running it across and down Mat's flank, caressing him, feeling the shudder that ran though Mat's body all the way to his bones.

Without him asking, Mat raised himself onto his knees so his ass was jutting toward Niall. He had to shut his eyes for a moment in order to regain a semblance of self-control. He'd had a plan—obviously poorly thought out—to take his time in the bedroom as well.

Leaning over, he ripped open the drawer to the bedside table and snatched up the container of lube. With shaking fingers, he opened it and squeezed the viscous liquid into the palm of his hand and onto his fingers. He thanked all the gods that he and Mat had been tested and decided to forgo condoms a few months ago.

Gently, he parted Mat's ass-cheeks, squeezing the tube so the liquid slipped down to his hole. With his free hand, Niall began to massage the ring of muscle, reveling in the feel of Mat's body, the way he moaned and tried to push back onto Niall's fingers.

Niall pressed his index finger inside Mat, twirling it, getting Mat ready for him. Using his knees, he forced Mat's legs even farther apart and reached underneath him for his cock. Mat groaned again, thrusting into Niall's hand, then backward onto his finger.

"More. Fucking. Right. Now."

Niall complied, first tugging his finger out and then returning with two. "Relax, let me in," he whispered.

Mat's cock was molten steel in Niall's grip. Niall swiped some of the precome up and used it to jack him, feeling Mat tighten in a way that meant he was close to orgasm. He let go then and concentrated his efforts on his fingers. Pushing deeper inside, he twisted them until he found what he was looking for. Mat shouted into his pillow and tried to grind himself against the sheets, against Niall's hand—anything, it seemed, to push him over the edge.

Niall pulled his fingers out and, with no finesse at all, grabbed his own throbbing shaft and tapped it against Mat's hole. Mat lifted his ass a little higher, and Niall pushed inside, holding the base of his cock with one hand—he was that close to coming. The heat of Mat's body, the way his muscles clamped down and then relaxed... Niall dropped his hand and pushed inside Mat until his balls were touching the back of Mat's ass. Niall was on the edge of coming within seconds.

This time, when Mat grabbed his cock and began to jack himself, Niall didn't even try to stop him. Sweat dripped down his forehead and onto Mat's back as he pistoned his hips, Niall's cock scraping over Mat's prostate, making him moan each time. Within minutes his balls drew up tight, and the spark he'd been holding back burst into full-blown flames. He pulsed into Mat, filling him with his come, marking him as Niall's inside as well as out.

"Oh, fuck," he groaned as he came so hard he saw stars.

Mat collapsed facedown onto the mattress and Niall followed, blanketing him with his body for a few moments. Then, gently, he pulled out and rolled off his man.

"Are you satisfied?" Mat mumbled.

"What are you talking about?" Niall asked, attempting to sound innocent.

"Mmm, I love it when you get all possessive and mark me. It makes me fucking horny."

"Good. In that case, mostly satisfied. I always want to mark you. I want everyone on this fucking island to understand you are mine."

"I am yours, Niall. You have nothing to worry about."

"Do you think the chili is done now?" Mat asked a few minutes later, his voice muffled by the pillow.

"It certainly will be by the time we get cleaned up again. You want to talk about the case, or should I keep distracting you?"

Mat laughed, a sound that sent shivers through Niall because he loved it so much.

"Pretty sure both. But, no, I'd like to at least lay out what we know, what we think is possible, and all the things we have no idea about—which I'm warning you is like 90 percent."

The main room smelled delicious. The blend of chilis, spices, and simmering tomatoes and beef made Niall's mouth water. Quickly, he poured the corn bread batter into his favorite cast iron pan and shoved it into the preheated oven.

Mat sat at the table, making notes on a yellow legal pad. Niall set the timer, then pulled a chair up next to Mat so he could see what he was writing. "Fill me in."

"Okay, here's what we know for sure. One, Cooper had his fingers in some illegal pies. I'm starting to think it was smuggling. Tom Bellows—the dockmaster for the Hidden Harbor Marina—said he, Cooper, was the guy to go to when you wanted a salmon out of season. I know that doesn't sound like much, but the fines are serious. Fishermen can go to jail, and the Native fishermen are very protective of their waters. As is their right. It's slippery-slope reasoning, but if he was the guy for this kind of stuff... what else did he offer?" Mat wrote, "Cooper—smuggling" at the top of the pad.

"Sure, I can see that," said Niall. "He certainly had the opportunity, and as a part of the police department he had some authority, so people who might have come forward might have been intimidated by his position of power."

"Right. Two, both Bellows and Sharleen Dixon claim to have seen Cooper more than once with a man they didn't recognize. Now, I'm sure the two of them know each other—it's possible that they're covering something up by both identifying some stranger—but I didn't get that impression. Whoever Bellows described, the man made him nervous. And Sharleen brought this guy up too." He ran a hand through his dark hair. "Like I said: they know each other, there is the possibility they've come up with this random stranger to throw us off, but I don't think so."

"Did they give a description?"

"It sounds like Sharleen saw him more than Bellows. He's between forty and sixty; he's big—she said he reminded her of you as far as size. He has dark hair. Bellows said he had a beard when he saw him, but the general description is similar enough for me to think it's the same person."

"Damn, can you get either of them in for a composite?" Niall asked.

Mat sat back in the chair, crossing his arms over his chest. "I think it would be easier to get Bellows in. Sharleen is a mess. Her place, man, it's bad."

"Yeah?"

"A nasty mess, like she doesn't care—probably she's suffering from depression. I don't like her much, but I don't want anything to happen to her. I'm going to have Birdy check on her again."

"What about the paperwork from Bellows you were going through?"

"It's a fucking nightmare. There could be information there, but… it's a mess. Sometimes it's just a first name, sometimes they write all the boat details down, but we have no, like, solid path to follow. So far there's been a few where I could tell it was the same boat registering only because of the handwriting. I don't know. I thought that after 9/11 better record keeping would be required, but I guess that's just in big commercial ports."

"Huh, me too. So, this stranger is the best lead you have?"

"Yes, I suppose."

"Still no idea where Cooper was hiding out?"

"No." Mat added, "His ex-wife is picking up the body fairly soon." He leaned forward again, tapping the legal pad with the tip of his pen before adding, "Where was Cooper hiding?"

"Who else might know about his criminal activity?"

"I already talked to Martin Reynolds. He knew about the fish thing too, but I didn't get the impression he knew more. I think Martin still didn't trust him because of Cooper being a cop—even a crooked cop."

"What about Jeffrey Reynolds? Is it possible he does know something? I mean, he thinks he knows something about your dad."

Mat tapped the sheet again. "Fuck, yeah, you're right. He would've been maybe in his late teens, early twenties, when Dad died, and he didn't grow up here, but he could've known Cooper."

"And..." Niall fucking hated Jeffrey Reynolds, "he was obsessed, is obsessed, by what he thinks is his birthright. He's made it his business to know a lot about Piedras—we know he didn't meet your brother by accident."

Niall took the pen from Mat and wrote, "4: What does Jeffrey Reynolds really know?"

"And then there's the bones." Mat pointed over his shoulder with his thumb in the direction of the remains outside. "Marshal called in the state, but they're all backed up, and since it's not a known homicide and no one has been reported missing, we're on the back burner. I need to put out a call to the community asking for information from the past twenty years. Ten of those were on my watch. The few runaways who were reported were found in Seattle or Portland." He released a gusty sigh.

The timer went off. Niall pushed back from the table and headed to the stove. Opening the oven door, he tapped the middle of the corn bread just like he'd watched his grandmother do a hundred times. It bounced in that slight way that meant the bread was done. He took it out of the oven and set it to cool on a rack.

Their bowls were already waiting on the counter. Niall ladled chili into them and carried them one by one to the table. Mat pushed aside the legal pad to make room for dinner.

When Niall returned with triangles of still-steaming corn bread, Mat looked up at him, saying, "Thank you for taking care of me."

Niall's heart skipped a beat and then began to pound as if he'd just finished a run. Loving Mat was the easiest and the scariest thing he'd ever done in his life.

"Of course," were the only words he could force past his lips.

FIFTEEN
MAT

Friday

"Is it too much to ask for more than one night of uninterrupted sleep?" Mat groused.

Niall squinted at him in the early morning light. "What is it?"

"Dispatch. There's been a report of violence at the Brooch."

"Don't they have their own security?"

"They do." Quickly he pulled on his uniform and sidearm, then made sure he had his cell phone and charger. "One of the seasonal workers, from what I understand, so I don't think it's theft or something simple. And they asked for no lights."

Mat couldn't recall the last time the sheriff's office had been called out to the Brooch. It had been at least a few years. They ran their business tight as a drum. The people who stayed there not only owned hundred-foot sailboats, they owned their own planes and multiple vacation properties across the globe. They did not visit Hidden Harbor or Killegen's Point; their money stayed at the Brooch.

. . .

When Mat pulled into the resort's parking lot, he saw that Patrick Radden had arrived before him and was waiting outside next to his cruiser. The dispatcher had said the caller requested they arrive quietly, so neither one of them had used lights. Mat assumed the goal was to not disturb the guests.

"Deputy Radden, thanks for waiting."

"I just got here, sir."

Mat rolled his eyes. "'Sheriff' or 'Dempsey' is fine."

Together they crossed the still-dark parking lot toward the boutique hotel. The structure had been built in the late 1800s and was one of the oldest on the island. Mat remembered from elementary school that the original walls were over a foot thick, built from trees a person couldn't wrap their arms around.

Before they reached the front doors, a young woman, maybe in her teens or early twenties, stepped out of the shadows and intercepted them.

"Are you from the police?" She was tiny, slender as a reed with long dark hair pulled back into two thick braids that swung across her shoulders as she moved.

"Yes." Mat moved forward to meet her. "I'm Sheriff Dempsey. This is Deputy Radden. Did you call?"

Instead of answering him, she whispered, "This way," and led them not through the front doors but around to one side and toward the back of the hotel, where a nondescript door was propped open with a rock. Next to it, a sign read Employees Only.

After slipping inside, she led them down a narrow hallway meant for the behind-the-scenes staff. When she pushed another door open, Mat saw stairs leading downward. She put a finger to her lips with a quiet, *Shhh,* her fear evident. Mat and Radden did their best, but inevitably some of the stairs creaked under their weight.

At the bottom of the stairs were obviously the original quarters for domestic help. The girl scurried to another door, opened it, and waited for Mat and Patrick to join her.

"Here." She pointed.

Mat stepped past her into a room about the size of a college dorm. Twin beds were pushed against the walls. A tiny fridge sat in between them, and a closet with no doors was situated at the foot of each bed. His attention focused on one of the beds, where a still form lay, covered with a thin blanket. It was that time of early morning when there was no color, and the tiny window between the beds probably didn't let much light in even at noon.

"What happened?" Mat asked.

It was obvious the second girl had taken a beating of some kind, or perhaps a bad fall. Mat crouched next to the bed. She cringed, and tears slid from the corners of her eyes. He couldn't tell if they were from fear or pain. One eye was swollen shut and the other very close to it. She likely needed medical attention, and he wondered why they hadn't asked for an ambulance.

"Is there a reason you didn't want management to know you called us?" Mat asked. "What are your names?"

"I'm Francine. This is Raisa." The woman—Mat now realized her size made her look young, but she was at least in her midtwenties—had slipped inside the room and pulled the door shut. She had her arms wrapped around herself as if the thin hoodie, jeans, and sneakers she wore weren't keeping her warm enough.

Mat turned back to the injured girl, wishing Birdy was with him instead of Patrick. This needed a woman's touch, not two imposing men.

"May I look?" he gently asked the girl on the bed.

"Please, sir, can you take us away from here?" Francine implored. "The man who did this, he is not a good man."

Mat wanted to tell her that any man who hit a defenseless person was not a good man. Raisa was possibly more slender than

Francine and, Mat was certain, younger. She had long blonde hair that was pulled away from her face in a ponytail. He stretched out a hand toward one corner of the blanket covering her, saying, "I won't hurt you. I promise. I just need to see your injuries."

The girl—Raisa, he reminded himself—turned her face into the pillow as if to distance herself from the physical trespass as much as she was able. She still hadn't uttered a word.

Mat didn't gasp, but some emotion must've shown on his face. Raisa had been thoroughly beaten. She wore an overly large, plain t-shirt and panties; what he could see of her was covered with bruises. Mat couldn't be sure in the dim light, but some of the bruising on her legs looked to be old, fading to a sick yellow, instead of just beginning to form like the rest.

"Who did this?"

"She won't say." Francine's eyes were wide.

Mat pulled the blanket back up to give Raisa a semblance of privacy in a not-very-private situation and stood up again. She still would not look at him or Patrick.

"Please take us away. I am afraid whoever did this will come back."

Mat glanced at Francine and then back at Raisa. The state of her bruising troubled him. She was the victim of abuse, that much was clear, but not much else was. Who would do such a thing in a public setting, a hotel, where anyone might see or hear?

"Raisa," he asked gently, "can you tell us who did this to you?"

"She doesn't speak much English," Francine offered.

Mat thought through various scenarios. Kneeling beside her bed again, he said, "Raisa, Deputy Radden and I can't just take you to the station or the hospital. We need you to ask us to take you. I know you are frightened." Taking a breath, he made himself ask the question he most didn't want to. "Were you sexually assaulted? If so, we can transport you to the hospital, where they can collect evidence." He hoped she was understanding at least a little of what he was saying.

Patrick spoke for the first time. "Francine, do you know what happened?"

"No." She shook her head. "We only share this room—she hadn't come to bed yet, and I was worried, but it's happened a few times before. I fell asleep, and when I woke up, she was trying to get into bed, but she was crying, and when I turned on the light she was undressed and I saw all the blood and bruises."

"Blood?" asked Mat.

"Yes." Francine pointed to a hand towel or shop rag lying half under the bed.

"Please." They all looked at Raisa. "Yes, hospital." Her voice was quiet, but Mat thought he detected an accent. He couldn't place it, though.

To Francine, he said, "Do you have anyone to call?"

"My sister," she said, "but she lives in Portland."

Mat nodded. "That's fine. We can put you up until she can get here—or help you get to Portland, if that's what you want."

"Maybe we should call an ambulance," Patrick said.

"No!" burst from Raisa, "No, please take me now." Her accent was pronounced. Where she'd been lethargic before, now she was stiff with terror and moved as if to fling the blanket off and run to the hospital herself.

"Raisa." Patrick's quiet voice stopped her frantic movements. "Mi ćemo se pobrinuti za vas."

Mat stared at his youngest officer, as did Francine—and Raisa, who quit struggling.

Patrick shrugged. "My mom is from Ukraine. I think Raisa is also. Or at least somewhere thereabouts. The accent was familiar enough I figured it was worth a try."

Eyes wide, Raisa allowed Patrick to wrap her in the blanket while Mat and Francine grabbed the women's belongings. There wasn't much: a set of uniforms, which they left, and their rucksacks. Quickly, Mat stuffed the few personal clothes close at hand into one of the bags and led Francine and Patrick, carrying Raisa, upstairs and back outside.

The hotel staff was starting to wake up. From somewhere down the hallway, Mat heard the sounds of dishes and pots and pans clinking. The sweet, oily scent of breakfast prep wafted toward them.

They made it to their cruisers without being stopped, but Mat felt like he had a target painted on his back the entire time. His shoulder blades twitched, and he wanted nothing more than to put Brooch Resort behind him. And yet he'd have to be back before the day was out.

Patrick carefully tucked Raisa into the back seat of his car, and Francine climbed in next to her.

Mat leaned in through the still-open door. "I'll follow you to the hospital, and we'll make sure you both stay safe."

Francine had her arm wrapped about the other girl, and Raisa leaned against her. They were both terrified, but Mat noted Francine's resolve and hoped it didn't waver. Almost nothing was worse than a sexual assault. As if the assault itself wasn't bad enough, dealing with the rape kit and the necessary questions was awful.

As he got behind the wheel of his cruiser, he pulled out his cell phone and called Birdy. She would meet them at the hospital, and they could start the rest of the process. *If* they could find an interpreter to help them interview Raisa.

He was tired already, but there was a long day ahead of him.

Birdy rode with Mat back out to the Brooch. They'd been unable to find a translator for Raisa, which Mat found extremely frustrating—though not surprising, really, on an island this size. They could, of course, interview her in English, but Mat wanted to avoid that. She was traumatized enough without having to talk with the authorities in a language she wasn't fully comfortable in. The sun had finally deigned to make an appearance, although it was fighting a heavy fog that had settled over the island since they'd been at the hospital. A few of the maple trees along the highway were anticipating fall and had started to change color. Random splashes of red, orange, and yellow caught Mat's attention as he drove.

"What do you know about them?" he asked Birdy. By "them" he meant the owners of the Brooch Resort.

"Well, sir, they have been on the island longer than most. The current owners descend from settlers who arrived in the 1800s to mine lime. There are actually two families, the Prescotts and the Jenningses." Birdy spoke just loud enough to be heard over the rumble of the road underneath them. "The Prescotts own the majority of the hotel, I think, but I don't know for sure. After a rough time economically in the 1970s and '80s, the resort rebounded as a destination for the 'very rich, but not quite rich enough to own their own island' rich."

Mat chuckled. It was a reasonable assessment.

"They have private security—except for the Customs office."

"I always forget there's a Customs office on the island." The sheriff's office had nothing to do with Customs; it was staffed and supported by the feds. Which was good. He didn't need more to keep an eye on.

"Well," Birdy added, "it's only there because all those rich folk come in from the north and the Brooch is the closest harbor to the border."

Boaters who arrived from Canada were supposed to pass through US Customs at the Brooch office, but who knew what percentage really did? There was a huge expanse of water between Piedras and the Canadian border, and Mat knew there was a population who chose not to declare their goods or persons. Which made him think about all the time Cooper had spent out on the water, alone or possibly with an accomplice.

"Right."

Birdy continued her summary. "There are only twenty rooms in the hotel, but they also have a private marina for hotel guests only."

"I imagine it's pricey to moor there."

"Very." She snorted. "Maybe they keep better records than Bellows does."

Mat huffed a laugh. "A preschooler keeps better records than Bellows. What else?"

"As far as island gossip goes, not much. There haven't been many complaints about them over the years. They seem to run a nice place. The few people I've known who worked there liked it enough."

"Do you know anyone who's there now?"

"Mmm, I think maybe Ona Lysk works in the pub, the one you can go to whether or not you're staying there."

"Is there one for guests only?"

"So I've heard, but I don't have that kind of cash, boss."

Mat nodded, braking as the road became narrower and windier and the fog thicker. "Me either." A mile or so later, the resort loomed up out of the half-dispersed mist, all but invisible until the profile of the roof touched the pale morning sky above the fog.

Even on the back of the building where the parking was located, permanent red, white, and blue bunting hung from the first- and second-floor railings, and an enormous American flag dangled, stripes vertical, in the center. He knew there was a matching set on the water side. Mat's first thought was that he wouldn't want to have the room with its view obscured, followed by, "I guess there's no way to think you haven't arrived in America."

"No, sir, there isn't," Birdy agreed.

This time, Mat parked in one of the visitor's spots close to the front door.

"Are you ready for this?" he asked.

"I guess."

The lobby was on the small side and dimly lit. The only outside light came from the glass panes in the front doors or from the picture windows on the far side of the dining room, which Mat glimpsed through a set of intricately carved doors. Otherwise, the interior was illuminated by hanging pendant light fixtures that, Mat mused, were probably original. The wood walls were dark and covered with black-and-white photographs of the property and early visitors from the early 1800s to, Mat guessed, the 1930s. He remembered that an American president had stayed here once, probably Teddy Roosevelt. Against one wall there was a large case displaying various artifacts; Mat spotted an old sextant, some mining tools, and small books that looked like maybe they'd been someone's personal property.

A man in his late forties or early fifties, around Birdy's height and with grizzled gray hair, was standing behind the reception counter. He looked up as they came inside. He wore a burgundy Brooch Harbor cardigan, leading Mat to deduce he was an employee.

"May I help you? Is something wrong?" the man asked, scowling at them. Mat understood that uniformed officers arriving at a person's business was perhaps not a favorite way to start the day.

He approached the counter. "I'm Sheriff Dempsey, and this is Deputy Flynn, from the Piedras County Sheriff's Office. And you are?"

"Paul Prescott. Has something happened I'm not aware of?"

With that last name, it was highly likely the man was related to the owners of the resort. The imperious way he posed his question made it seem it would be a shock for something to happen he wasn't aware of. Mat immediately didn't like him. He wasn't sure if it was the man's sneer or the way he completely dismissed Birdy, as if she were invisible—his attention was entirely focused on Mat.

Paul Prescott wasn't someone Mat knew. After living on the island almost his entire life, that was unusual. Prescott was older than Mat, but in any case, Prescott had probably been shipped off to private school instead of mixing with the local kids. He might claim to be island bred, but he didn't *know* the island.

During the car ride on the way over, Mat and Birdy had debated how to approach the resort management and, in the end, he had decided to go with his gut feeling.

"Another officer and I responded to a call here very early this morning, and Deputy Flynn and I are following up." Mat didn't let Prescott interrupt him, although it was clear the man wanted to. "One of your cleaning staff was assaulted, and her roommate called the sheriff's office. We arrived on the scene around oh-four-thirty, and after assessing the situation, we transported both the victim and the individual who called us to the island hospital, where the victim received care. They are both now in a secure location."

They weren't quite yet, but they would be soon. Deputy Radden was taking this very seriously. Neither of those young women would be harassed or injured on his watch.

Prescott's eyes widened and then narrowed. His imperturbable mask quickly slid back into place, hiding his emotions, but not before Mat recognized wariness mixed with unease. Not surprising, since his income depended on his resort being a safe place for guests.

"This is highly unusual. Why didn't the authorities check in with management?"

"I am the authority, and now I'm here giving you an assessment of the situation. Do you want to continue this conversation here, or would you like to take it somewhere more private? I'm perfectly happy to talk out here in front of your guests."

Patrons were starting to wake up. Mat could hear movement in the hallways and footsteps on the sweeping staircase to the second level. The sound of china clinking was audible from the dining room, where a few early birds were already having their morning coffee and dry toast, or whatever people in a place like this ate for breakfast.

"Let me call someone to watch the front desk." Prescott sniffed. "This is highly irregular. You can be assured I will be lodging a complaint."

"I love being assured of things," Mat retorted, feeling his patience stretch thin after an already long day—and it was only seven in the morning. "It makes me feel like I'm doing my job right."

"Sir," Birdy muttered loud enough only Mat could hear.

Prescott tapped a brass-plated call bell; Mat hadn't noticed it tucked near the edge of the countertop. Moments later a door behind the desk marked Employees Only opened, and a younger man poked his head out. "Yes, sir?"

"Cody, watch the desk while I talk to these... the sheriff," Prescott demanded.

Cody's eyes flickered to Mat and Birdy and back to Prescott, obviously wondering what this was all about.

"Yes, sir. Do you want me to finish pulling up the afternoon reservations first?"

Mat and Birdy's appearance was a nasty fly in the hotel's morning routine. Good.

"I want you to get out here and watch the front desk. Now." Prescott never raised his voice, but a threat was there. Mat could almost hear Prescott's teeth grinding.

The younger man blanched. He quickly exited the back room and pulled the door closed behind him; Mat heard it snick shut. Cody also wore a Brooch Harbor cardigan. His dark blond hair was cut short on the sides and spiky on the top—and his eyes were the same shape as Paul Prescott's. A son or nephew?

"This won't take long," Prescott said to Cody. "This way."

Birdy caught Mat's gaze as they followed Prescott, and she rolled her eyes. Mat had to stifle a laugh. Nothing about this was funny, but Prescott sure did have a stick or something else uncomfortable up his butt—and *this* would take as long as they needed it to.

Prescott led them down a short hallway. He opened a door, and they heard him say, "I need this room." Two workers garbed in kitchen whites, noticeably disgruntled, exited seconds later, and Prescott motioned for Mat and Birdy to follow him inside.

The uninspired space held a table, some cheap metal chairs, and a vending machine stocked with sodas and chips. It was obviously an employee break room, and Mat felt bad that Prescott had just kicked its occupants out.

"My office is too small for all of us," Prescott said. He took the chair at the head of the rectangular table and sat, motioning for Mat and, by proxy, Birdy, to sit as well. Mat was tempted to remain standing—everything about Prescott rubbed him the wrong way—but Birdy took a chair, so he followed suit. At this point he wanted cooperation. Hopefully he wouldn't need to get a search warrant.

Prescott began, "Explain what the police were doing on my property without my consent. We have private security to handle sensitive issues. I do not need my clients' private lives splashed all over the front page of the news."

Mat scoffed. "First of all, Prescott, we were called here. It doesn't matter who calls us—the sheriff's office responds. When we arrived, we found an injured young woman in distress and transported her, by her request, to the emergency room. Her friend who called us was too frightened to stay here. She seems to be very concerned about some kind of retaliation—you wouldn't know anything about that, would you? Why would your staff be scared to talk to management if they've been assaulted?" Mat knew the whys, but he wanted to see Prescott's reaction. "If by protecting your guests you mean keeping them from due justice, you have the wrong idea. Justice will come for them."

The color drained from Prescott's face. Mat continued speaking.

"The person the victim describes is male, possibly in his forties, dark hair, maybe five foot nine or ten. He's physically fit, but she smelled cigarette smoke on him. She was walking from the laundry to the basement staff quarters when he confronted her and forced her to go with him to one of the empty rooms—he seemed to know she carried a master key. He beat her, raped her, and then threatened to kill her if she told anyone. Does this sound like any of your guests?"

The room was silent. Prescott's mouth opened and closed as he processed the seriousness of the incident. "No, of course not. I —" He swallowed. "I mean, who would do such a thing?"

"Exactly. You don't know just by looking at people how good or terrible they are. This occurred in your hotel, on your watch, but this island is under *my care*, and you can be damn sure we're getting to the bottom of it."

"What do you need from us?"

"We're going to need to look at all the rooms that were unoccupied last night and get a list of all your guests. Including those using moorage instead of staying in the hotel. Please tell me you keep decent records."

Prescott frowned. "Of course we do. Everyone who stays at the hotel or in moorage has to fill out a guest form. We enter them all into the hotel database."

"We'd like to interview your staff and find out if this is an isolated incident or if it's possible something like this has happened before. And we'd like access to the moorage data." "Like" was a nice way of saying "we will," but Mat had learned over time it was helpful to let people like Prescott think they still had some say in a situation that was out of their control.

"I—" Prescott sputtered. "This is highly unusual. My staff has the utmost—"

Mat cut him off. "I'd think you'd want to get to the bottom of this. You don't want word getting out that your facility is an unsafe place to stay or work at, do you? It's hard enough keeping good staff, am I right? What if your guests find out about the assault? How do you know they're not in danger?"

Prescott nodded, his head bobbing furiously. "Yes, yes, you're right, of course. I'll send out a memo immediately and make my staff available to you." He looked around. "You can use this room. Who do you need to see first?"

"Send in the cleaning crew, please—I know many are likely just starting their shifts, but we need to talk to them first. After that, we can see the kitchen staff and grounds crew."

"What about the office staff?"

"How many of there are you?" Mat asked.

"Myself, Cody, and"—he looked up at the ceiling, probably counting his staff in his head—"five others. Also three bartenders, two full time and one part time, but they don't live on site and don't arrive until three, when their shifts start."

"Before we interview anyone, Deputy Flynn and I need to see the rooms no one reserved last night."

SIXTEEN

NIALL

Friday

"You don't live a boring life, do you?" Leo chuckled.

Mat had left far too early after a call from Dispatch, and Niall hadn't been able to fall back asleep with the other side of the bed empty, so he'd dragged himself up and gotten the coffee machine to do its magic.

"Did Ryder get in okay?" he asked, hoping to avoid the conversation about the bones waiting to be identified.

"Yeah, he got in late last night. But seriously, Niall, human remains?"

Niall sighed. It was no use. "Mat's going to have to call in the state. This isn't our doc's specialty, although Soper is the one who ID'ed them as most likely male. I'll be honest, Leo, the first thought I had was that they were my mother's. I know it probably seems terrible, but"—he shrugged, even though Leo couldn't see him—"I'd like closure someday."

"That's completely understandable," Leo said. "Let me talk to Kimball. We'll send Ethan Moore up. Before you argue with me, this would be a great way for Ethan to get more experience leading his own team. He's done a lot of extractions with a team but not been in charge of his own, and he needs the experience."

Niall hadn't met Ethan Moore yet. He had a contract with WCF, but when he wasn't in the field, he was an adjunct professor of forensic archaeology at Berkeley. Did Niall want another stranger up here tromping around his property? No. But he also wanted the bones removed and properly taken care of as soon as possible. He'd already decided if no one claimed them he'd pay for the burial himself.

"Okay. But this isn't an emergency. The bones have been out there for a while."

"No. But you know as well as I do that if there is family left— if we are able to identify the remains—they'll be grateful for the closure."

Niall did know. He was one of those families. A family of one —two now, he supposed—who would like to know what had happened to his mother. He'd like to put her ghost to rest.

There were people who'd say Ana didn't deserve Niall's forgiveness after the life she'd led and the way she'd treated her only son. A year ago, Niall likely would've agreed with them. But now he just wished her peace. Anger was a heavy burden to carry around, and he was tired of it.

"And what about this recent homicide?" Leo asked.

Niall had told Leo about Duane Cooper's showing up dead.

"I didn't do it." Niall was only half joking. "But if I'd gotten my hands on him after Mat was injured, I don't know…"

"What do you know about it?"

Niall sipped his coffee, wondering if Mat would be pissed if he shared information about an active case with Leo, and decided he was going ask forgiveness later. Besides, Leo was an ex-cop himself.

"Between you and me only, this case is active—though Mat

doesn't have a lot of resources. Still, I do my best not to interfere."

"How's that working?" Leo was laughing again. Niall rolled his eyes and waited for his partner-slash-semi-boss to calm the fuck down.

"Not well," Niall admitted. It took less than five minutes to fill Leo in on what Niall knew about Cooper's death.

"Huh," Leo mused. "It seems pretty clear he had a partner you guys never knew about. He wasn't acting alone. And now you say this Jeffrey Reynolds has come forward claiming that Dempsey's father's death wasn't an accident?"

"He wants a deal, but all he'd say is that July 3 wasn't an accident—which is the day Mat's dad was killed."

"This is… a lot of history converging at once."

"Yeah."

"Which leads me to believe Cooper's death is somehow also connected." Leo paused. "To the sheriff's death, I mean."

"But how would Jeffrey Reynolds know anything? He's almost ten years younger and he didn't grow up here."

"No, but from what you've told me, he's a creep. I'd bet my last dollar he made it his business to know everything he could about Piedras. He'd built the island community up in his mind as something he should have been a part of but that was denied him. If he befriended Mat's older brother, who else did he approach? Who else might have inadvertently shared information, thinking Jeffrey was a kindred soul—or not knowing he was bent on some weird self-serving justice?"

Niall had wondered that himself. A few people came to mind. Martin Reynolds was the first one—although, as an avowed QAnon supporter, he might not have been willing to give Jeffrey the time of day. Claribel Delacombe said she hadn't known of Jeffrey's existence, and Niall believed her. But there were plenty of others, including Chastity Reynolds, whom Jeffrey had strangled to death. Maybe Chastity had innocently shared how the older sheriff had died with Jeffrey? Niall hadn't known her, had never met her, but from what he'd heard, it was likely Jeffrey had used her for her inside knowledge—up until he decided she needed to die.

Fenrir bumped Niall's forearm with his nose, not hard enough to spill his coffee but hard enough to let Niall know that he'd been patient long enough and it was time to go down to the beach.

"Okay, okay," Niall said to the dog. "I need to go," he said to Leo.

"I'll text you when we have the details on Ethan and his team. Can you find somewhere for them to stay?"

"How many?"

"Three, maybe four."

Niall rolled his eyes. The team was going to have the same issue Ryder had had: fall was a popular time to visit the island. "Let me know the exact count and then I'll talk to Shay. He's rented a huge house for the time being."

Fog had rolled in from the water. It floated just above the ground, covering the grass, rocks, and trees, and making everyday things indistinct and amorphous. Niall had always been fascinated by fog. On the islands it could be clear at five in the morning, but by seven the fog would be so thick it was dangerous to drive.

After he pulled on a thick sweater over his shirt and slipped his rubber boots on to keep his feet from getting wet, he and Fenrir traipsed down to the beach for their morning communion with nature. The water was glass-like underneath the fog; no ripples marred the surface. If the sun had been out, it would've been blinding.

When he reached his favorite sitting-log, Niall pulled out his phone to see if Mat had replied to the text he'd sent. Nothing yet.

Which meant whatever the sheriff's office was dealing with required all his attention.

While he kept his eye on Fenrir—making sure the wolfhound did not disappear into the woods to visit his find from the other day—Niall pulled up Shay's number and pressed Call.

"Morning, Niall, what's up?" Niall heard the soft tones of classical music playing in the background.

"I have a favor to ask. I know I owe you, big time."

"Things come in threes. I'm glad you feel comfortable asking."

Just as Niall sat down, a huge blue heron squawked and launched itself into the air from one of the Doug firs at the end of the beach. The tree's branches swayed back and forth from the weight of the big bird as it disappeared into the mist.

"Yeah, well. Leo Zelinsky is sending a crew up here to extract the remains, and since it's a favor—even though he's calling it training—I'd like to save WCF as much money as I can. Do you have room for three, maybe four guests? I'm sure they'll reimburse you for any costs. I don't know how long they'll be here. Maybe a week, at the most ten days? I'd ask Soper, but he has Trevor and Caleb now."

"Sure," Shay agreed easily. "My place has four bedrooms and an entertainment room—I can accommodate them. The other day I got turned around between the garage and the great room."

Niall chuckled. "Thank you, Shay. I want to get this taken care of."

"Anything on Cooper yet?"

"Not yet, and Mat had an early call this morning."

"When it rains, it pours." Shay hesitated a second before adding, "Do you want to grab lunch today? We can hide out at Lulu's for a bit."

Niall rolled the offer around in his mind for a minute. "Sure, that sounds good. It's probably a good idea to get out. Leo and I are both off field duty for another week, so I've got nothing better to do than interfere in Mat's business."

They both laughed, but Niall knew Shay knew he was serious. The hardest thing—one of the hardest things—about being in a relationship with another cop was staying in his own lane. Mat didn't need Niall's help most of the time, and when he did, he was confident enough to ask for it.

"Noon?" Shay suggested.

It was kind of Shay to try to keep Niall out of trouble.

Mat replied to the text while Niall and Shay were at lunch. He wasn't very informative, just said that he was swamped, and on top of everything, he was meeting with the candidate he wanted to offer the open deputy position to. He'd be home when Niall heard his car coming down the driveway.

Shay chuckled at Niall's grimace. "Just one of the reasons I've never gotten involved. I was always getting ready for court, in court, or debriefing after court."

Niall was curious. He knew Shay was bi, but even when both of them had lived in Seattle, he'd never heard of him dating anyone seriously, female or male. Shay had a reputation as someone who had quick-and-dirty hookups with whoever caught his attention. "It's not too late. Look at Mat and me."

"Sure, now that I've moved to an even smaller dating pool—and you snagged the eligible bachelor." Shay took a bite of his burger, chewed, and swallowed before mumbling, "I'm happy enough single. Plus, I don't have the stress of worrying about someone. I'm a free agent."

SEVENTEEN

MAT

Friday

Mat and Birdy spent the rest of the morning interviewing the staff at the Brooch. All seemed properly horrified and had nothing to offer. No one had seen, or heard, anything. Paul Prescott himself took them to see the few rooms that had not been slept in. Two were no-shows, and one was a room they didn't like to reserve unless they were completely full, as it was located above the kitchen. Normally it was assigned to late arrivals, and there hadn't been any the day before.

It was in this last room that they found evidence of a struggle. Not only was the room over the kitchen, so noise was more likely to go unnoticed, it overlooked the employee parking lot and smoking area. Together, Mat and Birdy bundled up the sheets and stowed them in a large evidence bag. Somewhere he'd find money in the budget to have them processed. The perpetrator must've known about this particular room. Had he stayed in it? How else would he have known of its existence?

He considered calling off his meeting with Soren Jorgensen,

but, he reasoned, the sooner he got the man on board, the sooner the department wouldn't feel stretched quite so thin. Because right now Mat was feeling like tissue paper.

Just as he and Birdy arrived back at the station, Tom Bellows showed up. Mat had forgotten they'd asked him to come in to try and identify the man he'd seen with Cooper. They'd be bringing Sharleen in too, but after seeing her, Mat irrationally wanted to avoid it for a little while longer.

"Dammit," Mat muttered. He and Birdy were having a private meeting in the break room while Bellows waited at Birdy's desk, and Jorgensen was supposed to be arriving any minute. "Do you feel comfortable using the composite software?" It wasn't complicated, but Birdy hadn't had much experience with it. They usually recognized perpetrators based on a description.

"I'll be fine, sir. I've completed the training modules."

"I'll talk with Jorgensen back here for a few minutes. When we're done, I'll bring him out to meet you."

Deputy Radden interrupted them. "Sheriff? Raisa and Francine are in the interview room. I'm trying to sort out where to take them. Raisa refused to be admitted to the hospital, and sir, she will only give her first name. I brought them here after Raisa was, um, finished. I know you wanted them kept safe, but I didn't know where…"

Mat groaned. The closest women's shelter was in Anacortes. "Shit."

"What about the Spiritual Living Yoga Center? They might have a room available," Birdy suggested.

The center wasn't a hotel or a shelter, but the owner had been known to house people in need before. It had several small rooms where families or individuals who'd experienced trauma—last time it was a house fire—could stay for a little while.

"Radden, give them a call."

"Yes, sir."

. . .

"We'll talk in the break room," Mat said to Jorgensen when he arrived. "My apologies. We're short of space today."

"It's not a problem, sir."

"Still, I'm sorry. It's been a busy day, and, as you know, we're shorthanded." Mat pushed the door open. "Take a seat where you'd like. This is just a formality, and I'd hoped you could meet the other deputies, though again—busy day. But first..." He leaned against the counter facing Jorgensen. "Let me be clear: I prefer Dempsey or Mat or even Sheriff over 'sir.'"

Jorgensen drawled, "Okay... Sheriff."

"Deputy Flynn insists on 'sir.' I think it's just to get under my skin—but please, don't you do it too."

"Does this mean you're offering me the position?" Jorgensen leaned back and shoved his hands in the pockets of his slacks.

"It does. We wouldn't have had you come all this way a second time if we didn't think you'd be a good fit. I thought we could go over the offer and hopefully get some of the initial paperwork out of the way. What do you think? Do you want to join this backwater sheriff's office?"

"I do." Jorgensen smiled. "I think it's just the change I need. Please, call me Soren."

They spent a few more minutes going over a few things—including the salary.

"I'd like to offer more," Mat told him, "but this is what the council has authorized for now."

"When do I start?"

"Yesterday, but for now, how about I introduce you to Deputy Flynn? Deputy Radden is taking care of some last-minute details from an incident this morning, Deputy Jones is off until later today, and Holstrom is on Orcas. As far as an actual starting date—as soon as you can get here."

They shook hands. Mat had a good feeling about Soren Jorgensen. Not only were his references impeccable, the man emanated strength and reliability. Birdy Flynn had the same qualities, and they were characteristics Mat wanted on his team. Plus, Jorgensen came with experience. Mat wouldn't be training him from the ground up.

Birdy was still with Bellows, but Mat walked Soren over to her desk anyway. At the rate getting a hold of evidence they could really use on the Cooper case was going, they'd still be working on it when Soren arrived for his first day of work.

"Deputy Flynn, meet Soren Jorgensen, our newest deputy."

Birdy took in the big man with one glance. "Welcome aboard."

"Thank you." Soren shook her hand. At that moment Radden opened the door to the room where Raisa and Francine had been waiting, and they followed him out into the bullpen. When Raisa walked past them, she pulled her sweatshirt hood up over her head, concealing her bright blonde hair. As she had that morning, Francine had one arm wrapped around her roommate, offering both physical and moral support. Mat was glad Raisa had someone with her. Now he just hoped he could bring her justice.

"I need to get going," Jorgensen said abruptly. "I don't want to miss the ferry. I'll let you know when I can start."

"Sure," Mat agreed. "We'll give you the tour when you return."

Mat watched Jorgensen leave the building and then turned to Birdy. "How's it going?" he asked.

"Mr. Bellows and I are trying to get a handle on what the man he saw at the marina might look like. I'm wondering what you think: anyone you recognize?" She pulled her screen around so Mat could see it better.

The composite was, as they always were, a bit weird, the face not quite in proportion. The human eye wanted everything to fit like a finished jigsaw puzzle. The face on the screen had sharp, high cheekbones, a narrow nose, and a heavy brow. The top lip was narrower than the bottom one.

Mat shook his head. It was no one he could immediately place, although it seemed fairly likely that whoever this was had stayed out of Mat's orbit on the island. The longer he stared at it, the more he felt that he *should* know this person. Whatever it was about the image, though, it was too vague for him to put a finger on.

"Can you make the upper lip a bit wider?" Bellows asked. "And make the hair longer—straight, and almost to the shoulders." Biting the inside of his cheek, the dockmaster stared at the screen another second, then pointed at the screen and said, "Make the eyebrow shape a bit sharper—almost peaked in the middle, but thick."

As Birdy worked, Bellows kept looking at the screen, nodding slowly. "Now put a beard on him, a short one." Birdy complied. "Yes," Bellows exclaimed, "that's him. That's the man I saw."

Holy shit, Mat thought, their first real lead. All three of them stared at the new composite. The bullpen was quiet while they committed the face to memory.

"Sir?"

"Birdy?" He swung around to look at her.

"If we take the beard off and shorten the hair again," she proceeded to do so, then sat back and stared hard at her screen, "he could also be who the victim described this morning."

"Fuck." She was right. When was Birdy wrong? Not often.

"Send the composite to Radden's phone. Have him show it to the victim and text us back. Then we need to get back out to the Brooch and see if anyone there recognizes this guy. Shit, shit, shit."

By the time Birdy returned from escorting Bellows out, Mat had his answer from Deputy Radden: **YES.**

Mat had made a fresh pot of coffee—the good stuff—and Birdy had gone over to the bakery next door and picked up the last couple of doughnuts left before they closed for the day. Now Birdy sat next to his desk with Radden on speaker, calling from where he was settling Raisa and Francine in at the Spiritual Living Yoga Center.

"We need to try and identify this guy."

"Sheriff, Raisa is scared to death," Radden said, his voice raspy over the cell signal. "When I showed the picture to her, she said she didn't recognize it, but she did. If she was scared before, after she saw that picture, she was terrified."

"Crap," Mat muttered. Whoever this guy was, Mat wanted him behind bars. "The other girl, Francine, didn't recognize him?"

"She says no, but…"

"Okay." Mat nodded, his thoughts racing. "I want someone keeping an eye on the center at all times. There's no reason to think Raisa's attacker knows where she is, but I don't want him finding her if he's looking. Patrick," he asked, "do you think Raisa is here illegally?"

"Maybe?" Patrick replied. "I wouldn't be surprised. She's definitely scared to talk, but I think she understands a lot more than she lets on. The other girl, Francine, refuses to leave her. Madeline Roux has them tucked in at the center. But… they're not prisoners. They can leave, right? We can't make them stay?"

"Would you head down to the center and relieve Patrick?" Mat asked Birdy. "Keep an eye on the place, just in case. Dammit, I wish Raisa had agreed to stay at the hospital." He sighed and continued, "See if either one of the women feels comfortable enough to talk to you. Tell Madeline as little as you can… although she's smart, and I'm sure she's figured out those two are in more trouble than we know. Radden, I know it's been a long day, but go get some rest and relieve Flynn at midnight. I'm authorizing OT for this."

Birdy nodded and stood up, collecting her keys before heading out to the parking lot.

EIGHTEEN
NIALL

Friday–Saturday

Niall was thinking about his lunchtime exchange with Shay when he finally heard Mat's cruiser coming down the drive. His heartbeat sped up a bit in anticipation. It was hard to believe how much he'd changed since moving back to Piedras.

Shay claimed he was fine alone, but having someone to go home to—or someone to come home to you—evoked the most powerful feelings Niall had experienced in his life. It meant he loved and was loved. Scary as shit.

Maybe Shay had a point about being on his own. Some people really were happy that way. But there was no going back for Niall now.

He and Fenrir greeted Mat at the door. Mat was tired—exhausted. Niall could tell by the lines on his face and the way he carried his body. But also, Niall knew that something had happened. "Was there a break in your case?"

"I'm not sure. Maybe? A girl was assaulted out at the Brooch, and... I need to change out of these clothes first."

Niall followed Mat to their bedroom and leaned against the doorframe. He didn't want to miss Mat getting naked.

"Let's talk about your day instead," Mat said as he unbuttoned his uniform shirt.

"It was fine. I talked to Leo—he wants to send a team up to check out the remains. And by 'wants to' I mean he is going to, I just don't know when. Let's see, what else? I had lunch with Shay at Lulu's, and your mom dropped off another stack of wedding brochures."

"Jesus, I can't even think about the wedding right now. But"—Mat kicked his pants aside and began to pull on a favorite pair of thick cotton sweatpants, leaving his chest bare for the moment—"I want it done. I want to be married to you already, dammit."

Niall crossed the distance between them, grabbing on to Mat's hips and pulling him close. "I do too. I forgot one thing; Sage wants to perform a protection rite for us." With one finger he traced the new scars on Mat's chest. He was glad the scars were there, that he could touch them—it meant Mat was alive—but Niall could do without him getting blown up, shot, or stabbed again.

Mat pressed Niall's hand flat against his heart. The steady beat of that organ under Niall's palm was steadying. "Do I need to remind you that you were the one who was most recently in the hospital?" Leaning in, Mat pressed his lips lightly against Niall's. "Next time you see Sage, tell her we'll do it. Is there anything to eat?"

Mat left far too early again Saturday morning. Niall chafed at being the outsider *and* still officially on light duty for WCF, weekend or no. After a short work conference call, it was decided he'd return to the active roster Monday. When Ethan Moore and his WCF team arrived on Piedras—which hadn't been decided yet —Niall wouldn't be officially assigned to the investigation, but he hoped to stick around for it. Everything was a waiting game right now, and it was pissing him off.

Shit was happening, and all of it was out of his control. He was restless and twitchy, and there was nothing he could do about it. Not without pissing off his partner. But after several hours of getting up to pace around and then sitting back down at the table, Niall decided he needed to get out of the house. Even the relatively thin walls of the yurt were pressing in on him.

"Come on, dog."

Fenrir, who'd kept one eye on Niall all morning, stood up from his dog bed, stretched out his long body, and padded to the front door. Niall wished he had a copy of the printout Mat had shown him—but maybe it was for the better. He was already walking a fine line.

Niall directed his car toward Killegen's Point. He'd stop by Alyson's and see how she and Riley were doing. He could stop by Shay's place too; he hadn't seen it yet. If he kept himself busy, he wouldn't be tempted to drive the other direction and stop in at the sheriff's office to see how things were going. Last time he'd done that, it hadn't exactly ended well. Although he and Mat were together now, so maybe it *had* ended well.

If he just happened to head out to Brooch Resort, it would be to see if he and Mat had made the right decision earlier in the summer when they'd tossed the resort's information in the discard pile as too expensive.

The Kiln was the name of Brooch Resort's bar-slash-pub. The name was fitting, since the first White owners had been lime miners and then became lime barons. It was open every day, and Niall again told himself he was taking a tour of the property, giving the resort a chance to change his mind. It was, after all, locally owned and operated.

The Kiln was located waterside, facing Haro Strait. There was a breezy patio with tables and chairs looking out over the marina, and a gazebo to one side. A sign declared, "Pets Allowed on the Patio." Good to know, but Niall was still glad he'd left Fenrir with Alyson and Riley. It wasn't a hot day, but Fenrir would look askance at being left in the car. And, even if dogs were allowed, most people took a second look at Fenrir.

Inside, the pub was dimly lit. Niall stood in the doorway and took in the small space. A tall woman behind a mahogany bar was wiping it down and reorganizing the bottles of liquor behind her. There were several taps advertising both local and off-island beers. The Saturday lunch crowd had arrived ahead of him. Two men sat at the bar, pints in front of them, and a man and woman were at one of the tables reading over a paper menu together.

"Have a seat where you like," the bartender said. "I'll bring you a menu."

Niall sat at the opposite end of the bar from the two men. The bartender slipped a menu in front of him and rattled off the day's specials. "Let me know when you've decided." Her name tag read "Ona."

Niall nodded as he looked down at the selection. "I'll have a pint of the pale ale and a pub burger."

"Sounds good. Do you want me to charge this to your room?" Ona poured Niall's ale. With a practiced movement, she flicked off the extra foam before setting the glass in front of him.

"I'm not staying here, just checking it out. My fiancé and I are thinking about getting married here." Niall nearly choked on the word fiancé, but he managed to spit it out—it was true, after all.

She raised her eyebrows and smiled at him, nodding. "It's beautiful here. Have you checked out the wedding arbor yet?"

"No. I thought I'd have something to eat first, then see what the facility has to offer."

"Well, be sure to check out the chapel. And sometimes couples use the lawn above the marina too, where the gazebo is. When's the big day?"

Niall fiddled with a spare coaster, spinning it on the bar top. "We haven't set a date yet. Still trying to find the perfect place."

Nodding, Ona walked to the other end of the counter where a computer was mounted and, Niall presumed, entered in his order. "Your food will be up shortly," she called over her shoulder.

While he waited for his food, Niall stared around the pub, trying not to feel guilty that he was sort of interfering with Mat's investigation. Sort of. He snorted at his weak attempt to justify being at Brooch Resort: 100 percent completely interfering, 100 percent shouldn't be out here asking questions and trying to get the staff to talk to him. As if they'd just start talking about an investigation. Niall was certain the owner or manager had told them to keep their mouths shut.

"Here ya go." Ona slid his burger in front of him a few minutes later.

"Thanks." He took a bite; it was delicious.

While Niall ate, a few more people wandered in. The bartender greeted them and easily took care of them. She didn't seem nervous or edgy, and he couldn't come up with a way to ask if she'd heard about the assault. When he finished his burger, Niall dug out his wallet and left two twenties tucked under his coaster, as Ona was busy with a four-top.

"Thanks," he called out as he left.

Since he was here, he might as well take a stroll around the property. From the Kiln he walked to the gazebo, then down to the pier, where a lot of expensive sailboats were moored. A few people were doing things with the boats: pulling lines, adjusting this and that. No one who looked like the man in the picture.

He climbed up the hill to the main building and lobby. He'd seen the pictures in the brochure, but he might as well look in person. It too was dimly lit; he supposed it was because of the original light fixtures hanging from the ceilings. A young man behind the desk greeted him with a smile.

"How may I help you? Are you here to check in?" He seemed a bit confused at Niall's appearance.

"No," Niall said as he drew close to the big, old-fashioned reception desk. "My partner and I are getting married, and I wanted to check the place out."

"Oh, congratulations." The clerk beamed at Niall. "When's the big day?"

"No date yet—much to my mother-in-law-to-be's chagrin."

"What about your family?" According to his name tag, the young man's name was Cody. "I bet they're excited for you too."

"I don't have any," Niall said flatly.

"I'm so sorry." Cody turned bright red. "I shouldn't have asked. It's none of my business."

Niall shrugged. "I guess I do have family now. This is an LGBTQ-friendly establishment, correct?"

"What? Oh, yes. I'm gay, and... well, my uncle is the owner, but he's..." Cody shrugged. "He'll take anyone's money. Are—" He snapped his lips shut around the question he'd clearly been about to ask, the color in his face rising higher.

Niall suppressed a chuckle. "Is the resort busy right now? Is it okay if I take a look around?"

Cody's eyes darted around, as if he wasn't sure how to answer. "Um, we are full tonight, but not everyone has checked in yet. I guess it would be okay. My uncle is ill, or I'd show you around myself."

"I'm sorry to hear about your uncle."

"I think he'll be okay. He said it was his stomach. I hope it isn't catching, though."

As gently as possible, Niall extricated himself from the well-meaning but talkative Cody Prescott. "I'll just take a look around in the public areas."

It was interesting that the manager had called in sick, Niall mused. From the way Cody Prescott had acted—a bit twitchy—

Niall had the impression that this was not ordinary behavior from his uncle.

He wandered into the dining room located just off the lobby. A lone busboy was straightening the place settings, making sure the white linen napkins were folded into proper triangles and placing them atop the appetizer and dinner plates, which were bracketed by gleaming dinnerware. Niall picked up a fork. It was heavy in his hand. Not silver, but expensive. The worker studiously ignored him as he gazed out the windows. During the day it would be impossible for anyone to sneak around. Niall didn't see many security lights from where he was standing, directly in front of the windows; at night it would be much easier for someone to stay hidden.

A walking path from one side of the building led down to the water, meandering along the seawall until it was out of Niall's sight. Far to his right there was a sign for US Customs. Niall had forgotten that boats sailing in from Canada were supposed to officially cross the border here. He wondered how that arrangement had come about.

After poking his head into a few of the open conference rooms on the main floor, Niall took a hallway that led behind the kitchen to an outside exit. It opened up to what looked like an employee parking lot. No way did the wealthy hotel guests drive these cars; Niall's beat-up Subaru would fit in perfectly, though.

Feeling very much like he'd been doing something he shouldn't, Niall decided to head back toward Hidden Harbor. He debated stopping at Alyson's and picking up Fenrir, but he had this irrational thought that she would know what he'd been up to—and wouldn't approve.

He switched his focus back to Duane Cooper. The whole thing was bugging him. Why had Cooper been killed now? What had he been involved in that led to his death? In cop work, Niall had always asked himself who would benefit? Often money was involved in the answer—but as far as Niall knew, Cooper didn't have any.

There was Sharleen Dixon too. She'd been their only source of information about Cooper, and Niall had his suspicions about her. As dockmaster of the East Bay Marina, she would have seen Cooper around, probably more than she'd admitted to Mat. But… if she'd been in on Cooper's side business, she would likely be dead now too, right?

Out of the corner of his eye, Niall spotted the sign for the road Shay had rented a house on. Slowing down, he pulled a U-turn and headed back. Might as well make it believable when he told Mat about his day.

Niall rolled his eyes as he drove slowly down Rhododendron Street looking for the right address. This part of Piedras was exclusive: almost, but not quite, a gated community. It made sense, he supposed, with Brooch Resort practically next door. The beaches along here were privately owned and gated; the residents kept the riffraff and common folk off them.

Niall remembered that some of the land Mat's older brother, Sean, had been trying to buy up was around here—along with some on Orcas Island. Sean had planned to turn around and sell it all off to developers for a huge profit, but his death had put a stop to that. His murder.

Shay's house was at the end of the road, and nice, very nice. And far too big for a single man. Niall parked in the driveway and made his way up the steps to a bridge that crossed a damn gulch before he got to the front door. Looking down, he saw brush and large rocks below him. His half brother opened the door before he could knock.

"Afternoon. This is a pleasant surprise."

"I was in the area."

"Come on in," Shay said, opening the door wider.

"Nice place. You have your own moat," Niall commented. He

noticed Shay was in his sock feet and several pairs of shoes sat in a tidy line near the door. He toed his own shoes off and pushed them out of the way before following Shay.

"You want a tour?" Shay asked over his shoulder.

"Nah, that can wait until Mat is here too. What inspired you to rent this place?" Niall asked.

"You'll see. The kitchen and living room are through here." Shay led the way. "Coffee?"

"Sure." Niall followed him. The kitchen had been recently remodeled—had to have been, since the house was a prime example of 1980s architecture—and a deck the length of the house looked out over Haro Strait. *This* was why Shay had rented the house. "Gorgeous view."

"No fucking kidding." Shay turned to look out the huge picture window along with Niall. "So… why are you here?"

"Would you believe trying to stay out of trouble?"

"Is it working?"

"Mmm, not really." Niall stuck his hands in the back pockets of his jeans and leaned against the counter. He looked around. "Your place is primo."

"Yeah, and quiet too. Or it was. This morning some folks arrived next door."

"Oh yeah? Are you going to have to deal with a weekend of partiers?"

"I don't know. They seemed…"

"What?"

"I was getting my mail when these folks arrived, and they didn't seem like the type to rent a weekend place. Something is off. I mean, not everyone has to say hi when a neighbor greets them, but around here we do. Even visitors."

It was true. The island was friendly, and so were most of the people who visited.

"So they ignored you? Maybe you're losing your magic touch." Niall snickered.

Shay raised an eyebrow at him. "Four people: three men and a woman. Two big black SUVs. A lot of luggage, and then after unloading, one of the men and the woman left, and I haven't seen them come back."

"Peeking through curtains, even!"

"Niall." Shay frowned.

"No," Niall conceded. "I agree with you. That's odd." In his experience, two kinds of people drove big black SUVs: the feds and organized crime. "Show me."

He followed Shay out onto the deck that extended out over a sheer bluff—Shay's view of Haro Strait was similar to the one at the Brooch. They walked to one end, where they could look out over the small road that dead-ended here.

"The two who stayed behind have been here for hours and haven't even come outside to check out their deck. They haven't taken a walk on the beach."

"Maybe they're having wild sex?"

Shay threw him a laser stare. "It's turned out to be a gorgeous fall day. People may come to our islands to have wild sex, but on a day like this they at least walk the beach, have a glass of wine on the deck. They haven't left the house."

"There's no law against that. We don't have exact rules about how folks are supposed to enjoy themselves."

"And where did the other two go?" Shay grumbled. "That house is big enough for all four of them—and they'd get lost just like I do. Plus, none of them acted like couples. You know, no touches on the back, taking heavy bags, that sort of thing."

"You want me to tell Mat about them?"

Shay sighed. "No. It's just weird."

Niall had to agree with him. "Where is the SUV that stayed behind?"

"They parked it in the garage—who does that in a rental house? No one, that's who. Or, I guess, people who don't want other people to see their vehicle."

. . .

Niall stayed at Shay's long enough to finish the coffee Shay offered him. After leaving, he stopped in at Chester's to let Sage know that the protection rite, or whatever she called it, was on. And he grabbed another coffee—it was almost like being a cop again.

"That's wonderful, Niall," Sage exclaimed, smiling at him. "I'll contact Maddie Roux, and we'll look at the calendar together. I think it should be done as close to the equinox as possible. Will you be on the island?"

"You tell us the date, and we'll make sure to be here." He pulled out his wallet to pay for the coffee.

"So, you haven't set a date for the wedding yet?"

"No..." Comprehension dawned. "Alyson's been talking."

"Well," Sage said, "she's in all the time, and she may have mentioned a time or two that you and Mat still hadn't set a date."

Niall shook his head. "I guess we need to."

As he was slipping his wallet back into his pocket, a couple entered the store. That they were visitors to the island was immediately apparent; they looked like they'd walked out of an REI or L.L.Bean catalog. It wasn't unusual, Niall supposed. A lot of the Piedras tourists had money to burn and arrived ready to climb the highest mountain or something like that, despite there being no mountains on Piedras... but something about these two had him thinking about Shay's new neighbors.

The male was White, about six feet tall with bright red hair, and the freckles covering his face would make him recognizable anywhere. The woman was Latina, on the shorter side, maybe five three, with dark hair and dark eyes that took in her surroundings at a glance, and Niall thought they moved together like partners—but not lovers.

There was no doubt in Niall's mind that they were some kind of enforcement, but whether it was legal or illegal, he didn't know. Either way, the last thing Mat needed on Piedras right now was some kind of turf war. Casting one more glance at them, Niall hurriedly left the store.

He sat behind the wheel in the Chester's parking lot debating whether or not to call Mat and let him know about the odd visitors, but he had the feeling Mat would tell him he was imagining things. And maybe he was. Maybe he was seeing shadows where there weren't any. Those two could have been a normal couple taking time away from the rat race, recharging, having a romantic weekend. The thing was, Niall was certain the gleaming Ford Expedition belonged to them, and he really wanted to call in a favor and have someone run the plates so he could put his nagging suspicions to bed.

So what, he argued with himself. So what if this off-island couple drove a black SUV and seemed out of place? He needed to chill the fuck out. Mat was more than able to take care of himself and the citizens of Piedras—he'd been doing it for ten years before Niall showed back up and sort of accidentally insinuated himself into Mat's life. Mat had been a cop in San Francisco, for fuck's sake—a much more dangerous place than Piedras Island.

Duane Cooper, on the other hand… his death was something Niall was not going to ignore. It had been five days since he'd been found, and if Mat had any leads, he hadn't told Niall. There was something obvious they were missing, and Niall wanted to talk to Cooper's ex-wife.

Likely Mat would be pissed off, but Niall was going to do it anyway. The whole Cooper thing bothered him. Why hadn't he fled Piedras after the bombing? Why had he stuck around and gotten himself murdered?

Cooper had been through a divorce and, from what Mat and Birdy said, owed alimony forever, but he'd been able to afford several boats and the upkeep that went along with them. He'd still owned a house, even if it was small. Niall wanted to talk to the ex–Mrs. Cooper and maybe Sharleen Dixon. The ex lived in Anacortes, but Mat had said something about her taking charge of Cooper's remains. He shook his head. That wasn't the action of a bitter spouse, that was the behavior of a grieving widow.

The man and woman exited Chester's side by side, not speaking but with serious expressions on their faces. In tandem they opened the doors to the SUV and climbed in. Seconds later, the Expedition pulled out of the parking lot and headed down the road toward Hidden Harbor.

Niall tried calling Mat, but it went directly to voicemail. He clicked off without leaving a message, then tried a different number.

"Soper here."

"Marshal, Niall. Has Cooper's ex picked up his remains yet?"

"No…" Marshal sounded a bit confused, which, since it was Niall and not Mat calling, he should. "I talked to her a couple days ago. She's arranged for them to be picked up tomorrow."

Huh. He did not like this.

Niall checked the clock on the dashboard. It was just before two. If he sped and was lucky with the ferry, he could be in Anacortes around three thirty. He tossed off a request to Sol and her horses Árvakr and Alsviðr that the journey would in fact be swift—and that he would return to Piedras quickly with information that would put this case to rest.

NINETEEN
MAT

Saturday

Before heading to the station, Mat drove out to the Brooch to talk
to Paul Prescott and show him the composite. When he arrived,
though, it was Cody Prescott at the reception desk checking out
guests, and the elder Prescott was nowhere in sight.

Mat waited while Cody helped an older couple who kept
telling him how wonderful the resort was, that this was their
fortieth wedding anniversary and Brooch Resort had made it so
special. Cody kept glancing at Mat as he swiped their credit card
for the final bill and called a... bellhop, Mat supposed, to come
and help them get their luggage into the car.

From that interaction alone, Mat could tell that the younger
Prescott enjoyed his job and the resort.

"I'd like to speak to Paul Prescott," Mat said, once Cody was
free. "Is he your father?"

"He's my uncle."

"Your folks didn't want part of this?"

"Work for a living? No. When the 'rents divorced," Cody said wryly, "Uncle Paul got me." He shrugged. "Anyway, he's out sick today. What did you need with him?"

"He seemed okay yesterday."

"I think having the police out here really shook him up. Is there anything I can help you with?"

Mat pulled out the printout and unfolded it. "Do you recognize this man?"

Mat watched as Cody peered at the computer drawing.

"I'm not sure? I don't necessarily see everyone who comes to the resort. Maybe it's someone who visits but doesn't get a room. You know, likes to hang out at the bar or chat with the boaters. Could be a boater himself... but even then, I'd think I'd recognize him."

Mat nodded. "Thanks. When your uncle feels better, please have him call me." Putting the picture away, he pulled out his wallet and passed Cody a business card. "Here's my number in case you remember anything or your uncle comes in."

Mat started to leave but stopped, deciding he'd try one more angle. "I'm curious," he said. "Has anything seemed odd here lately? Have you had a lot of staff turnover? Is there, maybe, an incident that stands out to you?"

Cody looked thoughtful. "The hotel business is weird. All these different personalities, strangers, coming together, and we are expected to please all of them. Yes, we tend to attract a certain demographic, but there are differing personalities among them."

"But nothing recently that really struck you?"

"Well..." Cody lowered his voice. "What happened to that girl was terrible. Nothing like that has happened before—I mean, as far as I know."

"How long have you been working here?"

"This is my second high season. I worked part time, though, until I got my degree."

"Thank you," Mat said. "And do call if you think of anything."

Cody Prescott, Mat thought, was telling the truth. He hadn't recognized the man in the printout. Maybe Cody was right and he was someone who just came by for drinks, or maybe it had been a random attack. But Paul Prescott suddenly being sick worried him. He turned the key in the cruiser's ignition and drove out of the parking lot.

The multiple shades of gray that currently made up Chester's Grocery-Mart caught Mat's attention. It occurred to him that Sage saw a lot of people on the island, especially weekenders and seasonal folks who only came for the summer.

"Morning, Sage."

"Morning, Sheriff," Sage greeted him cheerily from behind the cash register. She was kneeling down organizing something, not currently helping a customer. Another employee had his back to Mat and was restocking produce.

"How are things?"

Sage stood up and faced him, crossing her arms over her chest. "It's been a busy morning already, and one of my part-timers started classes again, so I'm shorthanded. But business will die down soon enough. I shouldn't complain about being busy."

Mat walked over to the bagging area at the end of the cash wrap, pulled the now-wrinkled paper from his pocket, and showed it to her. "Do you recognize this man?" he asked.

She peered at the image for a long minute before looking back up at Mat. "I think so? I don't know his name, but he's stopped in once or twice. Funny…"

"What?"

"This is the second time recently I've been asked if I recognize someone. The first time it was a girl, though."

A mix of excitement and fear shot through Mat's chest. "What girl?" he asked, a tingle in his belly, knowing before Sage answered it would be Raisa.

"I'd never seen her before."

"How did they describe her? Who was asking?"

"It was a man and a woman I've never seen before. They had a head shot of her and didn't tell me her name. She had light hair, maybe blonde, and was in her late teens or early twenties. The man claimed she was his sister, but"—Sage snorted—"maybe *adopted* sister. They looked nothing alike."

Shit, shit, shit. What the hell was happening on his island? "If they come in again or anyone is asking questions like that, would you give me a call?"

"Of course. What's going on, Sheriff?"

"I don't know, but I'm damn well going to get to the bottom of it."

When he arrived at the station, he first checked in on the two girls. Maddie assured him they were fine and in the room she'd made up for them.

"What's going on, Sheriff?"

"I don't know."

"Same 'I don't know' that had a sheriff's department vehicle parked behind the building all night?"

"Yes, and I'm keeping it there as long as I can. Thanks for doing this, Maddie."

"Anytime. Although, this kind of thing—I'd rather have less of a need for my services."

"Me too. Me too."

Next, Mat and Birdy spent a few hours going to the businesses in town and showing the printout to people. No one seemed to recognize the man. Mrs. Tenny said maybe she did, but Mat pretty much thought she just wanted the notoriety—things were starting to die down after her discovery of Cooper's body. There were a few folks who thought maybe they'd seen him, and Mat tended to believe them, but they had no name, no other information. And, of course, a few places were closed. Mat marked them down to return to later.

Whoever the man was, it seemed likely he'd managed to go relatively unnoticed. If he was a visitor, he could have come by ferry, plane, or private boat. Mat was going to need to request the ferry terminal's video feed—but they didn't even have a date. They could be looking at months of feed, and something told him he didn't have that kind of time.

"Let's get back to the station," he said to Birdy. "You stay there and take any calls that may come in. Who knows, maybe someone we talked to was afraid to say anything but will call later."

"Yes, sir."

"When Deputy Jones gets in, have him relieve Radden."

"Yes, sir."

"Radden can take the night shift again, but if we don't get anyone in the next few days, we're not going to be able to keep this up, as much as I want to make sure they're safe."

"I understand, sir."

"Have we heard from Jorgensen yet?" Mat was anxious to get his new deputy on the schedule so his team could get a decent night's sleep.

"No. I'll let you know, sir."

"Sheriff or Mat," he reminded his favorite deputy.

At his desk, Mat powered up his desktop. Then he pulled out the legal pad with the list he and Niall had put together the other night.

Bellows had identified this man as the one he'd seen with Cooper. Patrick thought Raisa recognized him too, but she denied it. Raisa was likely in the United States illegally.

He tapped the pad with his pen, then added, "Unsub = Cooper's murderer."

It felt right, like when you found the puzzle piece that made the remaining bits practically fall into place. The pieces weren't quite falling into place yet, but they were getting close. Mat needed to figure out the connection between the unsub and Cooper, and who the mystery man was. That meant querying other agencies—and, regardless of what happened on TV, it was not lightning fast.

TWENTY

NIALL

Saturday

Niall sped along the roadway, keeping an eye out for slower vehicles. Of course, when you drove a twenty-year old Subaru, "speeding" was relative. He was pushing it at fifty-five, which was only five miles over the limit, but he needed to make the ferry. Niall couldn't help but think *if* it wasn't Cooper who blew up Mat's cruiser, it had to be whoever had killed him—and if the guy was still in the area, he might be starting to feel trapped.

Trapped animals were dangerous and would do anything to survive. But... why would he stick around? The only plausible reason Niall could come up with was that there was something the killer needed, otherwise he would've disappeared by now.

One of the multitude of reasons Niall hadn't had a regular partner during most of his time as a homicide investigator was *a failure to communicate*. Human resources had practically had it stamped on every page of his file.

Niall called it acting first and asking permission later. His childhood had taught him to listen to his instincts: to act, not to wait. Waiting got a person killed. If he was wrong, it was worth a slap on the hand—and he wasn't often wrong.

Therefore, if the ex–Mrs. Cooper was available to talk to, he was going to do it. He couldn't explain it, but he had a bad feeling and he wasn't going to ignore it.

When he arrived in Hidden Harbor, the ferry was just loading passengers. The line to board was fairly long, but he calculated he'd make it aboard. By some sort of luck, he managed to be the last car to board. He winced as he passed the sheriff's office, but he shoved his misgivings aside. Once Niall was parked on the deck but before they pulled away from the dock and he'd have no service, he called Ryder Mann.

"I don't have much time before I lose the signal—I'm heading to Anacortes. While I'm sailing, can you find everything you can about Duane Cooper—recently deceased—and his ex-wife? Shit, I don't even know her name, but she's the one I'm most interested in. But Cooper was a marine deputy out here for years."

"Uh, sure?"

Crap, Ryder was probably in the middle of something else.

"I should've asked, do you have the time? I know it's Saturday and an odd request."

"No, I can, shouldn't take long. I'll send what I find to your email. For this quick a turnaround, it will be pretty basic."

"That's fine. Just flag anything odd."

"Gotcha."

For the first time since Niall had moved back to Piedras, the slow pace of island life grated on his nerves. Instead of enjoying watching the islands slide by and wondering if they might see the J pod orcas swimming in the water, he wanted to be in Anacortes already.

Duane Cooper had been murdered a week ago. A long week for his killer to think and maybe realize he'd made a mistake, that by killing Duane he'd opened up a can of worms he hadn't known existed.

After what felt like hours but was only ninety minutes, Anacortes appeared in the distance. Niall's phone buzzed and vibrated as messages loaded. Luckily, there were none from Mat —what would Niall say if he called, anyway?

The email from Ryder was encrypted. Niall signed in, downloaded the file, and spent the last few minutes before the ferry docked reading it over. There were some interesting things about the ex–Mrs. Cooper he was certain Mat would like to know.

Guilt, a feeling Niall wasn't accustomed to, flooded him. He pushed it aside. He'd deal with Mat later. He had about two hours before the next ferry back to Hidden Harbor; he might as well use them wisely.

Cooper's ex-wife, Bonnie, lived near Alexander Beach, which, Ryder had noted, had a lot of high-end real estate. She paid her taxes on time and had money in the bank. She was self-employed as a bookkeeper, but that wouldn't account for her address or bank balance. Ryder had sent along the divorce settlement, and it wasn't much. The amount might hurt Duane financially, because as a marine deputy he didn't make money hand over fist, but still… where did Bonnie's money come from?

Niall had a feeling he wasn't going to like the answer… and that the money in Bonnie's accounts was why Duane no longer walked in this world. Even if the money wasn't the direct impetus, it was reason enough.

The address Ryder had sent him to was a one-story ranch-style house built in the 1960s or '70s, Niall thought, and well maintained—as in, freshly painted white with atrocious aqua trim. A gold, late-model Lexus SUV sat in the carport. Leaves from the maple trees that bracketed the house had blown across the driveway and underneath the car. It didn't seem like the car had been driven anywhere for a while.

The street the house was on was extra wide, like city builders had had a bit of space left over and didn't know what to do with it, so they'd added it to the road. The road also ran along the bay. All the houses here had incredible views and had to be pricey.

Niall eased himself out of the Subaru and shut the door. The street was quiet, and the sound seemed very loud. His was, he noticed, the only car parked on the street; everyone else used their driveways. Colorful leaves skittered down the street and sidewalk as the wind picked up; the fall storm the forecasters were predicting had arrived.

Duane's ex-wife must have seen him park—the door opened before he could knock.

"Bonnie Cooper?"

Mrs. Cooper was in her midfifties, probably five foot six, curvy, with gray-streaked auburn hair. She was wearing yoga pants and a white cable sweater that reached to midthigh. She looked tired, or scared. Maybe both. "Yes?"

"My name is Niall Hamarsson. I'm from West Coast Forensics." He showed her his badge before slipping it back into his pocket. "I have a few questions about your husband."

"I'm sorry—who are you?" She didn't automatically let him inside. On the one hand, he was glad she was questioning him. She shouldn't just allow random strangers inside her home. On the other, he didn't want to keep standing on the stoop.

"I'm with WCF. We're an investigative agency that assists smaller police and sheriff's departments in investigating cases." Oh boy, there was truth and there was him stretching it to the very limit.

"And?"

"And we have some questions about the death of your husband."

"Ex-husband." She remembered to correct him this time.

"May I come in?"

This time she stepped back to let Niall in. Like the outside, the inside of the house was sparkling and beautifully maintained. She led Niall into the living room, which had an enormous plate glass window that presumably looked out over Rosario Strait with a view of Lopez Island off in the distance—but since the shades were drawn, Niall couldn't see anything.

She gestured for him to sit in an overstuffed chair in front of the windows before sitting on the matching couch opposite him and clasping her hands together in her lap. "I should offer you something to drink."

"No, that's fine, I'm not thirsty."

"What do you want to know? We were divorced for many years."

"What was your relationship with your husband?"

"As I said, we were divorced for many years."

"You did, but it's not unusual for divorced couples to remain friendly or at least talk to each other. I'm wondering if you knew anything about Duane's business dealings."

Her hazel eyes widened, but she shook her head. "No, I wasn't involved in anything."

"But he paid you alimony, correct?" Niall steered away from her fear of Duane's business, coming at it from a different direction.

She nodded. "Yes, he did. He was very good about it."

"I'm curious, how he was able to afford that on his salary as a deputy?"

Her mouth opened and shut and opened again. "I don't know. I just know he paid me monthly, like he was supposed to."

"What do you do?" Niall asked, changing the subject again.

"What do I do?"

"Yes, I'm just curious."

"I freelance as a bookkeeper. Sometimes I help people with their taxes, but mostly bookkeeping here and there."

"Do you make a lot doing that?"

She wobbled her head. "Not so much. Enough, I guess."

"Did you know any of the people Duane worked with? Was there anyone you can think of who had a grudge? Maybe he owed money to someone? Because, I'll be honest here, Duane's finances do not add up."

The longer Niall sat in that room and talked to Mrs. Cooper, the more nervous she became. Instead of merely clasping her hands together, now she was wringing them, and Niall didn't think she realized she was doing it. She was scared about something and probably lying too, and it wouldn't take much to get her to break open. She was teetering on the edge, and he'd only been in the house for ten minutes.

"I think," Niall guessed, "you were closer to your ex-husband then you let on. Did you two get back together—unofficially, of course?"

"Who did you say you were with?"

"West Coast Forensics."

"And you're working with the Piedras sheriff?"

Niall did a half nod. "Consulting." If he were a praying man, he'd pray right then not to be struck by lightning.

Mrs. Cooper stood up. "I think I'm done answering questions," she said in a shaky voice. "I don't want to talk to you anymore."

Niall stood too. "Don't you want us to find out who murdered your husband?"

"Of course, but I don't know anything about it." Tears welled in her eyes, threatening to spill over. "Please leave."

He walked to the front door, then turned back to face her. "Out of curiosity, when was the last time you communicated with Duane?"

"Jesus Christ, I don't know. Maybe a few months ago? Now leave!"

Niall left. He got into his car and drove down the block and around the corner before pulling over again. Duane's ex-wife was scared; she knew something she wasn't telling anyone. Niall wondered if investigators had talked to her after Mat was injured. Probably. But one thing was for sure: a few months was less than the five months Duane Cooper had been on the lam.

Saturday

"Sir?"

"Yes?" Mat looked up from the notepad.

"Mrs. Tenny—"

"Jesus Christ, that woman is going to drive me around the bend. What now?"

"Sir." Birdy's voice had a tinge of displeasure. "She called to say there's some suspicious people asking around for a girl."

Mat sat up straight, immediately feeling guilty he'd bad-mouthed Mrs. Tenny. "What did she say?"

Birdy walked over to stand next to his desk. "She said it was a man and a woman, and they had a picture of a girl. She didn't recognize the girl, but she found the couple quite suspicious, so she watched them walk back to their car, and they drove down to the ferry waiting lot and they're still there."

"Did you take a look?"

"Not yet, sir."

Mat heaved himself out of his chair. "Let's go say hello to these guys." That they were the same people who'd been asking about Raisa at Chester's, he had zero doubt. They must have misread the ferry schedule, because the next one wasn't until after four.

Outside, he debated just walking the two blocks or taking his cruiser and decided he'd take the cruiser—it gave him more authority than walking up like a country sheriff. Which he was.

The second he spotted the big black SUV, he knew they were feds—or criminals, but more likely feds. And it pissed him off.

"What the hell are the motherfucking feds doing here? They didn't even have the courtesy to check in with my office. I hate it when they ride roughshod over local authority."

"They're feds, sir. It's kind of what they do."

"Yes, but normally they let locals know when they're around so we don't get in their way and they don't get in ours—which is what they're doing right now!"

He turned abruptly into the waiting lot and parked next to the Expedition. Why did they always drive the same fucking cars? Slamming his car door behind him, he stalked to the driver's side of the big car and pounded on the window.

The window rolled down, revealing a red-haired man in his early thirties. A woman sitting in the passenger seat leaned forward enough to see past her partner.

"What the hell are you guys doing here?" Mat demanded. "Don't you have the courtesy to call anymore? I have citizens"— okay, one nosy citizen—"calling because you're wandering around my island asking a lot of questions. In case you haven't noticed, this is a small community, and it's mine. I protect it, I take care of these people, and I want to know what you are doing here."

"I told you so," said the woman.

The man shook his head, reached into the center console, and pulled out a badge holder. Flipping it open, he held it through the open window so Mat could see it.

Nathaniel Richardson, FBI.

The woman held hers across the front of her partner. N. Gómez, also a special agent with the FBI.

"Do you guys want to explain yourselves?"

They glanced at each other and Gómez nodded. Richardson flipped open a file folder Mat hadn't noticed tucked in the console and pulled out a four-by-six photograph. He handed it to Mat. It was a picture of Raisa, and fairly recent, judging by the length of her hair. "We'd really like to know where this girl is."

"Why?" Mat demanded. "What has she done?"

"She's a witness. The only one we've got. We'd like her to stay alive and testify against a real shithead."

Mat still had the printout in his back pocket. Through his ire, instinct had him reaching for it and pulling it out. He unfolded it and handed it to Richardson.

"This guy?"

Gómez leaned over and snatched the paper from Richardson. "Franjo Petyr. Yes."

The name was unfamiliar to Mat. "I don't suppose Duane Cooper was on the feds' radar?" he asked.

Richardson shrugged. "Not as far as I know. Gómez?"

"Not a name I'm familiar with. We can take a look later," she said.

"Look," Mat began, "I don't want to talk here, and you can be assured that every eye in Hidden Harbor is trained on us right now. Come back to the station so we can talk in relative privacy?"

"Do you know where the girl, Raisa Melnik, is?"

"Come back with us, and we'll talk."

Residual anger still roiled beneath his skin, barely contained, as he drove the short distance with the Expedition behind him. It had been a damn long couple of days, and the arrival of the feds was going to make this day even longer.

"Sir?" Mat glanced at Birdy, who'd been remarkably quiet

during the exchange with the feds, not even mentioning his language. "Something tells me this is all connected."

"I would have to agree."

Yes, things were starting to come together. He hoped it would be nice and tidy, but with the way things had been going, he suspected it would be an unholy shit show.

"Good afternoon, Sheriff Dempsey. My apologies for not notifying your office my team was on the island. I'm Adam Klay." He held his hand out for Mat to shake. "Head of the FBI's Skagit field office."

"Only because he keeps turning down a promotion to West Coast lead," Richardson offered.

Klay and another fed, Sammy Ferreira, had arrived at the station minutes after Mat and the other two officers. Mat suspected Gómez had been on the phone to them the minute he pulled up next to their SUV.

If the station had felt small to Mat previously, now it felt like a broom closet with all four federal agents crowded in along with him and Flynn. There were rarely ever more than two of them in the building at any given time.

"Make yourselves at home," he said with barely any resentment, forcing a smile. "Would anyone like coffee?" It was almost five in the evening, but this day wasn't nearly over and Mat needed caffeine.

They all nodded.

"Do you have a room we can use?" Klay asked. He was around Mat's age, with short brown hair, a tight smile, and a build like a brick wall.

"I can give you a couple desks out here in the bullpen, or there's an interview room—but it will be a tight fit."

"We appreciate it. Thanks for accommodating us," said Klay, taking in the bullpen with sharp eyes.

Accommodating. Mat took a deep calming breath. He was still pissed and wanted a good explanation about why the feds were here, but he knew he likely wouldn't get one. And he wished he'd had time to look up the name he'd learned, Franjo Petyr.

He pulled out the battered composite and dropped it on his desk. "I want to catch this guy. I have a suspicion he's connected to more than one case here on Piedras."

"The Petyr family has always had their fingers in a lot of pies," Richardson said after staring at the piece of paper for a long moment. "We've had reason to believe he might be hiding out on the islands, but he's been careful not to be seen. More recently we narrowed it down to Piedras—the girl being here is not a coincidence."

Family. Wonderful. There was more than one of these fuckers.

Mat grabbed his bag from the back of his chair and pulled out the yellow pad he'd been making notes on.

Klay nodded toward the interview room. "Let's take it in there."

"Sure thing. Thanks for the recommendation on Soren Jorgensen, by the way."

"Jorgensen is a good man. You hired him, then?"

Mat nodded, flipping on the light in the small room and moving to the side so the agents could file inside. Once they were all seated, he took a seat as well.

Mat was reluctantly impressed by the feds' professionalism, as well as the team's general openness. Adam Klay was 100 percent in charge, but he listened to what Mat had to say, and they shared what they could about Petyr. The team didn't treat Mat and his department as lesser. In fact, they all went out of their way to compliment Mat and Birdy on what they had put together so far.

Mat had worked with the feds several times when he was in San Francisco, and it definitely didn't always go like this.

It seemed that Raisa Melnik was a witness, a human trafficking survivor who'd slipped through the feds' fingers last year. He wondered how she'd come to be working at Brooch Resort. Maybe Paul Prescott had been trying to cut corners with labor costs? Maybe she'd had legitimate-looking ID? They'd find out eventually.

"One of my deputies speaks a little Ukrainian, but not enough to fully interview Raisa. I put in an official request for a translator, but it might take longer than we want for the paperwork to go through. Is there anything you can do to expedite things?"

Richardson snorted, and his gaze darted to Klay, who tossed his fancy silver pen onto the desk with a clatter.

"What?" Mat glanced around the table at the amused faces of the other feds.

"Fucking Bolic," Klay grunted. "I should have thought of him."

"Is this a problem?" Mat asked.

"No." Klay picked his cell phone up from where it lay on the table and punched in a number.

"Seth. Adam. Have Sacha call me. No, I'm out on a case. Right. Hopefully. Thanks." This last was said a bit grudgingly. Mat had the impression it didn't relate to who Klay was talking to so much as who he was talking about.

Seconds later, Klay's cell phone buzzed, and he immediately answered, "Bolic. We have a situation over here on Piedras. If I tell you it involves Petyr, will you get your ass over here? Right. We're at the sheriff's office on Piedras. ASAP. Thanks." He looked at Mat. "He'll be here as soon as he can."

Mat's phone vibrated. Glancing at it, he saw it was Niall.

"I need to take this. I'll be back in minute or two."

"You're what?" Mat thought maybe they had a bad connection.

He'd heard Niall say he was in Anacortes, but last Mat knew, Niall was resting at home—like he was supposed to be.

"I'm in Anacortes," Niall repeated. "I just talked to Duane Cooper's ex-wife."

"Niall." Mat dug deep for patience he did not feel at the moment. Niall had fucking talked to Duane Cooper's ex-wife? "Say again?" he asked, knowing he sounded incredulous.

"You heard me."

Did he sound at all remorseful? Mat didn't think so. "Jesus Christ, you are not—" He searched around for the right descriptor. "You're not fucking Jim Rockford! You can't just go around interfering in an active case."

"I kind of am."

"What? What are you even saying?"

"I kind of am Jim Rockford. I'm a licensed PI who, apparently, can't keep his nose out of other people's business. I drive a crappy car and have terrible luck with women. Do you want to hear what I have to tell you or not?"

"Really? At this point, no," Mat ground out. "I'm pissed off. I didn't think I had to specifically ask you to keep your nose out of sheriff's office business. When I want your help, I'll be sure to ask for it."

There was a silence on the other end of the line, and Mat knew he'd gone too far. And shit, Niall was a good investigator. A great investigator, and he wouldn't be calling Mat right now if he hadn't found something.

"I didn't mean that. I'm sorry, Niall. The feds showed up today. They didn't even have the balls to tell me they were on my turf. They want the girl we brought in this morning; she's a witness in a human trafficking case."

"Okay," Niall responded, "but in case you missed the memo, Sheriff Mat Dempsey, I will do whatever it takes to keep you safe. I've never believed Duane Cooper acted alone. Therefore, whoever had him set the bomb is still alive and kicking, and"—he took a breath Mat could hear through their connection—"I can't fucking lose you. And I'm not sorry for coming down here."

Mat shut his eyes as he took in Niall's words, because he felt the same. He knew if push came to shove, he would do whatever it took to keep Niall alive and in his life. "I know. Just... What did you find out... Rockford?"

Niall snorted. "I just left her place. I'm actually parked around the corner right now. She's scared and hiding something for sure. I, uh, might have had Ryder look into her while I was on the ferry. She has money in various accounts, and something tells me the source was Duane's business. She's a part-time bookkeeper, Mat, in a relatively small town. She's never worked full time. Where else would the money come from?"

"Well, Cooper was paying alimony. I heard him bitch about it enough times."

"Was he paying her his entire salary? Because with what she has, he had to have been—and more. Yet he still had enough to buy boats, own his own house. The money trail is what we need to follow."

Mat didn't miss the *we*, but he chose to ignore it. "You say she's scared?"

"Yeah, the blinds were all drawn in the house, and her body language read terrified."

"Do you think she's going to run?"

"I've had some time to think about this, so let me just lay out some possibilities. Do you have the time?"

"A few more minutes. I like making them wait."

"Okay. Hear me out. We're pretty sure Cooper was smuggling something. Could have been drugs, whatever. He probably had a partner; he *had* to have one, in my opinion. And likely he'd been doing it a while. Maybe at first it was small stuff. Fast forward: somebody finds out. Your dad is my first guess. And they killed him for it—but Cooper managed to cover it up, make it look like an accident, and he's been flying under the radar ever since."

Mat nodded, even though Niall couldn't see him. The idea that something like this had been going on while he was sheriff really pissed him off.

"Then Jeffrey Reynolds comes along, and you and I both know he likes to find the dirt on people. I don't know exactly what he and your brother were up to, but somehow he ferreted out Cooper's secrets. Cooper panicked, but then Reynolds was arrested... and also the marina fire helped him out. I'll bet you a bag of doughnuts that speedboat he had moored out there was for picking up drops."

"Okay." This made sense to Mat.

"But I'm digressing. He's divorced, right? He can't have all this extra cash lying around; he needs to seem legit. A man who's hit some tough times and is struggling a bit. That's where the whale-touristy shit comes in. But there's no way he was making the kind of cash the ex-wife has from marine tours and low-grade smuggling. Along the way he got an offer he couldn't refuse—likely from this guy Petyr—that had him picking up much riskier cargo."

"Human trafficking." *Raisa.*

"One possibility. Drugs too."

Agent Klay stuck his head out the doorway of the interview room, raising a questioning eyebrow at Mat. He nodded back. "I'm gonna have to go, the feds are getting antsy."

"Okay, really quick. Bonnie claims she's a bookkeeper. What if she's been keeping the books for Cooper all these years—she was a money front. *Is*, since she's still alive. I don't know why she's still alive, but I have a feeling with Cooper dead, she's in a hell of a lot of hot water."

"Do you think the killer doesn't know about her?"

"Maybe, maybe not. If so, he may not know her level of involvement. Or he killed Duane only to find out someone else had the evidence he was after."

"And now he thinks she has what he wants," Mat speculated.

"And maybe even if he wants to get rid of her, that thing is still dangerous, so he can't just kill her. He needs whatever it is so he can destroy it. Maybe that's why Duane was killed?"

"Bingo. Records, electronic transfers, deposits, it could be anything. Maybe money too; maybe Duane was keeping too big of a cut. Who knows what it is, but he wants it or wants to destroy it."

"Back to my earlier question—do you think she'll run?"

"At this point, she's about to wet her pants if somebody looks at her sideways. She's cornered and doesn't know whether to run or dig a deeper hole and try to hide. In my opinion, I think she's going to rabbit. They always do—just when they should sit tight and ride out the storm, they run."

"I really have to go. Stay there for now. If she does leave, follow her. Don't let her out of your sight. And check in when you can. Oh, and Niall?"

"Yeah?"

"I'm glad you have bad luck with women."

Niall snorted and Mat clicked off, his mind swirling with the information Niall had given him. He was positive the man Tom Bellows had identified as Cooper's friend, who had been identified by the feds as Franjo Petyr, was the man who'd assaulted Raisa and killed Duane Cooper. There was too much pointing in this man's direction. It was circumstantial for now, but the hard evidence would come to light. It was trying to right now; they just needed a break.

Petyr had to have been Duane's partner all these years. Or maybe, like Niall had said, Duane had been the middleman, picking up goods in one place and depositing them in another— still illegal as hell. And what had they been smuggling? Mat hoped Duane hadn't knowingly stooped to human trafficking. The thought made him sick, that someone had so little regard for human life they reduced others to dollar signs and sold them as a commodity. In Mat's mind, people like that no longer qualified as human.

"Sorry to keep you waiting," Mat said as he eased back into the crowded interview room. Squeezing in between Birdy and Gómez, he sat back down and set his notepad on the table. They were all looking at him, seemingly waiting for him to speak.

"Well, what's the plan?" he asked.

"Sheriff," Klay began. "We've been searching for Raisa Melnik for over a year. She's the only witness we have against Franjo Petyr, and we want her back alive and safe. When Jorgenson saw her here, we knew we had to act fast, before she disappeared again."

"Well," Mat said stubbornly, "she's safe." As long as it was only him and his deputies who knew where she was, Raisa had little to worry about. Maddie Roux wouldn't say anything. It was when she stepped outside of the center that Raisa was going to become a target for Franjo Petyr.

"Where is she?" Gómez demanded. "We need her in protective custody yesterday."

"She's safe right now. I'm reluctant to tell you where, only because we promised to keep her safe, and that's something I take seriously. I run a clean station here. I'm sure you researched us—hell, probably when you wrote out your recommendation for Jorgensen."

Klay raised an eyebrow in silent acknowledgement, and Mat continued, "She's still on Piedras, in the safest place we could think of, and will be safe there for the night, at least. There's no ferry to leave on, and there's a storm headed this way. No one is going anywhere."

Gómez leaned toward Mat, interrupting what her lead had been about to say. "I understand. We all understand; we want nothing more than to protect her. Sammy and I can help whoever is with her now. She'll be doubly protected, and tomorrow we'll escort her to a safe house where she'll remain until the trial—because we are going to catch Franjo Petyr."

Mat glanced at Birdy. She was biting her lip and staring back at him. "Deputy Radden stays. He's been with her the most, and she seems to trust him."

Gómez held Mat's gaze for a moment before nodding her agreement.

TWENTY-TWO

NIALL

Saturday

That had gone about as well as Niall expected. Mat was pissed at him, and Niall deserved it, mostly. Even so, Niall still felt he was justified in his actions. He'd rather have Mat angry with him than dead.

He was parked around the corner from Bonnie Cooper's, where another street dead-ended at the bluff. He didn't feel as conspicuous here, as there were a couple other cars parked as if their owners had gone for a quick walk before dark. The wind had come up since he'd gotten off the ferry. An early fall storm seemed to be on its way.

Niall couldn't see the ex–Mrs. Cooper's house from where he was, but he had a feeling that something would be happening tonight. She'd reached the end of her rope, and if he waited until the morning, she would be gone. His visit probably hadn't helped, but there was nothing he could do about that.

Making sure the Subaru's dome light was turned off, Niall quietly opened the door and eased himself out of his car. The wind tugged at his clothing as he shut the door. He walked out to the edge of the bluff, hands in his pockets, and scanned the familiar view.

The wind buffeted him again. He looked to his right, the real reason why he was there. There were two houses between where he stood and Mrs. Cooper's. The closer one had a fence between it and the bluff, easy enough for Niall to slip along behind without being seen by the residents. The second had no fence and, like Mrs. Cooper's, had a large picture window so the home-owners could take in the view.

There weren't any lights on in the living room of the home, but there was light glowing from what was likely the kitchen, and Niall could see a shadow moving about doing something mundane like microwaving dinner or feeding the cat. Pulling the collar of his jacket up to protect his neck from the wind, Niall bent down and crawled the forty feet from one edge of the property to the other on his hands and knees. The cloudy half light threw weird shadows as the wind blew branches about, and at one point his foot slipped, sending a shower of leaves and rocks over the edge of the bluff. He froze, but with the wind and the waves below, he didn't think anyone could've heard him.

At the corner of the Cooper property there was a convenient cedar tree for Niall to take cover behind. Standing up, he brushed himself off as best he could, then peered at the back of the house from around the massive trunk.

Adjacent to the living room was a sliding glass door, and outside was a patio set covered with a tarp to protect it from the coming winter weather. Or maybe Mrs. Cooper was just the type who did that all the time. No outdoor lights had turned on since he'd left, and the shades were still tightly closed, but Niall could see that her car was still parked in the carport.

As he watched, however, a side door to the carport opened, and light spilled out onto the parking pad. Not a lot, but enough for Niall to watch Bonnie Cooper drag a suitcase out of the house and set it at the back of the car. She patted her pocket and darted back inside the house. Niall took the opportunity to slip out of the shadows and run across the lawn. He made it to the passenger side of her car, squatting below the window, before she came back out and unlocked the trunk with her key fob.

She opened the back hatch and heaved the suitcase in—and maybe another one; Niall couldn't tell from where he was crouched. The light in the house went out, the side door closed, and Bonnie came back to open the driver's door.

Taking the chance that when she'd unlocked the hatch all the doors had unlocked, Niall grabbed the passenger door handle and jerked the door open, launching himself inside.

Bonnie shrieked and tried frantically to get her key into the ignition. When that didn't work, she jerked sideways to get out of the car, almost falling to the pavement in her panic. Niall grabbed her by the long coat she'd slung over her sweater and pulled her back inside.

"Shut your door," he demanded.

"Don't hurt me! Please don't hurt me!" she begged, the fear clear on her face.

"I'm not going to hurt you. I was honest with you earlier. I am working with the Piedras County Sheriff's Office. But I have the distinct feeling you were not honest with me."

"I..." She took a deep shuddering breath.

"Pull yourself together," Niall said harshly. "You've managed to stay alive this long. Falling apart now will surely get you dead." While he spoke, he tried to think of what to do. When he'd told Mat she was going to run, he hadn't thought it would be twenty minutes later.

"Duane never told me anything. He said it was better this way. That the less I knew, the safer I was."

The interior of the car was dark, and Niall didn't like not being able to see Bonnie's face, but he sensed she was telling most of the truth. "Where were you going?"

"I don't know! I have a friend in Ashland. Maybe there. She said I could stay with her for a little while."

"And you think Duane's killer won't find you there? That he doesn't already know everything about you? As long as you don't run, he's not sure what you know—or if you know anything. But the minute you set foot off this property, you're dead too."

He was laying it on a bit thick, but he wanted her to accept what he was going to propose... and unless she truly believed the dark specter of death was on its way, he didn't think she would. She wanted to run *away* from danger, not into it.

"Here's what we're going to do." He checked his watch. "Instead of heading south, you're going to drive right up the road here and get in the ferry line. We'll catch the seven o'clock. It sails straight to Piedras without stopping—but I bet you know that already. And while we're on the ferry, you're going to tell me everything you know."

She stared at him, her eyes wide with fear and face wet with tears. "I can't go there. Duane said never to go there."

"Duane's dead," Niall reminded her.

"Why should I go to the island? It's never been anything but bad luck."

"There's some people who would like to talk to you. Sheriff Dempsey is just one of them."

"Oh, god, I don't know what to do," she sobbed.

"Do you know what Duane was involved in?"

"No." She shook her head. "He just sent me money to deposit."

"Nothing else?"

Her hesitation told him everything.

"Did he give you something, or maybe send you something, before he was killed? Or even earlier—before he went into hiding."

Her eyes widened and she bit her lip, tears still streaming

down her face. If she thought crying would make Niall feel kind-lier toward her, she was wrong.

"It's likely your husband was part of a smuggling ring that trafficked in human beings."

"What? No!" she protested. "Duane would never have done anything like that. He was a good man."

Niall raised his eyebrows. "I wouldn't be so sure, if I were you. Human trafficking is a very serious charge, and the authorities wouldn't be making it if they didn't have a great deal of evidence." They did have evidence, just not against Duane Cooper. "Did you and Duane have children?" he asked.

"No, we couldn't."

"Can you imagine, if you did have a child, that child being sold against their will into a life of slavery? You'd think it was impossible in this modern world, but in fact there are approxi-mately *forty million* human beings enslaved today. And your husband was likely responsible for some of them."

The car was quiet for a few minutes while Niall let Bonnie digest what he'd said.

"Duane sent me a package a few months ago." She sniffled and wiped her cheeks.

"What was in it?" Niall asked.

"A book. I didn't really look at it."

"Do you have it with you?"

She hesitated, then nodded.

Niall snatched the large handbag from the footwell. If he had something like, say, a record of some sort of illegal dealings, he'd want to keep it as close to him as possible at all times.

"What are you doing?" Bonnie screeched, jerking forward and grabbing for the bag, almost knocking their heads together. Niall held the bag away and turned slightly so he could look inside. She pulled frantically at his jacket, trying to get to her purse. "Stop it. I'm calling the police."

"That's complete horseshit. If you were going to call the

police, you would've done it already." He continued to rummage. Along one side, he felt something hard that was tucked into a zippered pocket. "Ah." He unzipped the pocket and withdrew a small, battered black notebook. Dropping the bag back to the floor, he opened the book and flipped through it. Page after page was filled with cramped handwriting noting dates, times, and locations. "You know, it's really hard for me to believe you had no idea what your husband was up to."

"He was my ex-husband," she hissed.

"Yeah, whatever," he scoffed, "Personally, I'm starting to think you and Cooper were trying to pull the wool over everyone's eyes." Spotting Bonnie's cell phone, he picked that up too.

"I hate you. Who do you think you are, anyway?"

Niall tucked the book and cell phone into the inside pocket of his jacket. If, in the process, he made sure Bonnie Cooper saw his weapon… well, so be it. He wouldn't use it unless he had to, but he also wouldn't hesitate. She let out a little gasp, and he knew it had worked. Hopefully she'd remain cooperative.

"Start the car. Take a left out of the driveway, and drive slowly down the street. Do not speed or do anything to catch the eye of the police or anyone else who might be watching you. Take the road to the ferry terminal. We need to make this run. Don't do anything foolish."

Bonnie did as Niall commanded. They drove through Anacortes and made it to the ferry terminal without incident, even though Niall almost gave himself a crick in his neck making sure no one was following them. He regretted leaving his Subaru behind, but there was no other choice. He didn't trust Bonnie to get on the ferry without him in the car. He flat-out did not trust her.

The line was long, and it was a toss-up whether they'd board the seven or the last sailing at nine. Niall kept his fingers crossed; the longer they were out in the open, the more worried he was that she'd try to flee. When he and Bonnie were on the ferry, he would feel a lot better.

Once they were in the line and Bonnie turned off the engine, Niall pulled out his cell phone and sent a quick text to Mat.

In line for seven o'clock run, not sure if we'll make it. Bringing Bonnie Cooper, grabbed her when she tried to run.

Moments later, Mat replied: **Let me know which one. Still at the station.**

"I have to go to the bathroom," Bonnie said into the silence.

Niall glanced over at the freestanding public restroom about fifty yards from where they were parked. Nope. No way. "You're gonna have to hold it."

TWENTY-THREE

MAT

Saturday

"We took a house out near Brooch Resort because we're fairly certain Petyr has branched out recently," Gómez was saying. "Land is a tad more respectable than human trafficking, and he likes nice things—feels he deserves them. He's here on the island under a newer alias. We think he's possibly using the last name of Lambert."

Why did that name sound familiar, Mat wondered. "That's not a terribly common name. Do we have Lamberts on the island?" he asked Birdy, even though he didn't think so.

"That name sounds familiar to me, sir," Birdy said.

"Do a search and see if anyone named Lambert comes up, or maybe a Lambert has moved here recently?" he asked her. "It's a long shot, but it's all we've got. If we don't find anything tonight, we can check with the real estate agency tomorrow. They have a 'Welcome to Piedras' mailing list."

Birdy pushed away from the table and left the room.

"We did a search as well," Ferreira added. "We didn't find anyone living here with that name who fit our profile. But several of the properties near the house we rented are owned by the same LLC, and LLCs don't have to reveal an individual's name. Doesn't mean we won't find it, just means we need to work a little harder. And... just because a handful of parcels are owned by the same LLC doesn't mean the owners are criminals, but this particular LLC uses 'vinók' in its name, which is a Ukrainian word for a type of wreath or crown traditionally worn by young, unmarried women. Maybe I'm reading a lot into nothing, but it seems like something Petyr would do. It's his kind of sick humor."

Mat thought about the real estate scheme his older brother had been involved in. Had Sean been involved in buying up other properties too? Possibly. Sean also liked nice things and had been in the process of trying to acquire them when he was murdered. It didn't seem far-fetched that he might have known about this Lambert person, or even been affiliated with him. Human trafficking? Mat wanted to believe that, even at his worst, Sean would never have been involved with the smuggling and selling of human beings. Maybe he'd never really known his brother, though.

"Sir?" Birdy poked her head back into the room. "It was a Sebastian Lambert who reported Chastity Reynolds's body, back in February. That's where I remember the name from."

Mat's heart began to pound. "What else do we know about him?"

"Not much, sir. He'd just moved here. I remember that he said he was at the marina because he was worried about wind damage from the night before and he'd been checking on his boat."

Right, Mat remembered. The man had said he'd taken early retirement and moved to Piedras. His sailboat had been moored at the marina where Chastity Reynolds's body had been found.

They'd never discovered where she'd been killed. Was it possible that Petyr had been involved in her death too?

Mat was going to have to talk to Jeffrey Reynolds again. Had he known Petyr? Damn. He checked the time; it was too late to get into the courthouse tonight. He'd need to go through Reynolds's lawyer, anyway. He pulled out his cell phone to find Amanda Tate's phone number.

She answered on the first ring. "Tate here."

"Ms. Tate, this is Sheriff Dempsey."

"What can I do for you, Sheriff?"

"I apologize for calling at the last minute, but I need to speak to Jeffrey Reynolds again."

"Are you bringing a bargain to the table?" she asked.

"Maybe, but I haven't run it through the DA. I need to talk to him, Jeffrey, first about who else might have been involved in his crime."

"He's never indicated anyone else was involved—other than your brother. I'll talk to him, but..." He heard the shrug in her voice. It was up to Jeffrey, but if he thought he might get a plea out of talking to them, Mat bet he would agree.

"Sooner, rather than later."

"I'm not on the island, so it won't be before tomorrow."

A thought struck Mat: Petyr/Lambert would likely know that Jeffrey Reynolds was being held at the Piedras County Justice Center. And, if Petyr was the cold-blooded killer the feds had painted him to be, he might very well want Jeffrey dead along with Cooper.

"When you talk to him, ask him about the name Lambert," Mat told her. "And make sure he knows Lambert is still on the island. I have a feeling he'll be more willing to meet with me then."

Clicking off, he looked back at the agents. "Being on an island has its pluses and minuses," he said. "I can't get in to see Jeffrey

Reynolds until tomorrow. There's not much more we can do tonight."

"Tell us about Reynolds. How do you think he might fit into the picture? We might be able to arrange something."

The clock ticked past eight thirty while Mat and Birdy rehashed what had been happening on the island since late winter. It was a little disconcerting to have the feds' eyes concentrating on him.

Agent Klay tapped the tabletop with his pen, the sound loud in the quiet room.

Richardson suddenly asked, "Do you think Reynolds really knows something?"

Klay looked up from his tapping. "What are you thinking?"

"I'm thinking Petyr must be feeling off-balance. The girl has disappeared, and he doesn't know where to. His back is against the wall, he's not thinking clearly, he's maybe as close to panicking as he was when he managed to elude us last year. He's felt safe here. Piedras wasn't on our radar until recently. But now he's feeling the pressure. And if this Reynolds person does know something or even pretends he knows something, he could also be on Petyr's hit list."

"Yeah, okay, but we don't actually know where Petyr is," Klay countered.

"I bet he's been mostly on the Brooch Resort end of the island," Mat offered. "I could be wrong, of course. But in addition to the LLC properties Ferreira mentioned, I'd expect him to choose that area because of its proximity to the Canadian border. Lots of unenforceable coastline."

They all looked at him. Mat cleared his throat and continued, "If he's smuggling, well, that's where I'd do it from. Hang on."

Out in the bullpen, Mat opened the bottom drawer of his desk and dug around to find an old paper map of the islands. He took it back into the room and lay it flat on the table so they all could see it.

He dragged his finger along the shoreline north of Brooch Resort. "This is the area with unobstructed shoreline. The houses here are big and fancy, and more than one of them has deep-water moorage. If I was doing what Petyr is doing, this is where I'd want to be."

"Several of the properties we've been investigating seem to be right along there," Richardson said after looking at his laptop again.

"What do you want to do?" Mat asked. "I have a pretty small department, pretty limited in the scope of assistance we can offer."

"First we need to pin down locations a bit more," Richardson said. "Where's the house we're staying in on this map?"

Klay rattled off an address on Rhododendron Street.

"That's right smack in the middle of the area I'm talking about," Mat said. "I'd check the properties here"—he moved his finger—"and along here. There'd be no reason for Petyr to have any inland property—unless he bought undeveloped land, and there's none on the coastline."

Someone banged against the station's front door. Birdy pushed away from the table to see who was outside and returned with two people. One was Niall, and the other was a woman Mat had heard about but never met. Duane Cooper's ex-wife looked terrible. She hadn't been sleeping well, if the bags under her eyes were any indication.

"Mat—Sheriff Dempsey," Niall corrected himself, "this is Bonnie Cooper. She has some information you'll want to hear."

The room was far too small for all of them plus Niall and Mrs. Cooper.

It was going to be a long night.

"Agents Klay and Richardson, this is Niall Hamarsson. He's with West Coast Forensics and also my partner. I'm going to step out of the room for a moment. Mrs. Cooper"—Mat took her elbow and led her to their interrogation room—"I'm going to have you wait in here for a few minutes. My apologies on the accommodations. I know they aren't the best."

"Am I being held? Are there... charges against me?" she asked.

"Mrs. Cooper," Mat began, "we just want to ask a few questions. You certainly aren't under arrest." With skill that came from a lot of practice, he eased Bonnie Cooper into the room, pulling out a chair so she could sit down. "Can I bring you something to drink, water or coffee?"

She shook her head.

"Okay. Please wait here. Someone will be with you in just a minute." Shutting the door, Mat headed toward the break room. He heard water running and suspected he'd find Niall there breaking into his coffee stash.

"I'm mad at you," Mat hissed when he came around the corner to, surprise, find Niall making a fresh pot of coffee.

Niall sighed. "I figured. Kinda hoped it would have worn off in the past few hours, though."

"Oh, it has. This is me totally calmed down."

"Mmm." Niall tossed out the old coffee filter, pulled out a new one, and reached up into the cabinet where Mat kept his special stash. He spooned fresh grounds into the machine and pressed the On button. Then he turned around and leaned back against the counter.

It was Mat's turn to sigh; he couldn't stay mad at Niall for long when they were together. Like thirty seconds was the maximum.

"I'm sure it's bad form to kiss the shit out of you in the station, but it's that or yell at you." After scanning to make sure no stray FBI agents were wandering around, Mat closed the distance between them, grabbed Niall's face, and planted a quick, hard kiss on his lips. Before Niall could properly respond, Mat stepped back, enjoying Niall's bemused expression.

"I definitely prefer that to being yelled at."

"Yeah, well," Mat groused. He'd much rather kiss Niall than deal with a bunch of feds, a dead fugitive, and a possibly hostile witness.

"So, what's the situation?" Niall asked.

Mat shook his head, not sure where to start. "I think we're close—and we were right, everything is connected." Quickly, he shared with Niall what he'd learned in the past few hours.

"They're across the street from the place Shay rented," Niall said. "I was over there just after noon. He'd seen these guys roll up and was totally suspicious of them. Which I find slightly amusing now. They came into Chester's when I was there too." He shrugged. "What else?"

"What did you learn from the ex?" Mat wanted to know.

"Well…" Niall grabbed a coffee mug. "You want some?"

Mat nodded, and Niall poured for him too.

"Bonnie Cooper is scared silly, or good at faking it. She was tossing suitcases in her car and ready to head for parts unknown when I stopped her. Duane sent her some kind of record a few months ago. She claims she hasn't really looked at it. But I have it right here." He tapped his pocket.

"Do you believe her?" Mat asked, holding his hand out for the evidence.

Niall grinned and handed over a small black book. "Six of one, half dozen of the other, really. If she has, she knows more than she's saying. If she hasn't, it's likely Petyr thinks she has and wants her dead anyway."

"Do you think Cooper told him he kept records?" Mat took a sip of his coffee. This already-long day needed more caffeine.

"Maybe as a last-ditch effort to try to keep Petyr from killing him?"

Mat thought that was very likely. But if so, it clearly hadn't worked.

TWENTY-FOUR
NIALL

Saturday

"So, the big question is—where is Petyr?" Niall asked, noticing how tired Mat looked, the lines on his forehead more pronounced. They were going to need more than a short vacation after this case was over. Maybe they needed to go someplace so far from Piedras no one would consider calling him.

Mat shook his head. "We don't know."

Mat's desk phone rang. Niall couldn't help but eye his ass as he strode over to answer it. The khaki uniform pants were pretty damn ugly, but Niall knew, firsthand, what was hidden underneath—and it was his.

"Sheriff's office, Sheriff Dempsey speaking."

The was silence while Mat listened to whoever was on the other end of the line. Then Mat began searching around his desk, grabbed a pen, and began jotting down information.

"Are you safe? Stay where you are—wait in your car if you need to, and lock your doors. I, or one of my team, will be there in just a few minutes. Don't call anyone else, okay?" Mat set the phone back on his desk.

In three long strides, Niall was next to him. "What?"

Mat looked at him. "That was Cody Prescott from Brooch Resort. He went to check on his uncle because he'd said he was sick and then wasn't answering calls. He's dead."

"Dammit, where?" Niall asked.

"His house is on Azalea Street."

"That's one street over from Shay's."

Mat crossed the bullpen and opened the door to the interview room housing the FBI team. "We've got a situation."

The feds immediately spilled out of the room. Niall would've thought it was funny, except someone was dead and a killer was on the loose.

"What's going on?" the agent who was obviously in charge demanded.

Mat and the agents would be heading to Paul Prescott's in minutes, and Niall knew he wouldn't be invited along. That didn't mean he was just going to wait at the station; that's not who he was. He thought for a second. The feds had the authority to close the tiny Piedras airport and the public moorages, but there was a shit ton of shoreline Franjo Petyr could disappear from—though possibly not right away. The ride in on the ferry had been bumpy, and there was a small craft warning through the next morning. Haro Strait in a storm was a death sentence. He punched in Shay's number and impatiently waited for him to answer.

"Hello?" Shay sounded sleepy, as if Niall had woken him up, or maybe he'd been reading or watching TV.

"Shay, it's Niall."

"What's up?" Shay was probably wondering why Niall was calling when they'd seen each other earlier that day. They were becoming friends, but not the kind that called every night to tuck each other into bed.

"Remember the folks who moved in next door?" Niall asked.

"Yeah. They took off a few hours ago. The garage door opened up, and they raced out of there. I thought maybe they'd changed their minds and were trying to get the last ferry."

"Yeah…" Niall glanced across the bullpen to where Mat and the agents were talking. "Look, Shay," he said quietly, "they're feds, and the shit is about to hit the fan. A perp Mat's been looking for—and it turns out the feds are too—he may be in your neighborhood."

"Do you know what this guy looks like?"

Feeling only slightly guilty, Niall snapped a picture of the composite drawing lying on Mat's desk and sent it to Shay.

"Just sent a picture. Not sure how close it is, but we're pretty sure this is the guy. If you see him, do not make contact with him. He is likely armed and highly dangerous." There was a pause. Niall presumed Shay was looking at the photo he'd sent.

"He looks familiar, but I can't place him."

"Well, he seems to have been on the island for a little while. Maybe not going to community events, but he's been around."

Niall couldn't stand the tension of inaction.

"I don't like this. I have a bad feeling. I'm coming over."

"Christ, Niall," Shay complained, "I don't need you to babysit me."

"It's not babysitting. I protect my family. Mat's busy with the feds; he's going to be working all night."

"Family, huh?"

"Family."

"Fine. I'll make more popcorn, and we can stream a lousy cop show."

"No way. I want to watch a legal thriller."

"We'll argue about it when you get here."

Niall felt in his pockets for his car keys and pulled up as he was heading for the door, realizing one problem with his plan. "Wait," he said to Shay. "I left my car in Anacortes—long story. Do you mind picking me up?"

Shay grumbled and muttered something about being "perfectly comfortable" but agreed to come and get Niall.

"Thanks, man. I'll be waiting outside."

Niall clicked off and shoved his phone back into his pocket. Not wanting to interfere—an outright lie because he did want to, but even he knew better than to mess with the feds—Niall sidled over to where Mat was getting ready to leave, talking to the fed with the red hair, and tapped him on the shoulder.

"I'm taking off." Mat frowned at him, but he was too wrapped up in the situation to ask any questions; for instance, "Where are you going?" Niall would let Mat think he'd headed back to the yurt. That *Rockford Files* joke Mat had made earlier was hitting a little too close to home.

"So, does Mat know what you're up to?" Shay asked in an irritatingly knowing tone.

"Know what?" Niall asked, attempting innocence. He'd never been a good liar.

Shay rolled his eyes at Niall before taking a right out of the station parking lot and heading up the hill. "All right. How about this, then—what's going on?"

"You mean what did I learn that I wasn't supposed to? Not much. Some asshole named Franjo Petyr is hiding out on the island, and he's a piece of work. It's likely that Duane Cooper and he were partners. Or maybe the guy learned what Cooper was doing and demanded a piece of the business."

"Huh."

"Yeah. Among other things, Petyr is a human trafficker."

Shay made a noise in his throat that Niall interpreted as him wanting to kill Petyr with his bare hands. He knew exactly how Shay felt.

Shay finally managed, "Do you think Cooper was too, or knew that Petyr was?"

Niall shrugged, even though Shay couldn't see him. They'd left Hidden Harbor behind, and Shay was navigating the dark road, his headlights illuminating the trees and shrubs along the roadway. Niall usually liked driving in the dark, but now it just seemed like there were too many places for Petyr to hide. "I didn't know Cooper at all. I talked to his widow tonight, though. That's what I was doing in Anacortes."

"Yeah?"

"She admitted she kept the books for Duane. He'd send her the money, and she kept track of it. He sent her some kind of record book last spring—she claims she doesn't know what it is. But I think it must be the reason Petyr is still on the island. Maybe he didn't know Cooper had managed to send it before he was forced into hiding."

"What kind of records do you think they are?"

"I really don't know, but if Petyr has stuck around looking for it, it must be important. It's probably dates, names, maybe coordinates. That sort of thing. Something that would implicate him. Cooper probably thought it would keep him alive."

"And yet... he's dead."

"Yep."

Niall checked his phone again; it was just past nine.

"Do you mind stopping at Alyson's so I can pick up Fenrir?"

"No problem," Shay agreed easily.

Niall quietly let himself into the Dempsey family home. Fenrir popped up from his dog bed and gamboled over to him, shoving his head against Niall's thigh in a hello.

"Did you miss me today?" Niall scratched right between

Fenrir's ears, where he liked it best. "Alyson, I'm stealing my dog back!"

He could hear the splashing noises of Riley's bath time coming from down the hallway. "Okay, see you later," Alyson called. "Maybe you and Mat could come to dinner this weekend?"

"Sounds good."

Niall let Fenrir out, locking the door behind himself. He opened the back door of Shay's car, and Fenrir gave him a "Whose car is this?" look before jumping inside.

They passed through Killegen's Point. It was quiet, the stores locked up for the night, even Chester's. Everything except the twenty-four-hour laundromat. Through the window, Niall saw a shadowy figure bent over one of the washing machines. The wind was gusting hard now. The trees lining the road danced wildly overhead, and downed branches already dotted the pavement like small offerings.

Shay broke the silence. "Where do you think he is? Where would you hide, if it was you?"

More trees and shrubs slid by. Red eyes glowed at them from the bushes: a raccoon, or maybe a coyote. Niall pondered Shay's question. Where *would* Petyr hide? He had to suspect that Paul Prescott's body had been discovered, that the police were on their way there right now or would be soon enough.

"If I were him," Niall said slowly, "I'd hide around the Brooch and try to get away by boat as soon as it's light enough or, I guess, when the wind dies down."

"There are Customs officials at the Brooch," Shay pointed out. "That would be pretty ballsy."

Niall nodded his agreement. "Ballsy for sure."

"Why wouldn't he try to get out tonight?"

"He'd have to be pretty desperate to drive a boat at night around here, even without the wind and especially with no spotter. I'm assuming he's on his own now, that he doesn't have anyone left to kill—except Bonnie Cooper. Before I called you, Mat got a call—Paul Prescott's nephew found him dead."

"I'm going to assume not by natural causes? I knew the guy, sort of, and while he might be the type to cut corners, he doesn't seem like a smuggler."

Niall wondered that himself. "My guess is because of the girl. Prescott was either also in on Petyr's operation or figured it out somehow and confronted him about it. We can speculate all we want, but I don't know if we'll ever learn all the answers."

Just as Shay took the turn to his house, the streetlights went out, as did all the porch and interior lights that had been on.

"Damn. Power's out," Shay grumbled.

"I'm not surprised, with this wind," Niall replied.

Shay approached the end of the street where his rental was located and slowed to a stop in front of the garage. "You think the kid is okay?" he asked. "Prescott's house is just over there." He pointed through the darkness to a house Niall couldn't see. "You said Prescott's nephew Cody found his body?"

"I'm already in enough trouble with Mat. I'm not going to check on the kid before Mat and the feds have a chance to interview him."

Shay fished a garage door remote out of the console and stared at it for a second. "Damn, that's not going to work." Instead he parked in front of the garage, blocking the door.

They had to cross the moat-slash-canyon to get into the house. At this time of night, with all the lights out, it was dark and especially creepy. The wind continued to gust, making branches scrape together ominously. Leaves were blowing off the maple and larch trees along the road. Niall couldn't see the water through the brush and shrubs at the end of the street; it was just a dark void. Even the stars were dark, hidden by a thick blanket of clouds. If there was a moon, it wasn't visible.

"I'm not saying we need to check on him," Shay grumbled.

"Just, he's a nice kid, and while I've never discovered a dead body, I figure it has to be unsettling."

"You've only officially been back on the island for a few days. How is it you know all these people?" Niall opened the car door for Fenrir, and the dog leapt elegantly out as if he were a celebrity.

"Niall, I never really left—not like you did. I've always come back to visit family and just to unwind."

"I suppose. Jesus Christ," Niall complained as he hunched his shoulders against the weather and began to walk toward the house, "this bridge is creepy.'

"I don't mind, and… I've always wanted my own moat."

Niall chuckled. Fenrir stopped to sniff something as they crossed the weird footbridge.

Shay fumbled with his keys for a second, muttering something Niall didn't quite catch before pushing the front door open. "Let me see, I think there's a generator," Shay said. "I'm trying to remember where it's located. There's a rental cheat sheet around here somewhere—it's probably in the garage." He dropped his keys onto a small table in the entryway and moved on, ahead of Niall.

"Wait," Niall murmured. Something was wrong. Even with the wind and the power out, things were too quiet, there was a stillness he didn't like. And where had Fenrir gotten to? Had he come inside? The dog did have a mind of his own.

"I've been waiting for you to get back." The words came out of the dark, chilling Niall to his soul.

"Shit!" Shay exclaimed, stepping back painfully onto Niall's foot.

The weapon Franjo Petyr held in his hand glinted ever so slightly, catching stray light from somewhere.

There was a popping sound, and they all blinked as the lights turned back on, the various digital clocks beeped, and the refrigerator rumbled to life. Either the generator had automatically kicked in or the power had come back on. Niall didn't know which it was, and he wasn't looking behind him at the street to find out while Petyr's weapon was aimed at them.

"There's two of us and only one of you," Niall growled. Where was the damn dog?

"I don't care." Petyr waved the gun between the two of them. "You are the one who will get me off the island." For just a moment he looked directly at Niall—sadly, he wasn't foolish enough to let Niall keep his attention.

"I honestly don't know how that's gonna happen," Niall said. "The island is locked up tight." At least he *hoped* the feds were doing their thing.

Petyr was an oddly indescribable person. He wasn't as tall as Niall and didn't carry as much muscle, but he looked strong—and he was the one holding the gun. Niall moved to stand between him and Shay, protecting Shay as much as he could.

"Such a sacrifice," Petyr said, noticing Niall's stance. "Willing to give yourself up for Delacombe."

"What do you want?" Niall demanded.

"I already told you, to get off the island. It's convenient your long-lost half brother is here to help me."

Petyr's dark eyes held a menace Niall hadn't witnessed in a very long time, not since a hostage situation when he was a beat cop. He was trying to come up with a plan, but—

"Get into the kitchen." Petyr waved his gun again. "I'll shoot the damn lawyer if you don't move fast enough for me."

Niall moved. Petyr kept his weapon pointed at Shay. He'd already killed one man today; another wouldn't mean anything to him.

Shay hadn't uttered a word since they'd entered the house and found Petyr waiting for them. Niall wanted to say something —to warn him not to do anything foolish. Petyr looked grim. Maybe he'd reached the end of the line, knew this was his final stand. That idea wasn't reassuring.

Niall's weapon was tucked into his shoulder holster under his jacket, but it would do him no good if Petyr shot Shay before Niall could pull it out. Petyr wasn't some petty criminal unused to using weapons, he was a cold-blooded killer.

Shay's kitchen stretched the width of the house. The cooktop and fridge were set against the wall opposite the picture windows that looked out over Haro Strait. The sink and dishwasher were fixed into the long, freestanding marble-topped island in the middle of the kitchen. On the other side of the island was a table with eight chairs around it—Niall thought that was overkill; he didn't have that many friends he'd want to spend a weekend with —and past the table was the slider out to the wraparound deck.

There were windows in all the exterior walls, reflecting their images back at them, the inky dark acting as a disturbing mirror. Still, Niall knew Mat was out there, at Prescott's house with the feds.

Petyr noted the direction of Niall's gaze and glanced over his shoulder, then back at Niall again. "Guess they found somebody dead over there."

"Yeah, you're a tough guy. Killing people who don't know how to fight back. Did you shoot Prescott in the back of the head, execution style? And assaulting a girl half your size. Did you feel better afterward? Do you think when they pull up your mug shot she won't be able to pick you out?" Niall was going to try the age-old "aggravate the perp as much as possible and see if he'll make a mistake" strategy.

It could work, or it could go horribly wrong. But he and Shay were both going to end up at the bottom of the moat, or worse, the bottom of Haro Strait if he didn't try *something*. "Of course you felt better. You're the kind of guy who likes to pick on people smaller than you are. It makes you feel strong, because deep inside you're just a scared little boy. You probably told yourself she deserved it... or maybe you were honest, and you told her—"

Petyr lashed out with his gun hand, striking Niall across the face. He was faster than Niall expected, and strong. The blow fucking hurt. Niall stumbled backward, folding in on himself, trying to reach his weapon. Shay made a little sound, but Petyr brought the gun up again, pointing it at him.

"Shut the fuck up," Petyr said through gritted teeth, then focused on Niall again. "Sit the fuck down before I put a hole in your friend. That fucking girl would be dead already if Prescott hadn't interfered."

The weapon was pointed directly at Shay, with no wavering. Petyr wore an expression men did when there was no way out. His plan was clearly to escape or die trying. Something perverse in Niall wanted to keep the man alive so the feds could get their hands on him. Petyr wouldn't be so arrogant then.

Limping around the island to the kitchen table with Petyr following him, Niall sat heavily in one of the dining room chairs facing the side windows, trying to make it seem as if the smack in the face hurt worse than it had. It *did* hurt. He still had scrapes from the damn building falling on him, and he was pretty sure Petyr's blow had reopened some of them.

As he sat, Niall paid attention to the house, trying to hear what it was telling him. He listened for Fenrir—shouldn't he be hearing his claws ticking against the hardwood flooring? Fenrir could be in the living room or somewhere else in the house that was carpeted—had he even come inside? Maybe Niall had imagined it.

"Tie him up." Petyr directed his command at Shay, waving at the counter with his other hand.

A nylon rope lay there. Niall hadn't noticed it until now. He had very little time to try to change the outcome of this situation. His gun was still in his shoulder holster, and Petyr hadn't noticed it yet.

"Hands behind your back."

As he began to comply, Niall's jacket gaped open. He hoped the holster was still hidden by his shirt but figured that was unlikely. From one of the other rooms he thought he heard something—a tentative step, a tick against tile flooring—but he couldn't be sure. The hallway? The kitchen? He prayed with everything inside of him for Fenrir to stay out of the way.

"What was that?" Petyr demanded, his eyes moving back and forth as he looked around the room but didn't see anything.

"I don't know," Shay responded. "The wind? Maybe a tree branch or something. Are you afraid of the dark, Petyr?"

"How do you know my name?"

Shay made a scoffing sound. Niall wanted to tell him to shut his trap, but he was trying to figure out how he was going to reach his gun, and Shay was a decent distraction. Petyr was going to kill both of them if he didn't do something. Niall had to get to his gun before his hands were bound. For the moment, instead of putting them behind his back, he carefully rested them on his thighs. Blood, or perhaps sweat, dripped down the side of his face, and his cheek throbbed.

"We know who you are and what you do," Shay said. "You won't make it off the island alive."

"For god's sake, Shay, don't aggravate the creep into killing us now."

Petyr chuckled; it wasn't a nice sound.

"You can't kill us both. You already said you need one of us to get you off the island." Shay's voice was calm and controlled. Niall knew, now, why he'd won so many cases. "And if you shoot us here, you'll surely get the attention of the police who are just a few hundred feet away. I can see police lights behind you, and they'd be over here in seconds."

If Shay was hoping Petyr would look the other way, it didn't work.

"I'm not worried about the police." Petyr's tone was arrogant. "The sheriff's department is looking, maybe for me, but I will be gone before their pathetic rent-a-cops can find me."

"You're not worried about the feds either?" Shay inquired. "They've joined the party, in case you were curious."

"Stop talking," Petyr ordered, spittle flying. "No more words from you."

It was now or never. Shay was as safe as he was ever going to be, behind him and slightly to his left, with Niall between him and Petyr. Slumping forward and moving both arms slightly back, as if he was complying with Petyr's demand to put his hands behind him, Niall instead reached for the Glock under his right arm. Being left-handed could be a pain in the ass, but it often took assailants by surprise, and Niall didn't miss the shock on Petyr's face when he pulled his gun out and squeezed the trigger.

He was out of practice, or maybe the blow to his face had done more damage than he realized. Niall's first shot grazed Petyr's arm and blew out the glass behind him. The second got him in the top of his shoulder as Niall dropped to the floor. Petyr grabbed at his shoulder but still managed to squeeze off several shots—at least one of which took out one of the windows facing the strait—before dropping to the floor on the other side of the island where Niall couldn't see him. He could hear him, though, breathing heavily and muttering in what was presumably Ukrainian.

"Shay, get down," Niall ordered.

"You think you could've warned a guy?" Shay's voice rose, incredulous. "I didn't even know you were carrying!"

"Shut it."

Niall was thinking he didn't know how badly he'd injured Petyr, when the lights went out and the house was plunged into darkness again. The wind, which had been strong all day, had picked up, and it started to rain. Niall could hear drops hitting the deck as the wind gusted in through the broken windows.

Playing with guns in the dark was never a good idea. He heard a shuffling sound and realized Petyr was likely trying to get to the front door while they couldn't see him. Did he have a vehicle?

Niall hadn't noticed one when he and Shay arrived, but that didn't really mean anything.

"What's your problem, Petyr? I thought you promised to kill us."

"Niall, do you really think you should be antagonizing the man? He's had a hard evening, what with the murdering not going his way."

Shuffle, shuffle. Rasp. The wind was making Niall hear things that weren't there. It was branches scraping together, not Fenrir.

Ignoring the pain in his head, Niall rose to his feet and rolled over the top of the island to the floor on the other side. Petyr was not there. Niall dropped into a crouch. If the power decided to come back on, he wanted to present as small a target as possible.

Tick.

Niall crawled on his hands and knees in the direction he thought Petyr had gone. He could hear someone breathing in the dark, but it was impossible to tell if it was Shay or the gunman. The way the wind was blowing through the shattered windows was making it hard to discern where sounds were coming from.

Something, a movement maybe, caught Niall's attention. Moving as fast as he could on his hands and knees, his gun digging into his palm, he crawled into the hallway leading to the front door.

A darker shadow against the black was making its way to the exit. Getting his feet under him, Niall leapt, landing half on top of Petyr and mashing him into the floor. Petyr's gun skittered off into the dark. Niall shoved his own weapon against the back of the man's neck. He struggled, but Niall had him in a wrestling hold.

"Shay, bring the rope over here and tie this jackass up while I hold him down." Because god fucking dammit, he didn't carry handcuffs anymore.

Petyr bucked underneath Niall, but Niall grabbed his arms and jerked them behind him, pushing one arm upward, discouraging him from struggling—his gunshot wound must hurt like a motherfucker, and Niall didn't have a problem with that. He had a height and weight advantage; the man wasn't going anywhere.

The electricity came back on again as Shay knelt behind Niall and began to tie Petyr's ankles together. After Niall was confident Petyr wasn't going anywhere, he rolled out of his way so Shay could wrap the rope around Petyr's wrists, cinching it so if the man struggled it would only become tighter.

Niall stood up, his heart racing. He took several deep breaths to calm himself. "Shay, find his gun and kick it over here."

Petyr spewed obscenities at them all the while, threatening to murder them, that he would send his men after them, that they would never know peace again.

"It's tempting to clock him so we don't have to listen to this bullshit," Niall said.

"As a lawyer, maybe not the best idea."

"He was trying to kill us. And he still wants to."

"As Shay, I'm with you."

The front door, which had never been properly shut, was unceremoniously nudged open, and Niall looked up, blinking at... his dog, tiptoeing into the house with a very guilty expression on his doggy face.

"What does Fenrir have in his mouth?" he asked Shay. "Has he been outside this entire time?" Niall groaned, remembering the last time Fenrir had brought him a gift. "This had better not be another bone."

Petyr started shrieking like a baby as Fenrir drew closer to him, and Niall snickered. He imagined that from where Petyr was lying on the floor, Fenrir looked enormous—and something was hanging from his fearsome maw. Plus he had leaves and twigs tangled in his coat, making him look like some otherworldly creature.

"Get it away from me!" Petyr was trying to crawl away.

"Scared of dogs, are you?" Niall sneered. "Maybe you've used them against people, and you know what they can do when they're mistreated or made to fear humans."

"It's a kitten," Shay exclaimed.

"He's pretty sweet, but I wouldn't call him a kitten." Niall was watching Petyr and enjoying the man's desperate keening. It was probably a terrible character failing on his part.

"No, Niall, Fenrir has a *kitten*."

Niall spun around to take a better look at his dog, who did in fact seem to be gripping something between his jaws.

"The hell." Niall stepped toward Fenrir, holding his hand out. "Whatcha got there? Can I see?"

Fenrir carefully stepped around the writhing Petyr. Niall could have sworn the wolfhound narrowed his eyes at the creep. When he got close enough to Niall, he opened his mouth and let Niall retrieve what was one of the most bedraggled kittens he'd ever seen. Until it moved slightly, Niall wasn't even sure it was alive; the creature was so small it fit in the palm of his hand.

"Really?" he said to the dog as he cradled the filthy beast against his chest, "I'm fighting for my life and you're... rescuing kittens?"

TWENTY-FIVE
MAT

Saturday

Mat's phone vibrated in his pocket. He ignored it. If it was an emergency, Dispatch would call the station. Birdy and Agent Richardson were there, having stayed back to interview Bonnie Cooper instead of accompanying Mat, Holstrom, Klay, and Ferreira to the Prescott residence. Someone needed to stay at the station with Cooper's ex, and they might as well find out what she knew while they were at it. Mat had handed Richardson the black book, saying, "I know nothing about how this was discovered."

Agents Gómez and Ferreira had left for the yoga center to talk with Raisa and Francine, and Deputy Radden, whom Raisa had asked to stay, would be sitting in. Birdy had stayed at the station with Bonnie Cooper, who wasn't under arrest but was also not going anywhere. And somewhere on the island was a stone-cold killer. There was little doubt in Mat's mind that Prescott had been gunned down by Franjo Petyr, and Mat thought he knew why. Until Petyr had put a bullet through his brain, Prescott must have been one of the few people left who could identify him. Mat suspected that Prescott had known more about Petyr than he'd admitted, and likely that knowledge had been his downfall.

The ambulance sat parked in Prescott's driveway, its blue and white lights flashing, but it was too late for Paul. He lay in his front room, open eyes staring at the ceiling, a red dot in the center of his forehead. He must not have been expecting Petyr to show up at his house. Perhaps he'd thought Petyr couldn't find him. Or maybe he'd hoped if he holed up at home, Petyr would forget he existed and just be on his merry way. Mat supposed it was possible the murderer wasn't Franjo Petyr, but the chances seemed very slim.

Nope.

The lights flickered, and the power went out for a second time. Cody Prescott was waiting in the kitchen for Mat to interview him while Holstrom guarded the front door. The kid was in a daze. He'd answered their knock without saying anything, just opening the door and pointing to the living room where his uncle's body lay.

The EMTs, Foster Jennings and Meredith Asher, pushed the gurney inside. They would be transporting Prescott's body directly to the morgue. There was no reason to bring Marshal out here on a night like this. Ferreira had been taking pictures of the scene, both with and without the body, while he and Klay talked quietly. Mat watched them work, envying their efficiency.

"What do you think, Agent Klay?" Mat asked just as his phone buzzed again. This time he glanced at it. "One second. I need to take this call." He swiped at the screen. "Niall, we're still working the Prescott—"

Niall interrupted him. "I'm at Shay's. We had a bit of a situation, and you and the feds are going to want to get over here. Shay and I are private citizens, and I think there's a good argument for putting this piece of shit out of my misery."

"What are you talking about?"

"Franjo Petyr tried to throw a little welcoming party for Shay and me. We took care of it. Don't worry—we're fine. He's here and still alive at this point." Niall rattled off an address the next block over.

"We'll be right there." Mat disconnected the call and turned back to Klay. "That was Niall. It sounds like Petyr was waiting for them. I hate being shorthanded like this." He sighed and ran a hand through his hair. If only he could clone Birdy or make time speed up so Jorgensen was already on the island.

Klay pulled out his phone. "Sammy can process the rest of the scene and interview Cody Prescott. You keep your deputies with the witness."

Mat nodded. He had no other choice, and the fact that Klay wasn't just kicking him off the case was something to be grateful for, at least. Foster and Meredith finished securing the body to the gurney and began to roll it out to the ambulance.

"Let Marshal know you're on your way."

Foster nodded, and they disappeared into the dark.

Shay was waiting at the door for them. He opened it wide so Mat and Klay could enter.

Mat did a double take when he saw Niall. An hour ago he'd been fine, but now he looked like he'd been hit by a truck. Blood had trickled down the left side of his face and dried there, one of his eyes was swollen, and he was holding one arm at a funny angle.

"What happened?" Mat demanded, his chest filling with emotion. Niall had a triumphant look in his eye, though—he might be bruised and battered, but Petyr was the one in handcuffs.

"Petyr was waiting for us when we got here," Niall responded. "He thought he could use Shay to get off the island—honestly, I don't think he thought it through. And I was a surprise addition."

"Do you need medical attention?"

Niall shook his head. "Nah, he knocked me on the head, but I have a thick skull."

"Your arm?"

Niall looked down. "Oh, my arm is fine." He turned his palm outward and extended it for Mat to see. Curled up in his hand was a tiny, filthy kitten. It was so dirty it was hard to tell what color its fur was.

"A kitten?" Mat squinted at the ball of fur.

Niall nodded. "Fenrir found it and brought it inside." Fenrir sat on his haunches next to Niall, a pleased expression on his doggy face.

"It's… alive?"

"Yep. I think I'm naming it Hel. Which is appropriate, because I suspect Fenrir found it at the bottom of the ravine."

"So it's really Fenrir's kitten?" No wonder the dog looked pleased with himself.

"Excuse me." Agent Klay's deep voice interrupted them, but Mat thought he detected a glint of humor in his dark eyes. "Let's focus on this POS." He nudged Petyr with the toe of his shiny shoe.

"Right." Mat turned away from Niall. All he really wanted to do was make sure his fiancé was okay, but right now he needed to be the sheriff.

They were still at Shay Delacombe's rental when the clocks ticked past midnight, and Mat was dead on his feet after a nearly twenty-hour day. He'd managed the last few hours on adrenaline alone—there wasn't anything much more thrilling than putting a big case to bed. But it wasn't fully put away yet. They needed to finish interviewing Bonnie Cooper and dig around in Paul Prescott's finances to fill out the paint-by-numbers murder case.

"Sammy has locked up the Prescott house," Klay was telling

him, "and Gómez is transporting Ms. Cooper to the house we rented for the rest of the night. That way we can keep her safe... and make sure she doesn't change her mind about sticking around to talk with us. Tomorrow we'll bring her back to the station and finish interviewing her there. Might as well see if we can get any more information out of her before she lawyers up."

Mat yawned and didn't even bother trying to hide it. "It's been an incredibly long past few days."

"I imagine. We'd like to get this wrapped up as soon as possible. Can we meet at the sheriff's office in the morning? Bolic will be here on the first ferry. He's fluent in Ukrainian and will act as interpreter."

It was nice of Agent Klay to ask and to keep Mat informed. The feds had total control over the case now. But Klay was playing nice and letting Mat feel like he had a say. And damn if Mat wasn't glad things were almost over. There were a few loose ends, but he was starting to see the big picture.

"I'll be there by eight at the latest," Mat said. "I'll have Deputy Radden bring Raisa."

"Have him bring her to the house tonight. She'll be staying with us as well. No offense, but I don't want any witnesses to go missing—again. She eluded us once before, and I'd rather not spend another year searching for her. I want this piece of shit put away."

Mat understood, he did, but it still rankled. He reminded himself that the important thing was putting the perp behind bars. Niall and Shay emerged from the bathroom, where they'd been attending to the kitten—which after a gentle rinse turned out to have faint gray and white stripes and, Niall said, was likely a girl.

"Shay, are you going to be okay? Do you want to stay with us tonight?" It killed Mat to offer, but he thought Shay might feel a bit odd after everything that happened and maybe shaky when his adrenaline wore off.

"It's late. The feds are just across the street. Surely they can keep an eye on my house too. Besides, I think everybody's been rounded up. There shouldn't be anyone coming for a visit in the next few hours, right?"

Klay agreed.

Before tackling kitten-bathing duties, Niall and Shay had found some plywood in the garage and nailed it across the broken windows. The weather was being kept outside where it belonged, and there was no chance of an intruder breaking in—at least, not through those windows.

"Pretty sure that's taken care of my damage deposit," Shay joked.

Petyr was spending the rest of the night at the Piedras County Justice Center; his wounds weren't serious enough to merit him staying at the hospital. Mat thought it fitting that Jeffrey Reynolds was getting to have a sleepover with him. They hadn't connected all the dots yet—hell, the case still looked like a three-year-old's line drawing—but he had a feeling in his gut that they were gonna have a nicely wrapped package when everything was said and done.

Most of all, Mat was looking forward to at least four hours' sleep, in his bed, with the man he wanted to spend the rest of his life with.

Mat wrinkled his nose at the odor permeating the cruiser. "Fenrir needs a bath. What the hell did he get into?"

Niall grimaced, settling himself into the passenger seat of the cruiser with the kitten tucked into his arm again. "No idea. The whole time Shay and I were dealing with Petyr, apparently he was on a mission of his own."

"Are you sure I shouldn't be calling Marshal to take a look at your face?"

"My face is fine."

"It really isn't. I like it without all the extras. You have a sort of black eye, and there's still blood in your hairline. Tell me again I shouldn't call Marshal."

"You shouldn't call Marshal. It's late. Don't you think he's been busy enough? We keep bringing him dead bodies to look at. We're as bad as cats."

As he turned the key in the ignition, Mat glanced at the kitten again. It looked quite comfortable, blinking sleepily back at him. "I take it we're keeping it?"

"Its name is Hel. And yes."

Mat backed the cruiser out of the driveway. "I don't like it when you get hurt."

"I don't like it much either. At least I didn't get blown up."

"You're splitting hairs," Mat protested. "You did almost get blown up."

"A building fell on us. Totally different."

"Are we really arguing about this?" Mat asked.

The empty roadway was half lit by the cruiser's headlights, the few streetlights doing their best to light the roadway. The wind had died down a bit but was still strong enough to cause branches to slow dance above their heads. A lot more debris had fallen to the ground. Mat saw something in the road ahead. He stopped and got out to pull a cottonwood sapling out of the way.

"No, I'm not arguing. But I think what you were really saying," Niall said when Mat climbed back into the car and got them going again, "is that you love me." Damn if the man didn't sound smug about it too.

"I do."

TWENTY-SIX
NIALL

Sunday–Monday

"Go shower. Seven is only a few hours from now. I'll get Hel settled and take a shower when you're done."

Really, what he needed was to take Mat into their bedroom and make sure he understood how much Niall loved him, how much he needed him. Mat was something Niall had never expected to have in his life—or even thought he wanted. Before Mat, Niall had been existing. Now he was living, and dammit if some of the living part wasn't hard shit to process.

The kitten squirmed in his hold. Niall set it down on the floor and watched as it wobbled toward Fenrir's bed. After sniffing a few times—the dog seriously did need a bath, but Niall wasn't giving him one tonight—the kitten curled up next to his chest, looking very pleased with herself.

Fenrir let out a *whuff* and rested his head on his paws, careful not to squish Hel. He didn't shut his eyes; instead, he watched Niall as if he could sense his inner turmoil.

"What?" Niall said to the dog as he heard the shower turn on.

Fenrir didn't answer, of course, although most of the time Niall half expected him to. Niall's gaze fell to the kitten again. The thing was tiny and definitely underfed. Next to Fenrir it was miniscule, and yet it trusted him completely. Hel understood already that Fenrir was its safe place.

"Are you trying to set an example for me? I'm not the one who disappeared into a canyon to rescue a kitten—but yeah, I'd do anything for Mat, so I guess you're right."

Niall crossed to the fridge, opened the door, and stared at the contents. Even though Hel appeared to be sleeping, she was probably hungry—and he was going to have to set up a makeshift litter box. He remembered a time when he was ten or eleven and his grandmother had found a kitten. She'd fed it scrambled eggs. The damn cat had grown to be twenty pounds and had still been alive when Niall left for Seattle.

He'd just finished scraping the egg onto a saucer set on the floor when Mat emerged from the shower with only a towel wrapped around his hips and—Niall hoped—nothing on underneath.

"That's a good idea," he said when he saw what Niall was doing.

Niall picked up Hel and placed her next to the dish. She sniffed at it and then began to delicately eat the egg.

"You're good at that," Mat said.

Niall frowned and looked at his partner. "Good at what?"

"Taking care of people. Taking care of those you love."

"I don't really feel like I am. I don't feel like I've ever done a good job taking care of… people."

Mat looked at him. His dark blue eyes were guileless and, as was so often the case, seemed to see right down into Niall's soul —even the parts he tried to hide, the parts he wasn't proud of, the parts that were scary that he didn't like to think about. "But you do. You've been taking care of me. I'd argue I don't need it, but I like that you take care of me. Does it bleed over a bit into my job as sheriff, which does put me in some danger? Yes. My job is inherently dangerous, and I like knowing that you have my back, Niall Hamarsson."

"I thought you were angry with me."

Hel had finished about half the egg and was waddling back over to tuck in next to Fenrir.

"Oh, I was." The towel started to slip from his hips and Mat caught it, tucking it in again. "I was angry, but then I thought… if our roles had been reversed, I would have done the same thing. And I think, correct me if I'm wrong, that you would maybe have not felt quite so protective if it hadn't been Duane Cooper who showed up dead."

"Maybe." He picked up the saucer, intending to put it on the counter.

"So, here's what I want you to do."

A certain tone in Mat's voice had Niall swinging around to stare at him.

"I want you to go take a shower and know that I will be waiting for you in bed. There're only a few hours before I have to be back at the station to meet with the feds and try to sort the rest of this mess out, but I'm fairly sure we'll be wrapping the case up. It feels like it to me. And if I'm going to be tired anyway, I'd like to also be recalling the epic sex we're about to have."

Hell fucking yes.

Mat was waiting, as promised, with his arms crossed behind his head, the covers only half covering him. Niall hadn't bothered wrapping a towel around himself. He climbed into bed completely naked, sliding his body next to Mat's and slotting himself where he belonged. "God, you feel good," he whispered.

"No, *you* feel good," Mat whispered back, tugging Niall so he lay partially on top of him.

The lovemaking started slow, as if Mat was new to Niall again.

He wanted to remind himself of the valleys and dips of Mat's body. Tracing and relearning each individual scar, from the old one barely visible under Mat's chin to the newest ones from April—even though Niall hated them, they were a reminder Mat was still alive and in his life.

Niall ran his nose along Mat's shoulder to his neck, breathing him in, filling his lungs with Mat's essence. One hand drifted downward, seemingly of its own accord, and Niall rubbed one of Mat's nipples until it was taut.

Mat's hands caressed Niall's shoulders before tracing his spine and ending up at the top of his ass, where he teased Niall's crease. Niall shifted so their erections were lined up against each other.

"Niall."

Maybe his adrenaline was still elevated from the fight with Petyr, but all Niall wanted was to be inside Mat, making sure he understood how much Niall desired him—needed him. Wanted to mark him as his own. And, as much as he would like to make this last all night, Niall wasn't going to make it; his cock was already rock hard.

"Niall," Mat said, a tad more demandingly, "hurry the fuck up. I need you."

Having his own thoughts mirrored by Mat was like dumping gasoline on a fire. His cock pulsed, and he ground down against Mat's body. "Prep yourself. I'm too worked up."

Niall lifted himself onto his knees, fisting his erection as he watched Mat ready his body. Grabbing the lube from the nightstand, Mat dripped some of the liquid into his palm before reaching between his legs. Niall had never been into this type of voyeurism before Mat, but watching his fingers rub around and into his hole as he stretched himself made Niall even harder.

While he was pushing a second and then a third finger inside himself, Mat teased one nipple with his other hand. His cock bounced, and a bead of precome oozed out onto his abs.

"It's my turn."

Mat, the love of his life, smiled at him and moved his hand. Crouching, Mat's legs half draped over Niall's thighs and Niall's hands gripping Mat's hips, he began to slowly push inside. As always, it was incredible: the pressure, the heat of Mat's body.

"Fucking hurry up—I thought we talked about this," Mat ground out.

Perversely, that made Niall want to move as slowly as possible, but even he couldn't stop the train now. For a minute he allowed himself to witness their union, his cock sliding into Mat's body, but the spark he'd been fighting—the goddamned electrical storm—couldn't be ignored. He pushed all the way inside and began pumping his hips.

Everything was too much: the lightning, his need for Mat. Niall tried to slow down, but Mat was no help, wrapping his long legs around Niall, digging his heels into Niall's ass and matching his every thrust. Niall tried to keep his eyes open, but it was too much; his orgasm hit, and he rode the tidal wave, pumping into Mat until, empty, he collapsed onto his lover with a groan.

"Every single time with you, it is fucking incredible," he whispered into Mat's ear. "Every fucking time. God, I love you so much." He felt stretched to his limit, the emotion he was feeling too big for his body. He shuddered, holding onto Mat's strong form like a drowning man.

Niall wasn't sure how long they lay like that, but Mat's soft, regular breathing had him gently pulling out and reaching for the tissues to clean them up.

Mat hardly stirred under his ministrations. Niall smiled, tucked himself in next to him again, pulled the comforter over them, and shut his eyes. It felt like a long time before he fell asleep—as if he couldn't convince his body everything was okay, that they were safe. But he did manage to, and morning came far too quickly.

. . .

He was the big spoon, one arm wrapped around Mat, keeping him tight against his chest. Unfortunately, there was a beeping sound neither of them could ignore.

Mat groaned and shut off the alarm. "I've got to get up."

Niall grunted and released his grip, rolling over onto his back. Mat followed him, kissing Niall on the side of the face before sitting up and getting out of bed to head toward the bathroom. And, yeah, Niall watched, because it was one of his favorite views. As he did, though, he heard his phone chime in the other room.

The text notification was followed by his phone actually ringing. Niall dragged himself out of bed to find it and kill it. He pulled on a pair of sleep pants, forgoing a shirt for now, and went to search the main room for his phone.

He found it in his coat—along with the cell phone he'd never returned to Bonnie Cooper. Glancing at his screen, he saw a missed call as well as a text from Ryder Mann. The message read: Call me ASAP.

Niall's first thought was that something had happened to Leo —or one of the other staff, but Leo was the person at WCF Niall was closest to.

Fenrir nudged him, asking to be let out. The kitten mewed, and Niall picked it up, cradling it against his chest as he opened the door for the dog.

"Make good choices," he called out as Fenrir disappeared around the side of the yurt. "Please don't bring anything back with you today."

Shutting the door, Niall quickly tapped Ryder's number. The phone only rang once.

"Dude, I am so glad you called back." Ryder's voice was breathy.

"What's going on? Why are you texting me on a Sunday morning? Is something the matter?"

Hel squirmed, asking to be put down. Niall complied and

watched as the kitten went to check out the saucer, which was empty. Niall opened the fridge, grabbing the milk and pouring some into a fresh saucer. It would have to do until they got to the pet store.

"What?" Ryder asked. "No, everything's fine on our end. But, hey, that woman you had me look into yesterday?'

"Yeah?" Niall tucked the phone between his neck and shoulder so he could start the coffee-making process. Both he and Mat were going to need a lot of caffeine today.

"Well, you know how it is." Ryder chuckled. "I just can't leave stuff alone sometimes. After I sent you that info, I got to thinking, and last night I had to run a deep check on her. And, ya know, if I'd hit a dead end, I would've stopped looking, but—"

Niall interrupted. Who knew how long it would take Ryder to spit out the information he was so excited about. "What did you find out?"

"Well…" He drew out the word, and Niall wanted to strangle him. "She's much more than an innocent small-town bookkeeper. I mean, I guess it's possible, but she manages millions of dollars. *Millions*, Niall. Her ex-husband's money was small potatoes, a front at the most. I didn't see it at first, because I was only looking at their connection and accounts, but once I went back and spent a few hours digging around, I discovered a snake pit. She's connected to some very bad people. Now, could it be coincidence? I suppose it's possible."

"Ryder."

"What?"

"Who is she connected to?"

"Oh, right. She's part of the Mogilevich family. Very tangentially, a second cousin or something, and that's worked for them because no one, say the US government, knew to look for her. The Mogileviches are part of the Ukrainian mob, and most of them are on the East Coast—New Jersey, Boston. I didn't know they were out here. But other crime families are moving west, and this was probably a way for them to diversify their portfolio."

"Bonnie Cooper?" She seemed as American to Niall as… apple pie, or something stupid like that.

"Her cover is that good, Niall, it's held for almost thirty years. But when she came to this country, her name was Bohdana Kovalenko. She was granted refugee status and then immediately disappeared, reappearing as Bonnie Cooper several years later, living in Anacortes and keeping her head down—at least enough that the feds didn't notice her."

"You're sure about this?"

From the silence on the other end of the line, Niall knew Ryder was offended by his question.

"Okay, sorry. You're sure. So, we have a situation." Niall ran a hand through his hair, trying to think. "The feds are already here on a separate thing—but maybe, after what you've told me, it isn't so separate. I'm gonna need to tell them about Bonnie, because I brought her back with me last night." Jeez, had it only been last night?

"Do you want me to send you what I found?"

Mat came out of the bedroom already wearing his uniform, his hair still slightly damp. He headed to the table where his jacket was hanging over a chair and began to put it on. Niall made eye contact and held up one finger.

"Ryder, I need to tell Mat about this. Send everything you've got to my email—and thanks, great work."

"Wait! Before you go. Ethan's team won't be able to get there for like a week. I don't even know why, all I know is there's a delay."

"That's fine. The remains aren't going anywhere, and they're protected."

"Okay. I'll keep you posted when I know more." He clicked off.

"What?" Mat asked after Niall set his phone on the counter.

Niall quickly shared what Ryder had told him. As he was talking, there was an impatient huff from the front porch. He crossed the room to let the dog in, nearly tripping over Hel in the process.

"Are you kidding me?" Mat asked, astounded.

Niall shook his head. "Not even a little bit." He picked up Hel again and held her against his bare chest.

"Why did she—Bonnie—let you bring her to the island?" Mat asked, a question that had crossed Niall's mind too.

"I didn't really give her much choice. Told her to drive the car to the ferry. Damn, she's a good actor."

"I need to get going." Mat patted himself, making sure he had his phone and other random sheriff paraphernalia. "I can't believe this," he muttered.

"Don't forget coffee." The machine had just finished gurgling and hissing. The carafe was full.

"Right." Mat grabbed his stainless steel to-go cup and filled it. Minutes later he was gone, and regardless of Fenrir and Hel, the yurt felt empty without him.

"Well." Niall looked down at Fenrir, who was eyeing him slightly askance and then looking pointedly at his food bowl. "Breakfast for you, and then what?"

Setting the kitten back down again, Niall poured dry food into Fenrir's dish and watched with amusement as Hel pushed in next to him and nearly tumbled inside the bowl. Fenrir just nudged her out of his way and continued eating.

Niall's cell phone pinged with a notification. He glanced at it and saw Ryder had sent over the files.

He was following this thing to the end. No way was he just sending the files to Mat and the feds and then sitting back and waiting to hear what happened. WCF had provided the information; Niall was going to see where it took them. Besides, he was the one who'd brought in Bonnie Cooper. And Mat hadn't specifically told him not to show up. If he'd thought about it, he might have, but he hadn't.

And that was an awful lot of justification.

Ignoring that last thought, Niall dressed quickly, pulling on a clean pair of jeans, a long-sleeved t-shirt, and a merino wool sweater. There was a chill to the air: fall had definitely arrived. After making sure he had everything he wanted—including the Glock tucked into his shoulder holster under his jacket—Niall left Fenrir in charge of Hel with a, "You brought her home, you have to take care of her."

He clattered down the front steps and turned toward where the Subaru was normally parked, only to stop in his tracks as he remembered he'd left his car in Anacortes.

"Fuck."

He stood there for a minute, his breath making puffy white clouds in the cool morning air. Maybe this was fate's way of telling him to let Mat take the case to the finish line. All the players were on the island. The feds had Petyr in custody.

"Truth will out," as the Bard had said, and its time was now. As he trudged back inside the yurt, Niall got his phone out, clicking on the email Ryder had sent. Then he selected Forward and sent it to Mat's work email.

TWENTY-SEVEN

MAT

Monday

Mat arrived at the station at the same time as Klay and Gómez, and there was someone with them Mat didn't recognize—as well as the two young women from Brooch Resort, who huddled together while Gómez talked to them in soothing tones. Raisa was obviously still terrified, and Mat felt for her. No matter how she'd come to the US or how long she'd been here, being under the scrutiny of the law was unnerving.

"Morning, everyone. I've learned something I think you're going to want to hear," Mat said as he shut the door of his cruiser and crossed the parking lot to meet the agents.

The new addition reminded him a little of Niall—the way Niall was edgy and wary, like he knew the world to be a cruel place and he would meet every blow with his own special brand of counterforce.

Klay introduced the newcomer as Sacha Bolic. "Bolic's an ex–US Marshal who also happens to speak Ukrainian," he explained. "He's helped us on a few other cases that required his expertise."

"Russian and Serbian too," Bolic added. He didn't have an accent, but Mat still suspected he hadn't been born here. He couldn't put his finger on what it was about him... just something.

"He's also my brother Seth's partner," Klay volunteered, "which for the life of me I cannot figure out."

Bolic threw Klay a quelling look, but Mat thought he saw the corner of his mouth lift in what could almost be called a smile. His eyes were hard, but when he shook Mat's hand he said, "Nice work. It's about time this scum was removed from the general population."

Mat agreed wholeheartedly. He opened his mouth again—surely the feds were going to want to know what WCF had dug up on Cooper's ex. "As I was—"

"Pardon me," Gómez interrupted him. "Bolic, the witnesses need some reassurance. Can we get this started?" The four of them disappeared into the same interview room they'd used the day before. Then Gómez came back out and went into the room where Bonnie Cooper was impatiently waiting.

"Where are Richardson and Ferreira? Not that it's really any of my business," Mat asked once it was just him and Klay.

"They spent the night at the justice center. Not that I don't trust you and your deputies, but we've been wanting to get our hands on this guy for a long time. They should be here any minute with Petyr—I want to see what happens when he gets a look at Bonnie Cooper."

Mat nodded. It made sense. His phone vibrated with an email notification; likely Niall had forwarded the information Ryder had discovered.

"Speaking of which, I learned—" The rest of his sentence was cut off by the entrance of the two agents who'd stood guard at the justice center. In front of them walked Franjo Petyr, in handcuffs and wearing a classy orange jumpsuit with the letters PCJC on the back. That both Richardson and Ferreira were on alert and ready to take Petyr down, hard, if he so much as batted an eye was immediately obvious to Mat.

Franjo Petyr was unassuming, something that probably worked well for him in his role as a human smuggler and who knew what else. He was five nine or ten, medium weight; his hair was the only thing about him that stood out, as it was jet black. Even the man's eye color was oddly indeterminate, and Mat had no problem seeing how he'd managed to escape capture as long as he had.

Just as they got to the middle of the room, Gómez opened the interview room door and ushered Bonnie Cooper out into the bullpen. She glanced around the room warily before her gaze landed on Petyr.

"You," she hissed, shrinking back against Gómez.

Petyr bolted from the agents. Mat didn't know what he thought he was going to do—the bullpen was on the small side, with desks and chairs at odd angles. Agent Richardson had a knee in his back before Mat could count to five.

Petyr still struggled, trying to get purchase so he could get to Bonnie Cooper. He was yelling in a language Mat didn't understand. Mat suspected this was the part where the criminal confesses all their crimes—and it irritated him he couldn't understand a word.

The door to the other interview room opened, and Sacha Bolic stuck his head out. When he spotted Petyr on the floor with Richardson on his back, a wolfish grin crossed his face, and he made his way over to the prisoner.

"Well, well, well, Franjo Petyr, here you are finally. Are you ready for your special time away at a federal facility? Keep talking so I can tell the nice officers what you were threatening this—" He stopped abruptly when he noticed Bonnie Cooper. "I know you. Is this a small-world coincidence I'm having? Bohdana Kovalenko, what are you doing here, so far from your cousin and all his friends? I mean"—Bolic stood to his full height, which was intimidating—"are you still running the books for him?" He turned to Klay. "You know who you have here, don't you? The gods must be smiling down at you, because in addition to Franjo Petyr—who, in my opinion, is a jumped-up piece of shit—you also have the numbers man, excuse me, numbers woman for the West Coast branch of the Mogilevich crime family. Or I assume she is. She's always been one of her cousin's favorites. Isn't that right, Bohdana?"

"Don't call me that. That is not my name."

"I'd cuff her if I were you, Gómez. She doesn't play by any rules."

"You can't prove anything! This is—this is a frame-up."

Mat's phone vibrated again, reminding him he'd received an email. It was from Niall, and as he suspected, it was the file that Ryder Mann had put together.

He held up his phone so everyone could see it. "Oh, but I think we can. Between this right here"—he shook his phone—"and the little black book Niall gave me yesterday, you will both be going away for a long time. When the feds get a good look at the ledger, I'm confident it will prove to be full of details about your wrongdoings."

"Fucking Cooper, he couldn't even kill you right," Petyr spat. "I give the man one fucking job, and he messes it up."

Richardson jerked Petyr up off the floor, probably a little more roughly than he needed to, but Mat would've done the same.

"Shut up, you fool," ordered Bonnie, as she tried to jerk out of Gómez's hold.

It seemed Petyr didn't like women telling him what to do because Bonnie's words only made him spew more.

"Well, that was an eventful morning," Mat said, repressing a yawn.

"I'm sad I missed the fun, sir," Birdy complained from where she was sitting at her desk.

"I know. Next time," he said, while also hoping that never again would he have human smugglers using his island as a drop-off point. That for the foreseeable future Piedras would be very quiet and boring, so he and Niall could get married and go on their honeymoon and come back to the island and find it the way they'd left it. For now, there were still a few things to clean up, and Cody Prescott was going to be burying his uncle in the next few days.

"You can come along if Jeffrey Reynolds agrees to see me."

"Sir?"

"I have a feeling he's not going to like it when I tell him I know Duane Cooper killed my father."

"Do we know that, sir? For certain?"

Birdy had missed Petyr's rant and Bonnie Cooper trying to shut him up, as she'd arrived about an hour after the feds drove off to the ferry, the girls safely tucked into one of the black SUVs with Gómez driving and Ferreira calling shotgun. Klay and Richardson had custody of Petyr and Bonnie—personally, Mat thought they'd drawn the short stick, because the two perps fought like an old unhappily married couple. Just before they pulled away, though, he saw Bolic lean in through the car window and chat briefly with Richardson. Then the two of them traded places, Richardson getting behind the wheel of Bolic's car.

"As certain as we'll ever be at this point, I think, and I refuse to bargain with Reynolds. I refuse to make my mother, or my sisters, go through his death all over again. He's gone, and having Reynolds 100 percent confirm Cooper was responsible isn't going to bring him back. I think my mom's been through enough with Sean's death too."

"A lot has happened this year."

"You're telling me."

"Oh, sir?"

"Yes?"

"Soren Jorgenson will be starting in two weeks." Birdy grinned at him.

"When did he call? Never mind, who cares—that's great news."

"Sir?" Birdy said again.

Mat leaned back in his chair and looked over at her, one eyebrow raised.

"I think you should take the rest of the day off. Now that the agents have left, surely you deserve a little personal time. I'll call Deputy Holstrom in a bit early, and we'll make sure the island stays safe."

Mat mulled over Birdy's offer for about thirty seconds. "Okay. I may take tomorrow too, depending." His mother's words about taking time when you had it floated back to him.

"Not a problem. With Jorgenson coming aboard, we're going to have plenty of coverage."

"Don't say that too loudly," Mat admonished. "You're going to curse us! But you know where to find me if something does happen."

"Yes sir, boss."

"Oh, hell no," Mat protested. "Not all in one sentence!"

Birdy chuckled while Mat shook his head and began to gather up his belongings so he could head home to his man.

Ten days later

"I think that went... well?" Mat said hesitantly, as he wasn't exactly sure what they'd just done. Both of them smelled slightly smoky, like sage (the plant, not the person) and the other herbs Sage and Maddie had used for purifying and then laying—he wasn't even sure if that was the right word— protective wards on Mat and Niall.

Niall shrugged. "It's not any weirder than appealing to Frigg and Freya, which, I'll admit, I do quite often.'

"Oh yeah? Norse gods?"

"Goddesses. Although I generally skip the sacrificial parts, I don't think they mind too much. So far it seems to be working. You come home to me every day."

Christ, when Niall said stuff like that, Mat didn't know how to respond.

"I love you. I'll never not want to come home."

"I know that. My heart worries sometimes, though." Niall glanced over at him, his light green eyes full of love.

Niall was driving their new-to-them car. When they'd finally made it to Anacortes to pick up the Subaru, instead of bringing it home, they'd gone straight to a dealership where they'd traded up for a larger SUV. The older car was too small for their family to pile inside along with Fenrir—who was also family—and tiny Hel, who wouldn't leave Fenrir's side. Buying a car together was such a boring domestic thing, but to Mat it felt like another comfortable milestone in their relationship.

"Hey." Mat pointed. "Turn down here."

Niall didn't ask why, just took the turn past Chester's that led to a lookout point facing the mainland. From here a person could see Lopez and, farther along, on a clear day, the North Cascades and even Mount Baker. There were no other cars there today. Niall parked off to the side, and they both got out.

There was an indignant *woof*. Niall shook his head and rolled his eyes before opening the back so Fenrir could hop out.

"Hel is not getting out," Niall muttered. She'd valiantly fought being tucked into a travel crate, though she seemed to have settled down a bit after her initial outrage. It was her own fault for not wanting to stay at home. Fenrir just wagged his tail and trotted off to sniff the tall grass on the other side of the road. Niall tugged his fuzzy wool cap down over his ears. He insisted the thing was called a toque. Mat begged to differ, but it wasn't worth arguing about—unless, of course, he wanted to tease Niall a little.

Zipping his coat up to his chin, Mat stepped around to the front of the car and leaned against the hood. Niall joined him, the SUV settling under their combined weight. The day was clear and cold. Mount Baker was magnificent, white with snow and gleaming in the sunshine. Niall slung one arm over Mat's shoulders and pulled him close. It felt perfect. They didn't need any words right now; together they gazed out at the wide world in front of them. Mat inhaled, then let the air back out, relaxing into Niall.

The past week or so had been a whirlwind of paperwork and phone calls between him and the feds, and Mat had somehow ended up spending a lot of time talking with Cody Prescott. He was Paul Prescott's heir, it turned out, and was very much struggling with the loss of his mentor and father figure. Funeral planning was not in Mat's job description, but it seemed Cody didn't have anyone else to turn to, so Mat had stepped up.

He'd also had the malicious pleasure of setting up a meeting with Jeffrey Reynolds so he could let the creep know he didn't have any information for Mat worth a deal. Had it been a petty move? Absolutely. Had Mat enjoyed making sure Reynolds knew he was going to stay right where he was for a very long time? Yes.

Mat knew it was ridiculous, but the fact that Reynolds had dated Niall before him rankled—even though he *knew* Niall was his now and nothing was going to change that. Jeffrey Reynolds was a person Mat could not find anything redeeming about. Hell, Birdy Flynn couldn't find anything good about him, and she found something good in almost everyone.

Then there'd been the arrival of the forensic team from WCF. It had taken Ethan Moore and his team just four days to exhume the remains. The group of investigators had done their best to be unobtrusive, but having strangers on the property digging stuff up had been an issue—especially for Fenrir, who'd taken an instant dislike to *his* forest being invaded.

Niall had complained the entire week about the low-grade grumbling and growling that had occurred whenever Fenrir heard the team's voices outside, apparently also paired with pacing to the front door and back to Niall asking to be let out so he could, what? Dismember the archaeologists? Mat had no idea, but the entire household was glad when the team finally packed everything up and left. The results would likely land in Mat's in-box in a few days, something he both dreaded and looked forward to.

It was also far past time to sit down and talk to his mom about his dad's death, about Mat's all-but-confirmed suspicion that Duane Cooper was the one responsible. In a sense, justice had already been served, however late—and neither man would be coming back—but Alyson Dempsey deserved to know what Mat thought had really happened: that his dad had, inadvertently or through investigation, discovered Cooper was smuggling and confronted him about it.

Over the past few days, Mat and Niall had come up with all sorts of scenarios about how it might have gone down, but he figured it was likely fairly straightforward. They'd been out on the water together and Cooper had straight-up hit his dad in the head, pushed him overboard, and then lied about not being on the boat—there'd been no witnesses to dispute Cooper's claim that Sheriff Dempsey had been alone, checking on a distressed boater. It had been that simple.

"Get back here." Niall's voice pulled Mat from his thoughts, and Mat realized Fenrir had wandered to the cliff side of the logs that kept cars from driving over the edge. The dog gave Niall a look but obeyed and ambled over, sitting on his haunches on the other side of Niall and leaning against him.

"It's a Niall sandwich." "Sandwich time" being Riley's new favorite joke.

"You are such a goof."

"Are you talking to me or Fenrir?"

Whatever Niall responded with was whipped away by the wind. Maybe he hadn't said anything. Niall pulled him even closer and pressed his lips against Mat's in a gentle kiss. Mat couldn't help but part his lips and dart his tongue out so he could taste Niall.

Too soon Niall pulled back, his arm still over Mat's shoulders and other hand against Mat's cheek. Mat stared into his eyes. Love and just a tinge of uncertainty swam there.

"I can't believe"—Niall's voice broke—"of all the people in the world, you picked me."

"It goes both ways, believe me."

"I love you, Mat Dempsey. I love your family too—because of them I have a family now." He traced a long finger down and along Mat's jawline. "I love you and everything you bring to my life."

Mat couldn't help but kiss him again. Their cold noses bumped against each other. Leaning away, Mat smiled at his man. "I guess we should get going. Mom's expecting us."

Niall nodded. "Come on, dog, get back in the car."

Once the conversation with Alyson was over, he and Niall were leaving Hel and Fenrir with her and Riley for the afternoon and driving into Hidden Harbor, where Mat had an appointment for the beginning of a tattoo that, he hoped, would cover the scars on his chest.

"You don't think it's a ridiculous, me getting a tattoo?" he asked for the hundredth time, as he opened the door and settled into the passenger seat. He felt like a teenager, getting his first tattoo at an age he didn't want to think about.

"You saw what Kim drew you. It's amazing." Niall started the engine, maneuvering the car around so they were heading the right direction.

"It's beautiful. I'm not sure I'm worthy."

Kim had sent over the design, an intricate Celtic knot with a sword running through it. The whole thing would be done in black ink. Mat was thinking he might add a little color at the end, but the design had to be inked on in black first anyway.

"You don't have to get such a big one, though," Niall continued. "You could start out a bit smaller and see how it feels."

"That's not how I roll."

"Oh?"

"When I decide on something, I want the whole thing. Not a section, or a slice, or a taste. The whole damn thing."

"The whole thing, huh?"

Niall's wicked chuckle did *something* to Mat's dick, and he shifted to adjust himself.

"Yeah, the whole thing. The good—the reasons for that should be obvious. The bad—because you can't have good without bad, and bad makes the good even better. And all the stuff in between, because those are the things that make life, right? Life isn't just one thing, life is all the things. Life is…" Mat cast around. "Sitting out on the porch with you watching the waves. Cleaning up the mauled toilet paper rolls." Hel was costing them a lot where toilet paper was concerned. "Taking the trash out. Getting up at three in the morning to watch meteor showers. Doing dishes knowing I'm washing two plates and two sets of silverware—even laundry. It's all those things." He trailed off, glancing at Niall.

"I'm starting to believe you might like me okay," Niall said with a grin.

"You know I do."

"Does that mean you'll help design a new cabin?"

And, yeah, Mat had been holding back: afraid to make any decisions, to influence Niall, because the old cabin hadn't been Mat's space, not ever. But if he was going to pontificate about love and how it was everything, then he needed to accept that Niall wanted to build a new cabin with him, with both of them in mind, *together*. The new cabin would be a home where he and Niall would move forward as a couple, syncing their lives.

Mat released a satisfied sigh and couldn't help but smile. "Yeah, okay."

EPILOGUE

Seven months later—Mat

"You may now kiss your husband," Shay Delacombe solemnly announced.

Mat took another half second to contemplate his husband, the tall, dark, and broody man he wanted to spend the rest of his life with. They'd both shed tears during the ceremony. It had been more difficult than Mat had expected speaking his vows, and hearing Niall say his own back to Mat, in front of approximately sixty of their friends. But they'd managed it. They had declared their love and promised themselves to each other. It was... overwhelming, and wonderful and a whole host of emotions he couldn't name at the moment.

"Well?" Shay teased. "Second thoughts already?"

His joking words lightened the mood that was close to suffocating Mat. In tandem he and Niall leaned in, hands still clasped together. Their lips barely touched. Mat breathed in the scent of Niall's cologne. Beneath it he could smell Niall himself. Mat would know his woodsy-cinnamon-coffee essence anywhere.

The audience collectively sighed. Mat heard someone sniff from the front row. Ending the moment, Mat moved to stand shoulder to shoulder with his husband, facing their guests.

"Everyone," Shay said to the crowd, "refreshments will be served in a few moments. Please make your way to the main hall." So only Mat and Niall could hear, Shay added, "But let the grooms get there first, because they both need a drink."

"Hey!" Mat protested.

"Am I wrong?"

No, he wasn't.

They'd decided to hold the wedding at Walker Winery and Tasting Room in Skagit, so there was plenty to drink. And after the dinner and reception, Mat and Niall were heading to Sea-Tac, where they'd board a plane headed for Thailand. Neither one of them had traveled much outside the US before, and Thailand seemed perfect—and relatively LGBTQA friendly. They were spending a few days in Bangkok before heading to Chiang Mai and then Phuket. The trip of a lifetime with the man he loved. He couldn't wait to get started.

Niall, who hadn't let go of Mat's hand since they'd slid the rings onto each other's fingers, tugged him toward the first group waiting to greet them. They'd decided against a formal receiving line. They'd mingle and greet all the guests over the course of the evening.

"Uncle Mat!" Riley cried, "You look handsome. Are you really going to see the elephants? Can I have a piece of cake now?"

Mat eyed his sister Ella. "Did you tell her she had to be polite before she could eat?"

Ella laughed. "I did my best to set some ground rules."

Mat ruffled Riley's hair with his free hand. "Let's see… Thank you, yes, we are going to see elephants, and there'll be cake after dinner."

"Hmph."

Riley looked adorable in purple cowboy boots, denim skirt,

and red shirt. The ensemble was paired with a pair of bright orange tights covered with multicolored flowers. One thing Mat and Niall had insisted on was casual attire; they did not want their guests to dress up if they didn't want to. Plus, since it was in an old barn, fancy dress seemed ridiculous.

His mom had been right when she said Skagit was far enough away to deter drop-ins. But everyone they'd invited had come. Including Niall's new coworkers Leo Zelinsky, Kimball Frye, Ryder Mann, and Scarlett Weaver. Of course, Birdy Flynn was there, along with Patrick Radden and Theo Jones. As the newest, Soren Jorgenson had drawn the short stick and was in charge of the Sheriff's Office while everyone else was gone. Even Fiona had planned to be there, but she'd had to cancel when the twins came down with a nasty flu.

"You're going to take good care of Fenrir and Hel while we're gone?" Niall's rumbly voice sent shivers down Mat's spine. Their flight didn't leave until the wee hours of the morning, so they'd gotten a hotel room close to the airport. Mat didn't plan on using the room for sleeping. They could do that on the plane.

"Yes, Uncle Niall, I promise. We have plans. I'm going to go on an adventure too."

Mat could practically feel Niall melt at the casual way Riley called him "uncle." The man was tough and grumbly, with walls built so high most people gave up, but Riley had snuck around them.

Caleb Collier raced up to them. "Hi, misters." He slid to a stop and looked at both of them, then Riley. "Riley, come on, I want to show you something!" Everyone snickered at Caleb's lack of interest in the grooms. He obviously wanted to explore the barn, and the property owners had a kid too, so there were plenty of kid things to do.

Riley and Caleb dashed off, Shay and Ella following them, leaving Mat and Niall alone for the moment.

Mat took Niall's other hand and turned so they were facing

each other, as they had during the ceremony. "Husband," he said, staring into Niall's agate-green eyes.

"Husband," Niall repeated, one corner of his mouth curling upward in a rare smile.

"We did it. I kind of can't believe it," Mat said.

Niall huffed and rolled his eyes. "Me either. I thought we might have to elope after all."

"I kind of wish we had, but at the same time it was nice being surrounded by family."

"Huh," Niall grunted.

"Yeah, 'cause now you have one, with all the warts and sunshine."

"Warts and sunshine?"

Mat shrugged. "I'm no poet. I'm just your husband."

Letting go of Mat's hands, Niall grabbed his lapels and shuffled closer, so they were toe to toe, foreheads touching.

"Mind the suit," Mat protested, but he wasn't serious. Niall could handle him however he wanted.

"I love you, Mat Dempsey," Niall growled. "We didn't need to do all this. No matter what, I love you. You're the only one for me. You always will be."

"That's a long time, always."

Niall released one of Mat's lapels, bringing his hand up to cup Mat's cheek. "Forever. That's all I need."

Continue on with *Full Disclosure,* book 4 in *Veiled Intentions*

He thought he didn't care what had happened to his mother after she disappeared all those years ago. But, the past has a way of rising from the, er, dead when least expected.

~

If you haven't already, consider going my newsletter and grab your copy of Get Real which features Kim Carr, our local tattoo parlor owner and new to you character, Winston Parsons.

For more of Elle's Piedras Island world, head over to West Coast Forensics, starting with Real Trouble, Dany and Soren's story! Dany and Soren first met in the Shielded Hearts series. If you need a timeline (I do!) there is a series order page on my website: ElleKeatonAuthor.com

~

Check out The Last Grift, Elle's latest book and first in in the Subtle Deceptions series.
Somewhere between right and wrong, the truth lies.

The Last Grift is first in the Subtle Deceptions Series and is part of the Piedras Island/Veiled Intentions universe. Written in third person, Subtle Deceptions follows the unplanned adventures in the life and love of the disreputable Gabriel Karne.

ABOUT ELLE

Elle's characters are snarky, a tad damaged, and definitely have minds of their own, but the mystery is always solved and hearts crossed. Currently, there are over forty Elle Keaton books available for you to read and many have been produced into audiobooks.

Romantic Suspense and Mystery Romance by Elle Keaton
Shielded Hearts
Veiled Intentions
West Coast Forensics
Reclaimed Hearts
Subtle Deceptions

For more information, to purchase signed paperbacks or audio, please visit my direct sales website!

ElleKeatonAuthor

Thank you for supporting this indie author!

AFTERWORD

This is a work of fiction, created without use of AI technology. Any names, characters, places or incidents are products of the author's imagination and used in a fictitious manner. Any resemblance to actual people, places, or events is purely coincidental or fictional.

Elle Keaton's creative body of work cannot be used in any manner for the purpose of training AI.

The author, Elle Keaton, supports the right of humans to control their artistic works. No part of this book has been created using AI-generated images or narrative, as known by the author. The primary style sources used in the writing of this book are the online versions of the Merriam-Webster Dictionary and The Chicago Manual of Style. Due to their inherent limitations for fiction-writing and the author's personal style choices, there are instances where other style guide rules have been consistently applied. Region-based idioms, age- or era-appropriate slang, UK spelling and style rules, and other deviations based on specific dialects may inform some of these choices. Should you have questions, please contact the author at: dirtydogpress@gmail.com